BROKEN GIRL VS FIX-IT BOY

FOREVER LOVE #2

JORDAN FORD

NOTE FROM THE AUTHOR

Dear Reader,

Writing this second book was such a roller-coaster ride. One of my main goals with this series is trying to write deep, realistic characters that really capture the experience of loss and then recovery. I've experienced loss and heartache in my life, and I know each person deals with these emotions in different ways. It's such a privilege to watch these characters work their way through this tragedy.

I'm truly honored to write this series for you, and my prayer is that you'll come away with something to warm your heart, touch your life or inspire you in even the smallest way.

As I did with *City Girl vs Country Boy*, I've put together a **Behind the Scenes booklet** (https://dl.bookfunnel. com/2mo6l1qp7u) for you. It gives you a little more insight into some of the other characters on the farm and within this series.

Being able to set these books in New Zealand and share a part of myself is really special. I know there will be words and phrases you may not understand, so I've put together a KIWI DICTIONARY for ya. If you come across something that doesn't make sense, you'll no doubt find it here. You can download your copy by **following this link** (https://dl. bookfunnel.com/gtguyptohn).

I hope this book satisfies all your reading needs. You can look forward to some laughter, some tears and a whole lot of heartwarming romance.

Thank you to my awesome team: Rachael, Lenore, Beth, Kristin and Emily. You guys are all so creative and talented. Your input into my books is a treasured gift.

To my review team and reader group - I love you guys. You make this job so incredibly brilliant.

Greg, Rose and Terry - thank you for your advice and support with getting details right. It's so awesome to be able to talk to people and nut out scenarios that are realistic for my characters.

Thank you to my family who are so incredibly dear to me. I'll fight for you guys whenever I have to. You fill my cup to overflowing, and I'm so grateful.

And to my Lord Jesus - thank you for creating this

world in love. Your life force flows through everything. Your constant, unconditional love is in the very air we breathe. You shelter us when we're in pain, you carry us when we're too weak to walk, you bring comfort in our darkest hours. All good things come from you, and I'm so very grateful. I love you so much.

1

BIANCA

T he book in my hand feels rough and brittle, like the pages might disintegrate if I turn them too quickly. The spine creaks when I shut it and hug the book to my chest. I'm finding it hard to read, and I can't really concentrate with strains of Vivaldi filling the air. Oma has her stereo turned up so the music can float throughout the entire house.

But I've always needed silence to read; otherwise, I lose track of my place.

Leaning my head against the window, I gaze down at the vibrant trees below. It's a sticky, hot day in Sydney. No breath of wind to revive the trees, just a heavy humidity set on melting all in its path.

I went for a walk this morning and came home saturated. Oma made me shower immediately and put on a fresh change of clothes. I shut my eyes, exhausted by it all. I can barely breathe in this house without it being monitored.

"A lady never does this."

"A lady always does that."

"We don't slurp our tea, Bianca."

"Sit up straight, dear."

The constant scrutiny would drain even the strongest soul, and I now have a very clear idea of why my mother couldn't handle it. She left with Papa when he and Oma got divorced. Unfortunately he passed away before Stacey and I were born, something that broke my mother's heart. She tried to connect with her mother, keep the lines of communication open, but the woman made it impossible.

She makes everything impossible, yet I don't have the strength (or courage) to do anything about it. So I comply. I practice the piano for an hour every day. I meet with a maths tutor so I won't be behind when school starts. I wear the clothes Oma has picked out for me. I straighten the cushions on the couch when I stand up.

Pressing my forehead into the glass, I'm suddenly reminded that Oma will tell me off for leaving a smudge on her perfectly clean window. This old colonial I've been living in should inspire me. It was built in the 1800s and looks like it belongs in the pages of *Little*

Women or *Anne of Green Gables*. But all the magic and wonder of a house this old has been sucked dry by cleanliness and an order so neat you'd think Oma was raised by a drill sergeant.

I miss Mum. I miss her crumpled-up sweater at the end of the couch and the coffee mug left on the table with her pink lipstick marks staining the rim. I miss the cluttered bathroom sink in their en suite and dishes left to dry in the rack in the kitchen.

There's no drip-drying in this house. The kitchen must be spotless before any relaxation can begin. The thing is, Oma doesn't know how to relax.

Even when reading or watching an educational show or listening to her favorite classical composer, her back is ramrod straight, her bony fingers clutched together. I don't know what drives that woman, other than the fact she wants to make me her replica.

I don't know what to do.

Part of me yearns to head back to New Zealand, to that white farmhouse filled with just a little chaos and a whole heap of despair. I thought escaping it might make me feel better, but the sadness just followed me across the Tasman. Turns out sorrow is an international thing.

"Stacey." I whisper my sister's name, tapping my short, rounded nail on the glass as I picture my reckless sister. I can see her up in that room we were meant to share.

Her side would be piled with multiple changes of clothes, while mine would be neat with just the odd thing left out every now and again. My bedside locker would be filled with books and diaries, my watch and hair tie resting beside the lamp. Hers would be covered with all the junk from her pockets—a packet of gum, a few coins, an earring she's lost the back for.

I miss her.

She betrayed you!

My inner voice always likes to slap at me when I start feeling soft. When my defenses start to slide and the warm fuzzies tickle my heartstrings.

She made out with Riku—my big crush from our school in China. She knew how much I liked him, but apparently that didn't matter as they played tongue-twister at the Christmas party. When I found out a few weeks later, I was so angry and hurt. I *still* am.

Stacey doesn't care about me, yet I miss her. That stupid dance she does when she's happy, that little squeal when she's excited. I thought time would help me hate those things. I thought maybe if I listed all the awful, thoughtless stuff she'd done throughout my life that I'd be able to stop caring about her.

But for every annoyance, I think of something that makes me smile.

She's my twin.

And I'm a lost cause.

A lost cause who is stuck and too afraid to do anything about it.

"Bianca?" Oma calls as her quick steps echo on the stairwell.

She finds me in the sunroom, her tight lips pursing the second she spots my feet on the bay window seat.

"Those cushions are very expensive, dear. We don't put our feet on them."

I swivel and rest my feet on the polished wooden floor. It's hard and unforgiving as I press my bare toes into the timber.

Oma walks across the room, plumping the cushions back up and brushing her hand across the squab I was illegally using.

"What are you reading?" She points at the book, and I show her the cover. "Ah." She smiles. "*Emma.* A Jane Austen classic."

"I took it off your shelf." My voice is tiny. It always is around her. "I hope you don't mind."

"Of course not. Just be very careful. These books were passed down from my grandmother. They're very old and delicate."

"I'll be careful."

"I'm sure you will be." She nods and looks at me like *you better be.* At least that's what it feels like.

I swallow and run my thumb down the hardcover spine.

"Your piano lesson is in thirty minutes. I'll drive you there, and then we can go past the uniform shop on the way home. I called this morning, and all the alterations have been completed. They assure me the uniform will fit you perfectly this time, although I'm still going to insist that you try it on while we're there so we can double-check."

She seems kind of triumphant about this, so I try for a smile. I know that will make her happy, but my lips can barely twitch. I don't want to go to a snobby private school where I'll be surrounded by rich girls who I have nothing in common with.

Starting a new school is hideous enough, but to go it alone will be a million times worse.

I need Stacey!

But I left her. I've treated her like she isn't family anymore, and the more time that passes, the harder it is for me to do anything about it.

I want her, but I don't.

It's so confusing.

All I do know is that I want to be rescued from this

nightmare. I want Mum and Dad to magically appear, to bust in the door and take me away from this.

But they won't.

Because they can't.

They're dead, and no amount of wishing is going to resurrect them.

Tears clench my throat, making it swell uncomfortably. I grit my teeth and look away, not wanting Oma to see my tears. She doesn't like me talking about my parents.

"You need to leave the past in the past."

That's what she says. Like they're some kind of event that happened, not part of who I am.

The doorbell rings, followed by a repetitive rapping.

"What on earth?" Oma stands up with a tut and bustles out of the room.

I return *Emma* carefully to the shelf, nearly dropping the book when I hear the one voice I've been yearning for.

"Where is she? Where's my sister?" Stacey's words are clipped and determined.

I press my hand into my stomach and rush for the doorway, forcing myself to stop at the top of the stairs.

What am I doing?

Am I forgiving her? Am I running down those stairs and pretending like she didn't break my heart?

I swallow and grip the frame.

"I don't care if you don't want me in your house! I'm here for my sister, and you can't stop me from seeing her!"

"Please, Ms. Graf. Let us in."

"Beck," I whisper, the sound of his deep, gruff voice like a country song calling me home.

Beck came.

Beck's here.

Why does that make me feel so relieved?

"Bianca!" Stacey shouts. "Bee!"

"Oh, stop your hollering," Oma snaps. "She's up in the sunroom."

I hold my breath and listen to the clatter of footsteps as Stacey rushes up to find me.

She jerks to a stop when she spots me in the doorway. The sunlight behind me streams against her face. She's still gorgeous, her model features perfect and unscathed, even with the wide-eyed look on her face.

I swallow, trying to find my balance. Part of me wants to crumple into one of her bear hugs, but I need to stand strong.

She hurt me.

"Stacey, what are you doing here?" I gape at her, pressing my fist into my stomach to quell the jumping sensation. But it does nothing.

Stacey's eyes drink me in like I'm special.

"I'm here to take you home." Her voice shudders, and her blue eyes glass with tears. "Because that's what I am. I'm your home. Your sister. And we have to stick together."

But she hurt me.

She doesn't respect me.

She never sees me.

"I know what I did was wrong. And I'm sorry, okay? I was a jerk, but you can't just run away from me. We're family. We have a forever love. A forever bond that can't be broken."

Where is this coming from?

I've never heard her talk like this before.

The tears on her cheeks tell me she's being real. The look in her vibrant blue eyes is practically begging me.

"I don't know what you think you're playing at, Beckett Connell, but you can't just show up here and kidnap my granddaughter!" Oma spits a little fire at the man Dad wanted me to live with.

Stacey whips around to look down the stairs.

Vivaldi crescendos into the air as we wait for Beck's reply.

It comes in typical Beck style, slow and easy. "It's her decision, Adeline."

"I did not give you permission to call me by my first name. It's Ms. Graf."

"Oh good God," Stacey mutters and turns back to look at me. "You've been living with that?" She throws her arms wide. "How?"

I look down, fighting a smile. Stacey's incredulity has always cracked me up.

With a loud sigh, Stacey steps toward me. "Look, I know I screwed up, but you can't stay mad at me forever. I need you, Bee. We need each other."

I glance up from the floor and stare at her, not exactly sure what to say.

My insides are shouting out a firm "Let me pack my bags!"

But another part of me is scared.

What if I follow her back to New Zealand and she just hurts me again?

Stacey's always been so good at looking out for number

one. I don't want to be the puppy following her around again.

Catching my bottom lip with my top teeth, I try to figure out how to play this, how to safeguard myself. I want to go with her. I want out of here. And she's right; we are each other's home. Each other's family.

But she broke my trust. She hurt me when I was already so wounded.

She didn't know how wounded you were going to be. She couldn't see into the future.

But still, she made out with a guy I liked.

My forehead bunches, uncertainty writhing inside of me.

Stacey can obviously see it on my face, because her expression starts to match the pleading in her eyes. A tear spills free, but she slashes it off her cheek before it even reaches her mouth. With a couple of determined sniffs, she wards off the tears and blinks at me.

I wait it out, wondering what she'll say to win me over.

Am I being mean? Making her work for it?

My insides shudder as I let out a breath, and then she smiles at me. It's a familiar smile, a hopeful one, and I think I almost know what she's going to say before she even says it.

Sucking in a shaky breath, she rasps, "I saw a pineapple at the airport this morning."

Pineapple: our code word for when we saw something really weird or funny.

"It was a guy in his like sixties, maybe. White suede jacket with tassels, skintight leather pants, and this wild hair that I swear he stole off Bon Jovi in like 1988 or something. Do you remember that CD of Dad's…"

Her voice trails off, but I know the cover she's talking about. Bon Jovi's *New Jersey* album. Released in 1988. One of Dad's favorites.

My lips turn up at the corners before I can stop them.

"I so wanted to WhatsApp with you, but I just…" She blows out a breath, shaking her head. "I wanted to surprise you more. I needed you to see my big gesture. So you'd know how much I mean what I'm saying right now."

"You really missed me, didn't you?"

"Like a mountain misses the snow."

I grin. "Like a princess misses her crown."

"Like Uncle Beck misses his cows." She giggles and I join her as we both say in unison, "Like Mum misses her Pinky bars."

We share a knowing grin as an array of Dad's comparisons swirl through our minds. He always did love them. And Mum always loved a good Pinky bar, something she could never find outside of New Zealand.

"I love you, sis." Stacey closes the space between us, wrapping her arms around my neck and squeezing tight. "Now you need to go pack your bags. I am officially rescuing you from Prison a la Graf, and I'm taking you home where you belong. And I promise that I'll take care of you. I won't hurt you and I'll help you at school and I'll be the best sister in the world." She pulls back and holds my shoulders, her strong fingers clutching tight. "And you have to promise that you'll never take off on me again. When I piss you off, you kick my ass. You don't just run away. You promise?"

I hold her elbows, a touch of fear and doubt whistling through me as I whisper, "I promise."

2

HARPER

A promise is a promise.

That's the thought that won't stop humming through my brain. I can't decide if it's an irritation or a comfort. All I know is it's a fact.

I promised Mum and Dad that I'd take care of Willow and Oscar while they were away.

Well, just because they're gone for good doesn't mean I shouldn't hold fast to what they hoped for. I need to take care of my siblings, which is why leaving them to travel down to Wellington on my own is such a harrowing thing to do.

I tell myself that's the only reason as I cruise down State Highway 1, but I'm actually full of crap. This trip is going to be harrowing for so many reasons I don't even want to think about right now.

Turning up the volume, I hum along to a little Kenny Chesney. Having the car to myself is actually kind of nice. I can listen to whatever I want, as loud as I want. The freedom of that helps me to relax, and the sun heads for the horizon as the landscape grows more and more familiar.

My insides tickle when I descend the hill into Wellington.

Home, I think, turning right at the intersection and taking the long way to my house so I can cruise through downtown and capture a glimpse of the water. I stop at the traffic light and watch the throng of pedestrians cross the big intersection. People are heading home from work or maybe going out to dinner. The group of young executive types who are clipping past me are maybe on their way to a bar or an early evening yoga session. I watch their sophisticated butts disappear down the street, the wind lifting their ties, ruffling their hair and making their skirts dance.

I don't realize the light has turned green until someone honks at me. I quickly accelerate, then check my speed. I don't want to rush this moment. I want to cruise, soak in the city sights and sounds, glance up at the buildings, stare for a moment too long as I pass Dad's favorite cafe. The place where he introduced me to lattes with a shot of vanilla.

My throat swells, sending a dull ache down to my stomach.

I grip the wheel and tap my finger to Thomas Rhett's "Don't Stop Drivin.'" Country music has always been my guilty pleasure. I'm the only member of my family who likes it, which is why I always play it when I'm alone. Pausing for the pedestrians, I wait for the red arrow to disappear off the lights before turning and finally heading to my house.

I was hoping that being back here would fill me with this sense of warmth and comfort—City Girl is back where she belongs. I mean, it sort of does. There's something nice about the familiar, but as I pass the row of fashion shops, my mind is infiltrated with thoughts of gumboots, thick calf muscles and a solid farm boy wearing nothing but a pair of black stubbies.

Why is my pulse picking up?

I frown and clench the wheel, dodging thoughts of vast blue skies, paddocks of green, star-scattered nights and logs around a fire.

"Logs around a fire," I murmur, coming back to my promise and why I'm here.

My family.

My only living family.

I have to focus on them and nothing else.

Shunting thoughts of Tane aside, I pick up my pace and soon pull into my street. The late afternoon light is a dark, bright gold bathing the side of number 27. My breath hitches as I spot our red letter box and am flooded with one memory after another—Dad and Oscar playing rugby in the front yard, Willow twirling in the driveway, Mum laughing on the top step while she slips off her heels and I tell her about the ridiculous catfight I witnessed at school.

I jerk to a stop in the driveway, my fingers wrapped around the wheel as emotions clog every pore in my body. I can feel them swelling, threatening to take me out. A snowstorm of sadness and pain swirls inside of me and all I can do is sit there and stare at what was, knowing my home of thirteen years will never be the same again.

"Harper!" Mrs. Clancey from next door comes running across her yard. Her smile is broad with delight as she rushes up to the car and pops my door open. "Oh, honey, it's good to see you."

She practically hauls me out of the car so she can wrap me in a fierce hug. I gently pat her back and try to ease out of her clutches.

She won't let go, and I'm forced to stand there with her hands on my waist while she looks up at me like I'm the granddaughter she always wanted. The wind nips at my hair, and I tuck it behind my ear.

"How was your drive down? You must be exhausted."

"It was okay." I force a smile. "And I'm fine. I'll probably sleep well tonight, though."

Forcing cheer is so damn hard sometimes. I probably don't need to do it with Mrs. Clancey, but it's kind of automatic. I want her to think I'm strong enough to handle it. Because I have to be strong enough. There is no other choice.

"Well, do you want to come for dinner? I doubt you feel like preparing a meal after all that driving."

"Actually, my friends are meeting me here soon." Thank God I have a valid excuse.

"Okay, well, good. I'm glad you're not going to be on your own. It's a shame Willow and Oscar couldn't come down with you."

I hitch my shoulder and turn out of her grasp, opening the back door so I don't have to look at her. "It's a bit too much for them."

"Understandably. If you need any help packing up the house, you just give me a holler. I'll make myself available."

I grab my bag, my insides spasming at the words *packing up*. Forcing a breezy tone, I spin with a smile. "That is so sweet of you. I appreciate the offer, but I think I'll be okay. Zoey and Alaina will be here to help me, so…"

"Of course." Mrs. Clancey brushes a gray lock of hair across her forehead that the wind is insisting should be in her eyes. Her blue eyes that are starting to glass over.

Don't cry! Please!

I clear my throat and stare down at the crack in the driveway. It was on Dad's list of things to deal with. The crack appeared about five years ago and has steadily been getting worse, inching its way toward the garage door.

"I'm going to miss you kids. I know moving up north is probably the right decision— you never do anything without thinking it through—but there'll be a big old hole in this street without the Hughes family here."

I nod but can't find my voice.

"You'll get there, sweet girl. Your parents were always so proud of you, and they had good reason to be."

"Thank you," I rasp. It's all I can manage through the swelling in my throat.

Sniffing through my tingling nose, I press the lock on my keychain and the car beeps.

"I better…" I point to the house, and Mrs. Clancey steps away so I can pass her.

"Of course. You just call me if you need anything. Alf and I are retired old fogies now, so we're free at the drop of a hat."

I force out a laugh and head for the house. She's watching me. I can feel it. My fingers tremble, making it hard to slide the key into the lock, but then I hear that familiar clunk of the deadbolt and I push the door open and step inside.

My shoes sound loud on the oak floorboards; the lack of bodies in this place seems to make every sound echo.

I stand still in the entrance, waiting for the silence to dissipate, for Dad to come skipping down the two wide steps that lead into the lounge and suddenly spot me.

"Hey, Caramel. How was school?"

His voice is still so real in my head, I can almost conjure him. He'd still be in his shirt and pants from work, but he would have taken his tie and shoes off.

"Lance, can you make sure Ozzy's doing his homework? I'm going to get a start on dinner," Mum would call from the hallway.

"On it!" Dad would give me a quick eye roll. "Wish me luck. I'm about to enter the lair." His spooky voice and wriggling fingers would make me laugh.

But I can't laugh now.

Because he's not standing in the lounge.

Mum's not about to bustle into the kitchen, rolling up her sleeves and asking if I can help out with dinner.

No one's going to call me Caramel anymore. No one's going to listen about my day and actually be interested.

The silence descends like a thick blanket, smothering

me, wrapping me in a cocoon so cold I think my legs might buckle.

I can't.

I can't fall apart like this.

They need me to be strong!

Oscar and Willow need me to get over myself, pack up this place and return to them.

A knock at the door makes me flinch. I let out a short gasp and turn to face the wood.

"Harper! It's us!" Alaina shouts.

The bag slips from my fingers, landing on the floor with a smack. I rush to the door, grappling with the handle and flinging it open.

"Hi!" Zoey stretches out her arms with an excited laugh before pulling me against her.

Alaina encircles us both and I cling to my friends, closing my eyes and focusing solely on the act of hugging.

I think I hear Zoey sniff, and I quickly say, "No one's allowed to cry. This is a cry-free zone."

"Okay." Zoey's voice wobbles.

"I mean it." I squeeze her around the shoulder.

"I'm just gunna miss you. I can't believe you're moving

to stinky old Hamilton."

Pulling out of the hug, I look between my two best friends and force a smile. We all look so different, yet we've been sisters since starting high school.

Zoey's the short little pixie with her cropped hair and large blue eyes. Alaina's the exotic beauty with her olive skin and waves of luscious black hair, and then there's me. The tall one. The sensible one.

Rubbing their arms, I bolster a smile. "It's not forever. I'll be back before you know it. Ozzy and Will need me right now."

"We know." Alaina groans. "It's just so unfair."

Pulling my shoulders back, I dodge the pity train and try to keep my voice firm. "It is what it is. I just have to focus on doing what needs to be done and not feeling anything."

Zoey cringes. "Not feeling? Babe, that sounds really unhealthy."

"I need to survive this," I choke out. "I can feel later, once this is done."

"Okay." She nods and taps the little dimple in her chin. "Fine. We'll pack up this place, sort everything out, and then we can get you drunk and you can have a good cry."

I scoff and shake my head. "I'm not getting drunk."

"It's our mission in life to get you drunk at least once." Alaina winks, and I just roll my eyes and turn away from them.

"Come on, if you don't let loose every now and again, you're going to snap." Zoey clicks her fingers to emphasize her point, but I ignore her, walking into the sunken lounge area.

Clapping my hands together, I spin back to face them. "Right. The plan is to eat, and then I want to start in Oscar's room and work my way to the front of the house. I have a meeting with a real estate agent in the morning who is going to help me find someone to rent this place. It needs to look freaking amazing as soon as humanly possible. I'm only taking a trailer load of stuff back up to Hamilton. Everything else is going into storage. If you see something you're not sure about, let me know."

Alaina salutes me. "Ma'am, yes ma'am."

I smile at my ridiculous friends who I love so much.

I don't know what I'd be without them. A burst of love blooms inside of me, and I race back up the stairs, enveloping them in another group hug and clinging tight.

This week is going to be shit, but at least with them here, I might have a chance of making it out with my sanity still mildly intact.

3

BIANCA

T he fields flash by as we drive back to the farm from the airport. The grass is glistening with a rain that must have fallen while we were leaving the airport. We drove through light, intermittent showers until we reached the Bombay Hills and then the weather cleared, rays of sun burning a chunk of the clouds away.

No one's really talking, and that's fine by me. I'm too tired to talk. Getting out of Oma's house was a bigger fight than I expected. She was livid that I wanted to leave her.

Beck stood up for me, but her nasty words about throwing my life away made me cry. That pissed Stacey off, and she pulled her sassy pants on and made the situation a hundred times worse. By the time Beck led us out of there, Stacey and I were *both* crying. Dragon Oma spat fumes at us the whole way to the car, but I can't get the thought out of my head that once we drove away, she probably shuffled back into her big empty house with only the strains of Vivaldi to keep her company.

The thought makes me feel bad. How sad and lonely must her life be?

But it's not like she does much to entice people.

I sigh, wondering if I should still try and keep in touch. Wondering if she'll even let me. She didn't let Mum. Every time my sweet mother tried, she got cut down that much harder until Dad put his foot down and told her enough was enough.

"You can only try so hard, Leanne. I hate what this is doing to you. Let her go, and focus on the people in your life who love you."

Mum tried, but I bet she never fully let go. I bet she still thought about her mother sometimes and wondered how to make it right. I understand completely, because I'm just the same. Conflict stresses me out. Running from Stacey the way I did was so unlike me. I usually bend over backward to make things right. But this time she had to bend for me. I guess there's something kind of empowering about that, but I'm also totally exhausted.

I just want peace. Calm.

According to my friends back in China, I should never

forgive Stacey for what she did. But Greta and Ellen never really liked her anyway. They thought she was a snobby bitch. They never understood how she ticked. I don't always and I'm related to her. They were my allies at our international school, but they're not here. And even though we've been keeping in touch a little, it's not the same. They're getting on with a life I'm no longer part of. Our WeChat messages seem to be fewer and further between, fizzling out faster than they used to. I haven't exactly been putting in much effort, but it's hard to know what to talk about when they're busy at school and I'm still busy mourning.

It's easier to hide away than deal with change sometimes.

Rubbing at my swollen eyes, I blink and focus on the blue sky. White, cotton ball clouds dot the blue expanse. I rest my chin on my hand and soak in the idyllic picture, not even minding the whiff of silage when we drive passed it.

Beck lets out a satisfied sigh from the front. "Nearly home."

I smile at him in the rearview mirror, then turn back to look out the window.

Home.

Still doesn't feel quite right.

How can anywhere be home without my parents? I

wish they were with us. It hurts so much knowing they never will be again.

It makes me want to run and hide.

But I've done that already, and it didn't change anything. I just took my misery with me. So here I am again, back with my sister—my family—ready to make things work.

I don't know how I'm going to do it, but I have to try.

Stacey promised she'd take care of me, that she wouldn't hurt me again.

And I promised that I'd stay with her.

Biting my lips together, I try to quell the anxious ghosts howling inside of me.

She won't be able to help herself, Bianca.

I close my eyes and ignore the little voice, praying it's wrong. Praying I can find the strength to stay put, to—

Beck pulls into the long driveway, and I catch sight of the white farmhouse at the top of the small rise.

"Wow, garage looks good," I murmur, noticing how pristine white the square structure opposite the house is.

"Yeah, Beck made us sand and paint it." Stacey pulls a face.

Beck snickers from the front. "It was good for you."

As the car pulls to a stop outside the garage, I can't deny this weird sense of something settling in my chest. It's a good feeling that I can't explain. Relief, maybe? I'm not sure, but as I step out of the car and find Tane striding toward me with a big grin on his face, I wonder if it's also a touch of happiness.

"Hey." He pulls me into a bear hug. "Good to have you home, Bee."

"Thanks," I murmur against his shoulder.

Holding me at arm's length, he gives me a cheeky smile. "I don't think I could have handled Stace if you'd refused, so thank you. You've done us all a huge favor."

"Haha. I heard that you, you big munter!"

"Ooo, she's getting her insults on." Tane wiggles his eyebrows, and I can't help a soft snicker. It's really nice to see him again. It's nice to be welcomed back with such enthusiasm.

I glance over my shoulder, wondering if everyone else is around.

Tane reads my mind and gives me the low down. "Oscar's having his screen time, so don't expect to see him for at least another thirty minutes, and Willow's gone for a walk."

"Where's Linc?" Beck grabs my suitcase out of the boot and starts walking for the house.

"He's tinkering in the machinery shed."

Beck whips around with a frown.

Tane raises his hands. "Don't worry. He knows what he's doing. The small tractor was making a weird noise this morning. He's just giving the engine a tune."

"Righto." Beck walks up the stairs, obviously doubting his new worker's abilities. "I'll just dump this stuff and go check in with him. Everything else running okay?"

"Smooth as. We've had no issues."

Beck gives Tane the kind of smile my dad used to give me when I aced an exam or a piano recital. It kills me that I'll never get that look again.

Swallowing hard, I follow Tane inside and ask about Harper.

"She left for Wellington yesterday."

"That's right." I place my backpack on the floor by the stairs. "Stace told me."

"And you're leaving for Upper Hutt when?" Stacey asks Tane as she walks up to me with a glass of water.

"Thanks." I give her a surprised look, not used to her serving me.

"I'll head off first thing tomorrow. Want to get it over with so I can then go help Harper with the final pack-up."

"Cool." Stacey nods, then looks to me. "Speaking of packing—or in this case *un*packing—let's go get you sorted, sis."

I swallow my mouthful of water and bob my head, trailing my sister up the stairs. Looking at the glass in my hand, I wonder if all my doubts are for nothing. She's obviously super keen to have me here, to make this work.

Aw, man, I hope we can.

I guess I kind of like it here. If I'm going to be sad, it may as well be in a beautiful place surrounded by pretty cool people.

4

TANE

I miss my family already.

I've only been away for one night and I'm already pining to go home. Mussing up my hair, I wrinkle my nose at the stale smoky scent lingering in the kitchen. Mum must be at it again. Beck never let her smoke in the house, but I saw her stealing cigarettes out near the chicken coop and around the back of the garage when she got a chance.

Grant obviously doesn't mind her slowly killing herself.

Plunking into the hard kitchen chair, I glance around the pokey space. Pizza boxes from last night's take-aways are still piled next to the sink. I bet the last few slices are now hard, crusty lumps sticking to the cardboard.

Dax wanders in, his shaggy tail wagging as he takes a seat at my feet.

"Hey, boy." I rub his soft ears and grin down at him. "You missed me, didn't ya?"

His tail goes nuts, his tongue lolling out of his mouth while I give him a good scratch behind the ears, remembering all of his favorite spots.

I miss having a dog on the farm. Beck's border collie died about three months before Grant arrived. He brought Dax with him, and the collie/heading cross took to the farm with no worries. He loved it out there. It's kind of sad that Grant took him when he left. I wonder if Beck will get around to replacing the dog. He hasn't mentioned it, but I bet it's in the back of his mind. Seems wrong not to have one, but I guess Beck's been dealing with a lot of stuff lately.

"Morning, boy," Mum mumbles as she shuffles into the kitchen, her pink slippers scuffing on the worn lino floor.

"Hey." I force a smile, still trying to figure out our relationship.

She gave me a pretty tight hug when I first stepped out of Beck's ute, clutching my shirt like she was worried I might float away if she let go. It was good to see her again. It's obvious how much I still mean to her, but it doesn't change the facts.

Hanging out with her and Grant last night was kind of hard work. Conversation was stilted, and in the end we watched a movie. She snuggled up with her new man on the couch while I shuffled in the single armchair, trying not to be annoyed by it.

One of the things that ate at me most was the fact that I couldn't remember the last time Mum and Beck had snuggled. Beck's not a cuddly guy. I just figured that was his way, but now that he admitted to never really loving Mum, I have to wonder if it was more. What's the bet he used to hug Abby all the time? He probably couldn't get enough of her. But something died in him the day she did, and my mum wasn't enough to bring it back to life.

I hate that she couldn't.

I hate that he's partly to blame for this situation.

But it still didn't give Mum the right to cheat. She should have just been honest.

So should have Beck.

I scowl and jerk out of my seat to fill the kettle and get it boiling.

"Coffee?" I ask Mum.

"Yep. It's in the cupboard." She points. "I'll have one too."

I start preparing two mugs, thinking of Harper and her lattes while I measure out a teaspoon of instant granules. I wonder how she's doing. Man, I wish I could get to her right now, but I promised Mum a few nights. I can't bail after only one.

The kettle pops, and I focus on pouring the bubbling water into the mugs. Trying not to think about Harper is basically impossible, so I've let myself dream. Let myself imagine what life could look like this year. I know I have to take it slow, but there's no point denying my feelings for her. The way she kissed me in the barn, the way she looked at me across the fire after agreeing to stay in Hamilton...I want to believe those things meant something.

I have to find out.

So, I've decided that I'm not going to be shy about it. I'll pick my moment and tell her just how I feel. Hopefully it won't freak her out or make things awkward between us, but life is too short to let a moment like this pass by.

Adding in the milk, I tap my spoon on the edge of the mug and try to ward off the fear that she might put me in my place with a scornful look or a polite *not in a million years, buddy.*

"What's that frown?" Mum laughs at me while I hand her the coffee. She takes a sip and puts some bread in the toaster. "You look so like him when you do that." She snickers, but her words make my blood run cold.

"What did you just say?"

Her shoulders stiffen, but she gives me an exaggerated eye roll. "Now, don't get all tizzy about it."

Thumping my mug onto the table, I give her a hard glare. "Don't ever compare me to that loser."

"I wasn't." She chucks me a cloth, and I wipe up the spill I made. "I just said you looked a little like him."

"That's no better." Throwing the cloth into the sink, I plunk down in my seat and scowl at her. My insides are going nuts. Why the hell did she have to bring my father into this? As if this little visit isn't hard enough. It kills me that I even look one microscopic bit like him.

Thankfully I was born with my mother's brown eyes and dark skin. Well, my skin's not that dark, thanks to my idiot father and his pale white flesh.

"Hey, I'm sorry. I shouldn't have said that." She starts playing with the curls on the top of my head. I want to slap her hand away, payback for hurting me, but instead I clench my fists and press my knuckles into the table. "He wasn't always bad, you know? He—"

"Don't!" I snap, flicking her off me. "No history lessons. No excuses." My voice starts to tremble as black memories writhe inside of me—pain, fear, blood and bruises. "There are *no* excuses for what he did to us."

"Yeah. Fair enough." Mum swallows and then sniffs. "Don't worry. You never have to see him again. I made you that promise, right?" She gives me a closed-mouth smile. "He's locked up for who knows how long anyway. Knowing that idiot, he'll do something to screw up any chance of parole."

"He should have been locked up for more than just armed robbery," I spit, still annoyed that we had to sneak away in the darkness. If he hadn't been busted, I'd be looking over my shoulder when I walked down the street, waiting for him to jump out of the shadows and punish me for running away.

That man is nothing but a bullyboy loser who liked to beat on his wife and kid. He didn't even have to get drunk to do it. It was a sport for him—taunting me, scaring the shit out of me, and then springing when I least expected it.

I reckon he would have killed me that night if Mum hadn't threatened to call the police. He left the house, ranting obscenities before tearing off in his car. He no doubt expected to come home and find me tucked into bed, where I'd stay until the bruises didn't show anymore. He probably thought Mum would be waiting for him in their room, where he could have his way with her because she was too scared to say she didn't want to.

But he pushed it too far that night.

He triggered something in my mother, some flight instinct that had her grabbing her wallet and me, and that was it. She ran to the outskirts of town, and we spent the night under a bridge, my blood soaking into her shirt while she stroked my back and hummed something. I can't believe I still remember that. Her arms were shaking, but it wasn't cold. I couldn't figure out why she was shivering when it wasn't cold. Once she stopped singing, she started muttering things. Things my ringing ears couldn't capture.

After that, it all gets a little blurry—or at least the memories merge, screwing up the timeline in my head. All I remember is never feeling like I could settle. Never feeling one hundred percent safe. Different beds, short-term housing. Mum had who knows how many jobs. And then she met Beck in that lunch shop on Victoria Street. She served him coffee while I sat in the corner playing with the only toy I owned—a cheap-ass plastic Spiderman.

I remember Beck looking at me, and I thought he was kind of scary with his big beard and sad eyes. But Mum saw something different. She saw a man who could save us if her husband suddenly found out where we were. So she played nice, and he took us in, provided the kind of home I could only dream of.

We'd been living with him for over a year when we got the news about my father. Mum read it in the paper and started bawling. I didn't know what the hell she was going on about, but Beck explained it all to me later, after he'd calmed Mum down.

I remember that flush of humiliation. The shame of

having the same blood as that man. The same dirty DNA inside of me.

The amount of times I've wished, *prayed*, that I could somehow magically be Beck's kid. Beck's flesh and blood.

I'm smart enough now to know that it's impossible to change my heritage. But I can control some things. Like the fact that I don't want to be *anything* like that asshole, and I'll do whatever it takes to be a better man. A man like Beck.

5

HARPER

The house is empty.

It feels so hollow and cavernous without the furniture. But it all went yesterday, packed into a moving van and then a storage facility near the wharf. It's a pain having to pay for storage, but I'm not willing to sell the furniture when I'm hoping to be back here in a year. I might want some of it, and besides, second-hand furniture isn't exactly a cash cow.

I've thought through every decision meticulously, trying to channel a little of my father. He was a details man—analytical, practical. I always loved that about him. Hopefully he's proud of each yes or no I've said, each option I've weighed and decided on.

I sold my little car yesterday. That hurt. It took me ages to save for my yellow Suzuki Swift. I loved that thing, but it's not the smart option when I have siblings to cart around in Hamilton. The family wagon is the better choice, so I'm holding onto it.

Wrapping my arms around myself, I grip my elbows and walk out of my empty bedroom, refusing to look in Mum and Dad's doorway when I pass. Packing up their room was torture. Zoey and Alaina were in there with me, quietly asking what I wanted to take or store. I managed to answer them through gritted teeth while agony clogged my throat, burned my eyes, and made my hands tremble.

The house has been cleaned from top to bottom. We've worked our asses off, and it's never smelled so fresh or looked so shiny. Mum would be proud, and that makes me feel a little better. I want to make them proud. Even though they're not here anymore, I don't want to do anything to let them down.

I can't fail them.

I can't fail my siblings.

It's driving me in this weird way, motivating me not to fall apart, to hold strong. If I have to do this, delay my dreams of uni and freedom, be a parent to Oscar and Willow, then I'm going to do the best damn job I can. I have to make this mean something, and succeeding will mean something.

Biting my lips together, I check the time on my phone and head down to the kitchen. The real estate agent said he'd be bringing someone through at four. I don't want to be here when he does. He's pretty confident he'll have this place rented out within a week or two. I wish I could stay for that, but I have to return tomorrow. School starts on Monday, and I want to be there for that. Even though Stacey and Bianca are there to monitor everything, and Beck will look after everyone, I still need to be there.

First day of school is a big deal. First day of a *new* school is even more important.

"So, orientation is only like three weeks away," Alaina says.

I stop in my tracks, resting my hand on the wall as I listen to them.

"It's going to be so fun! I can't wait to check out the schedule. Hopefully we'll have some of the same time off so we can catch up for lunch and stuff."

"Hopefully there will be some hot new guys in my classes."

Zoey giggles at Alaina's comment, and a tight ball of jealousy knots my stomach.

Clenching my jaw, I try to ward off the feeling. I have a mission, a really important one. There is absolutely nothing for me to be jealous about.

With a little lift of my chin, I step into the kitchen, pretending I haven't been eavesdropping.

Even so, Alaina and Zoey both jolt like I've busted them doing something wrong.

I smile at them, hopefully saying that everything's cool. I don't want to actually have to say it, because I don't think I can. I wish I *were* strong enough to brush my hand through the air and assure them, "Just talk about it, you guys. It's fine."

But I'm worried my voice will tremble, that a little of my envy might spurt out.

Alaina swings her arm around my shoulders and kisses my head. "Come on, pretty girl. Let's take you out for dinner. Then we'll hit a club for a little bum wiggling, and then you can spend the night at Zoey's place again."

I nod. "Good idea." A nice city dinner will be just the ticket. I'm going to relish some tasty food and indulge in a dessert. Then I'm going to dance until my feet hurt. I think I've earned it.

I should probably shout the girls a thank-you for all their hard work this week.

I'll surprise them at the restaurant.

Following Alaina out the front door, we head to Zoey's place to get ready. I go for a simple black dress and borrow a pair of her mother's heels. As clothes pile up around us and the smells of perfume and moisturizers sweeten the air, I start to relax.

It's fun putting makeup on and getting dolled up.

"I booked us in at Ortega."

"Ooo, yum. They have the best seafood." Alaina fluffs the back of her hair, then opens up her compact.

I squeeze in beside her and apply some black eyeliner. I love the way it makes my eyes pop. I'll plump up my lashes with a little mascara too.

Wish Tane could see me.

The thought makes me stutter, and the liner slips out of my fingers, clattering into the sink.

"You good?" Alaina glances at me.

I hope she can't see the flush on my cheeks. I feel like my skin's on fire.

I've been dodging thoughts of Tane all week. I don't know why I can't get him out of my mind. It's insane. The amount of times I've wished for his presence is ridiculous. It would have been helpful to have him around while we were grunting and shifting furniture, stacking boxes by the front door.

But it's not just that. I've actually missed his lazy smile and easy manner, the kindness that makes his brown eyes so warm and inviting.

Don't go there. Just focus on his bod. That's way safer.

At least I'll get to see his muscles ripple tomorrow

when he turns up with the ute and trailer. Hopefully he'll be sporting one of those loose singlets that doesn't hide any of his yumminess.

His yumminess? Harper, shut up! You're not allowed to like this guy. He'll only distract you from your mission. You're stronger than this.

I pick up the eyeliner and try to apply a little more, but my fingers are shaking, so I give up and reach for the mascara instead.

Thank God my girls won't be at the house tomorrow. For some reason, I don't want them meeting Tane yet. I haven't said a word about him, other than casual comments that make it sound like he's just another body in the farmhouse. I can't even figure out why I don't want to spill.

"Harp, you're looking hot, babe." Zoey slaps my butt, nearly making me smudge my makeup. I give her a dry look and she giggles. "You know what I think?"

"Do I want to know what you think?" I tease her.

She grins and leans her butt against the bathroom counter. "As sucky as it will be not having you around, I'm thinking this whole farming thing could be a cool adventure."

"Totes." Alaina snaps her compact shut. "Farmers are hot. All strong and muscly from working their land. I reckon you're going to fall hard for some Waikato boy."

I roll my eyes, trying to hide the fact that my heart is racing. Tane's flashing through my brain—a thousand images of him, from his smile to his tousled hair to those arms that protected me in the storm.

"I'm only in Hamilton for a year. There's no point falling for anyone."

"Are you kidding me?" Zoey gasps. "A year is plenty of time to hook up and get yourself some nooky. You need to take advantage."

Alaina's eyes narrow as she turns to look at me. "Unless you're still hung up on Dylan."

"We broke up." I shrug.

"Only because he was going away. It was a purely logical decision, which I still think is dumb."

"You can't live by your emotions." I unearth the old argument we had just before Christmas.

Zoey takes the mascara off me and touches up my right eye. "I think there's a balance required."

"If she was really in love with Dylan, she wouldn't have broken it off. If he was the one, she would have made long distance work." Alaina's always so sure of her arguments.

I blink and check my appearance in the mirror. "It was too much pressure. I didn't want to hold him back. And after everything that's happened, it's... it's a good thing."

"It sucks that he didn't come back." Zoey hands me her cherry red lipstick.

"No." I shake my head and point at the muted pink one. "You guys, I told him not to. He'd been planning this trip for too long."

"He should have come back to support you."

"We're not together anymore. It's not his responsibility." I stretch my lips to apply the color and hope to God this conversation wraps up soon.

I don't want to talk about my ex...or some sexy, hot farm boy.

I just want to go out with my girlfriends and pretend for one night that life is normal. That the people I cared about most haven't been ripped away from me and I'm not floundering in the wake of their sudden departure.

6

TANE

These Wellington suburbs are flash. I lean over the wheel and check out some of the houses, impressed with their size and sleekness. So different to what I'm used to. I hate this, but I kind of feel like a country bumpkin right now, which is dumb, because Hamilton is a city (okay, a big town) and it's on my back doorstep. I go in there all the time.

But Wellington's the next step up.

It's no Auckland, but it's still got a few high-rise buildings downtown, and there's a fast-paced bustle that doesn't exist in Hamilton.

Checking my phone screen, I prepare for the right turn before Siri tells me to take it. The wipers screech across the windscreen, and I wince. It's that annoying kind of weather where one second it's raining enough for wipers and within a minute, I'm switching them off again. I just hope these light showers don't get any heavier. I don't want Harper's stuff getting all wet and then stewing in the trailer on the drive home. We're on a bit of a clock today. School starts tomorrow, and I don't want to be pulling up to the farm at midnight, so it's not like we can wait for the right weather conditions.

About ten minutes later, I've traveled out of the high-class suburb and am now driving past moderate homes. Two more left-hand turns and I'm pulling in behind Harper's station wagon.

"Mmm." I gaze at the house in front of me. It's all straight lines and funky angles. The large tinted windows that dominate the front corner are speckled with raindrops, but I bet a lot of light still gets into the house. It looks like a high stud too. It must be pretty airy in there.

I wonder if Harper finds the farmhouse dark and dingy in comparison. It must be compared to this piece of modern architecture.

Slipping out of Beck's ute, I check that the trailer I'm towing isn't sticking out in the road, then spin and head for the front door.

I can hear the music before I lift my hand to knock. It's country and blasting.

Country music?

Do I have the right house?

I knock and no one answers. If I've got the address right, which I'm pretty sure I do, I bet Harper can't hear me over that country beat.

Checking the door, I ease it open and call out, "Harper?"

Someone is singing as I slip into the house, moving left until I spot her in the kitchen, belting out lyrics to a song I don't recognize while mopping the floor.

What a crack-up.

I let myself laugh, because she can't see or hear me, and then I let myself just watch.

Her red shorts are snug around her butt, highlighting the sweet curves. And then those tanned legs that seem to stretch for miles do a little shuffle as she dances to the tune. She's got one of those loose-fitting shirts on again; it's draping off her shoulder and making my mouth water.

I swallow and wipe my lips, not wanting to be pervy.

"Hey, Harp!" I shout.

She spins, sees me, yelps and then rushes to turn off the music. Her feet slip on the wet floor, and she ends up falling and catching herself against the kitchen counter, whacking her elbow pretty soundly in the process.

She hisses and gives it a rub.

"You okay?" I wince and move toward her, but she holds up her hand.

"I'm fine, and don't stand on the clean kitchen floor." Obviously embarrassed, she slaps her hand down on the speaker and the music suddenly cuts off. She tucks a loose lock of hair back into her messy bun and then forces a smile. "Hi."

I grin at her and cross my arms. "So, City Girl likes country music. That's interesting."

Her cheeks flush a pretty pink before she rolls her eyes. "It's my secret guilty pleasure, and you're early." She tries to scowl at me, but it just looks cute and makes my smile grow even wider.

Her lips twitch and she blushes again, shaking her head and muttering something under her breath while collecting up the bucket and heading for what I can only assume is the laundry.

"The house is sparkling!" I call to her. "Looks real good."

"Yeah, I want it to be spotless for the tenants who move in."

"Found someone already?"

"Maybe. The real estate agent is sorting it out for me. But even if these people don't take it, the house needs to look awesome for other potential renters."

"Yeah, good call." I wander into the living room, liking the sunken-in lounge and slight retro feel of the place. I wonder if Harper's parents designed and built the house. It doesn't have that standard, kit-set feel.

I want to ask but am worried it might unearth a little more pain, so instead I settle for, "I'd rent this place."

"Thanks." She appears in the angled archway and gives me a closed-mouth smile. It's tinged with sadness, and my heart twists for her. This must suck so bad.

Drying her hands on a small towel, she then throws it into an open box and looks at me. "Did you manage to get the trailer okay?"

"Yep, it's in the drive. I'll start loading up."

She nods and grabs a box after me, following me out to the trailer. Spots of rain speckle our exposed skin and make us blink. Thankfully, there's not too much stuff here. We should be able to fit it in easily enough, and it won't take too long to load up.

We chat about storage and furniture as we work, catching each other up on the past week. I give her the rundown on Bianca returning and then gloss over my time with Mum.

"It was okay. I'm glad I did it."

She watches me carefully but doesn't press for more when I start talking in clipped sentences. I'm kind of grateful. I don't want to get into that shit, not when she's dealing with her own stuff.

She tells me about her fancy-pants dinner from the night before and dancing until her feet hurt. I can't imagine her letting loose like that. I wish I could have seen it. I bet she looked smokin' in whatever outfit she put on. I can still see the light remnants of makeup around her eyes. I bet she was a stunner. She's gorgeous when she does nothing, so I can only imagine the effect she must have had on any guy with eyeballs last night.

The thought twists my gut in a funny way, so I stop thinking about it and focus back on the jigsaw puzzle that is the back of this trailer. Shunting a box into the corner, I step back and figure we can slide Oscar's sports equipment down the side and that'll leave enough room for the last few boxes.

Turning back for the house, I pick up my pace when I spot Harper straining to lug a massive box down the front path.

"I've got it." I run forward with my arms outstretched, but she just grunts.

"Nope! I'm good. I've got it."

I don't believe her and hover nearby as she carts the box to the back of the trailer, practically dropping it when she finally reaches the thing. I catch the edge and steady it, shunting it into the back.

Giving Harper a sideways glance, I resist the urge to tell her off. I can see her rubbing her lower back as she heads back into the house.

What the hell has she got to prove? I'm here to help!

I'll be pissed off if she hurts herself because of stubborn pride. That's one of the stupidest ways to get an injury.

"That's everything," she calls from the front step.

"Cool." I shove a rolled-up blanket into the final space so boxes are forced to stay put while I drive. Stepping back, I close the door, glad I went for a covered trailer. It'll keep their belongings nice and secure...and dry. The rain has only eased while we've been working, so I'm confident that only a few boxes are mildly damp. They should be dry soon enough.

Locking the back, I wander around to the driver's door and pause when I spot Harper in the front yard, gazing up at the house. Although the rain has stopped for a moment, tears of water still amble down the surface of the house. A sad farewell to a family that wasn't ready to leave.

My heart curls with affection and sorrow as I quietly make my way to Harper's side.

"You okay?" I whisper, gently placing my hand on the back of her neck.

It's so long and delicate, her skin smooth against my thumb.

She kind of relaxes under my touch, leaning her head to rest on my shoulder, like the weight of sadness is too heavy to bear. I run my arm across her shoulders and lightly down her back before hooking it around her waist. I belong here, by her side. She fits perfectly against me.

I brush my lips across her forehead and instantly regret it.

The move makes her jerk and stiffen.

Standing tall, she steps away from me and shoots me an edgy smile. "We should go. It's a long drive."

I gaze at her for a moment, saddened by her jitters. Hating the way she jumped away from me.

With a thick swallow, I nod and shove my hands in my pockets, jingling the keys as I walk to the ute. "You want to follow me?"

"Sounds good." She slips into the station wagon, and I try not to feel so deflated as I start the engine and carefully back onto the road.

I don't know why she reacted to me that way. It's almost like she wants me but feels like she can't or something?

I'm going to have to call her on it.

When we stop for lunch today, I'm telling her how I feel.

Nerves dance through me—a mix of anticipation with maybe just a little dread. What if she rejects me on the spot?

But I have to try.

I can't do the whole guessing game bullshit.

I care about Harper, and she needs to know it.

7

HARPER

The cafe in Turangi is crowded with a Sunday late-lunch crowd.

Tane and I take a seat opposite each other at a small corner table. It wobbles when I lean my arms against it, and Tane immediately grabs a cardboard coaster, folding it in half and fixing the problem.

"Thanks," I murmur, rubbing the back of my aching neck.

I feel like the full-on week is catching up to me, exhaustion nipping at my heels. But I can't crumple yet. We still have to get back to the farm and unload everything. I'm making Oscar and Willow help, even if they don't want to. Hopefully they won't complain. It'll be nice for them to unpack and set up their rooms properly. It'll make the farm feel more like home.

My stomach clenches and I rub at the ache.

Delicious smells waft through the air as the two waitresses deliver meals to hungry customers. I see our coffees coming and feel like a puppy about to get its first meal of the day. Yes! Coffee!

"Here you go." Our waitress places the two mugs down, and I can't hide my grin as Tane pulls a latte toward him.

"You didn't want to order instant?" I pick up my teaspoon.

He wrinkles his nose at me and skims the froth with his spoon. "Don't think they serve that here. You have to order this fancy stuff."

"Whatever." I shake my head, but my snicker gets cut off by the look in his eyes.

It's impossible to deny it.

The guy likes me.

He likes me big-time, and I'm not sure what to do about it.

Alaina would tell me to stop being such a moron and go for it. Zoey would tell me not to deny my feelings. But they don't understand.

When Tane touched me outside the house in Wellington, put his hand on my neck and I instinctively rested against him, I felt my insides begin to melt and soften—

to crumble. I could have wept right there in his arms, and I know he would have held me.

Thing is, that's a dangerous place to be. His arms around me? Me crying on his shoulder?

That can't happen. I'm terrified that if I even let one tear fall, I won't be able to stop. The floodgates will be permanently opened and I'll be a useless, sobbing wreck.

Right now, I don't have the luxury of weeping or softening. I have to stay strong. There's too much to do. I can't cry. I can't feel right now. I just have to serve my family the best way I can.

Which means no lovey-dovey emotions, no tears. No new boyfriends.

"So, you excited to get back to school tomorrow?" I set the conversation on a safer path while we wait for our food to arrive.

Tane rests his cup back on the saucer and licks a little foam off his lip. I avert my gaze, trying to forget the feel of his tongue against mine. My insides vibrate with desire and I rub my stomach again.

"Yeah, it'll be good. Year 13. Last year. Cam and I are prefects, so that'll be interesting."

I nod. I was a prefect and loved the leadership challenge. "You in charge of any particular area?"

"Yeah. Sports and well-being. So, I think that means we're in charge of encouraging students to get active and involved, being up front for school-wide events— swimming sports, athletics day, that type of thing—and amping up the different house groups. Plus, we'll read out the weekly sports reports at assembly."

"That'll be fun."

"Yeah, I think so. Hopefully it won't be too much extra work. There's a chance I'm going to be team captain this year, so between that, being a prefect and studying, it'll be a busy one."

"I'm sure you can handle it." I smile while my insides go nuts. He makes it damn near impossible not to like him. Man, if he was leading cheers for my house group, I'd be screaming at the top of my lungs while swooning in between chants.

I'm so ridiculous.

With a little sniff, I focus on drinking my coffee and try once again to scramble onto safer ground.

"How was the time with your mum?"

Tane's lips flatline, a muscle working in his jaw while he looks away from me. I asked him this already, but he kind of got busy with sorting out boxes in the trailer and I never got a decent answer.

"Really bad?"

"It was all right." He shrugs. "It meant something to her."

"I'm really sorry. It must suck."

"I did the right thing. It's not always easy, but you know…" His nose twitches as he sniffs and picks up his coffee. The cup looks so tiny in his broad hands.

I wrap my narrow fingers around mine and glance up when the waitress appears at our table again.

"Aw, mate." Tane chuckles. "That smells so good."

I love that easy smile he gets on his face. It's so adorable.

The waitress grins at him as she places the all-day breakfast in front of him. It's got everything from grilled tomatoes to scrambled eggs and bacon and sausages.

"Those sausages look good." I sniff the air.

"Want one?" He grabs a small link with his fingers and plops it on my plate before I can say no.

It rolls around next to my beautifully stacked eggs benedict.

"Thanks." I clear my throat and pick up my cutlery.

"So, what are you going to do to keep yourself busy while we're all at school?"

"Not sure." I shrug, hating the question. I've been

trying to avoid thinking about it. "I guess grocery shopping and laundry and you know... keeping the house running. I need to sit down and chat with Beck about what he wants. I'm pretty good with numbers and accounting. If he needs me to do any computer stuff for him, I can."

"I'm sure he'd appreciate that. He hates that kind of thing."

That makes me feel a little better, and we spend the rest of the meal chatting about the farm. Tane's really passionate about the place. It shines through as he talks, almost makes me buy into the idea that it's the best place in the world.

His goal is to work there after high school, although Beck's insisting he also do a part-time degree in agriculture or business or something that will enhance his work on the property.

Before I know it, both our plates have been wiped clean and collected. I finish the last of my coffee and am about to say, "We should hit the road," when Tane stops me with a look that freezes my heart.

"What?" I stupidly whisper, not really wanting to know the answer.

His eyes start to glow with a look that makes me want to melt against him. "This year ahead of you... I know it's scary, but you don't have to do this all alone. You just have to take one step at a time, one task at a time. It doesn't need to be this giant thing to worry about, and I'm here for you. I'll help you with anything you want me to."

I swallow and splay my fingers on the wood, pressing the tips into the hard veneer. I thought I was doing so well at hiding my tension. Can he seriously see through me so easily?

"I wish I could I say I wasn't worried at all, but I guess that would be a lie. I don't know how to be a mum."

"No one's asking you to be a mum. We're all there to help and look after each other. It doesn't all come down to just you. Don't carry that weight. We have to share this."

I feel like he's saying more without actually saying it.

His gaze softens a touch further, the edges of his lips curling up. "We could share a lot of things. I could be good for you, City. Real good."

A breath catches in my throat, and I don't know what to say.

Shuffling in his chair, Tane rests his arm in front of mine and draws a gentle line down each of my fingers. "Let me in. Let me help you, show you how much I care."

Desire whips through me like a tornado, but I curl my fingers and gently slide my hand away from his.

The move injures him, but he does a pretty decent job of trying to hide it. His smile is still kind and sweet.

I try to soften my retreat with the best explanation I can. "I'm not myself right now, Tane. This whole situation is… I feel like I'm barely keeping it together. You don't want me. I'm not good for anybody at the moment."

His lips dip into a thoughtful frown before he softly disagrees with me. "You'd be good for me, City. We'd be good for each other."

8

BIANCA

"I don't know where it is!" I hear Harper calling up the stairs. "This is why I asked you to get ready last night, Oz, so we wouldn't have this rush in the morning."

I glance into the short hallway and spot Oscar shuffling to his room, doing up his uniform shirt and muttering under his breath. I catch a whiff of his deodorant and wrinkle my nose. I think he got a little heavy handed with the Lynx this morning. I guess subtlety doesn't rank very high on the awareness scale when you're twelve.

Biting my lips together, I tuck my side fringe behind my ear and head for the bathroom.

The house is insane this morning. The kitchen was like a Shanghai train station while we all bustled around each other trying to get toast and cereal ready. It's safe to say that the kitchen is pretty much made for two bodies, three at a push.

I managed to bump Oscar from behind, and the milk sloshed out of his Weet-Bix bowl, dotting the floor.

"Thanks a lot," he snapped.

"Sorry." I offered to clean it up for him, and he thumped to the table while I crouched down and wiped the lino.

"Toast!" Harper called. "Whose toast is this?"

"Mine." I shot up and crashed into Tane, who managed to catch his flying marmite sandwich before it hit the floor.

"We're all good." He stopped me from apologizing and took a mammoth bite before grinning at me with a mouthful of food.

It gave me the nervous giggles, which were quickly cut off when Harper shoved the plate at me and quietly begged, "Please take this and get out of the kitchen."

I prepared my toast at the table and ate quietly while Stacey and Harper bickered over who would get to use the coffee machine first.

"I have to leave first," Stacey snapped.

"It's my machine! And I need a caffeine fix, pronto."

"You could always try instant," Tane called from the table.

"Shut up!" the girls replied in unison, then ended up snickering at each other.

"Fine." Harper stepped back. "I'll make your coffee first. Just watch how I do it. I don't want anyone breaking this machine. There's a little trick to it."

Harper explained the "trick" to death while Stacey rested her hand on her hip and rolled her eyes at me.

What did she have to complain about? She was getting decent coffee.

You should have heard her squeal when Harper walked into the house with it.

Yesterday afternoon and evening were taken up with unloading boxes from the trailer and helping Willow and Harper unpack. They didn't get through everything, but already their room is looking awesome with personalized blankets on the beds and embroidered cushions. We now have a coffee machine and other little knickknacks in the kitchen, plus an awesome stereo that Tane said he'd hook up after school today.

It makes me anxious for our boxes to arrive from China. I mean, kind of. It'll be so weird and heartbreaking unpacking Mum and Dad's stuff. I don't want to think about that. But it will be nice to have my books and posters to make our room in the farmhouse feel a little more like me.

"I hate this uniform. It's so freaking ugly." Stacey storms past me, adjusting the navy A-line skirt and grumbling about the way it sits.

What the hell is she on about?

She looks amazing.

She could wear a potato sack and she'd look incredible. She has no idea how lucky she is.

Slipping into the bathroom, I look at my reflection and frown. My big breasts strain the buttonholes on my shirt—not too badly, but enough to make me self-conscious about it. I untuck the pinstripe material and try to readjust it before doing a re-tuck and puffing out the part around my waist. It's a lame attempt to hide the pudginess of my stomach. School uniforms are not designed for girls who carry a little weight.

It's always been that way for me. I'm soft around the edges, just like my dad. He said there was nothing wrong with it, but when you're standing next to your supermodel sister, it's hard to feel pretty.

I run a hand over my red hair, another thing I scored from my father. Mum always loved it. Apparently I was born with red fuzz, and that's why my middle name is Rose. But Mum's not around to love my carrot top anymore, and for some reason it looks so much brighter and more orange in this bathroom mirror.

I wrinkle my nose and smooth my hand over it, running it down my ponytail before tucking my side fringe behind my ear.

With shaking fingers, I reach for my toothbrush and finish off my morning routine.

North Ridge High School.

Help!

I hate starting a new school. It's always so stressful.

Stacey has promised she'll look after me and that I can hang with her new friends who are so awesome, according to her. I shouldn't be worried, but dread still froths in my stomach as I spit the paste into the sink and wipe my mouth.

Running my fingers down my rounded cheek, I wish I had some magic way of deleting these freckles off my skin.

"Hurry up, Bee! I need to brush my teeth. Tane wants to leave in five minutes!" Stacey raps on the door.

More than happy to spin away from my reflection, I pull the door open. "I'm done."

Stacey rushes past me so fast I'm kind of flung out the door and end up bumping into Willow, who whacks her shoulder on the doorframe.

"Oh my gosh, I'm so sorry. Are you all right?" Humiliation burns as Willow rubs her shoulder and smiles sweetly.

She doesn't say anything, just spins on her toes and flits toward the stairs. It's hard not to notice how thin and delicate she is. The uniform sits perfectly on her hips, the tucked-in shirt accentuating her narrow waist and tiny breasts. The sandals that wrap around her ankles make me think of Meg from the cartoon *Hercules*.

I gaze down at my leather sandals and cringe. I've always hated wearing sandals. Why did I even agree to buy these? My pale, freckled feet are gross, and the gap between my big toe and crooked one next to it…ugh!

Racing into my room, I fling off the sandals and grab a pair of ankle socks out of my drawer. I feel better once I'm lacing up my black leather shoes. At least I can hide one thing I don't like about myself.

"Get moving, you lot! You can't be late on your first day!" Beck hollers up the stairs, and I fight the urge to wet my pants as nerves spike through me.

Grabbing my bag off the floor, I double-check that I've got everything I need. Harper made me lunch, which was really sweet of her. I told her she didn't have to, but she said she was already making everyone else's. I must make sure I offer to help next time. We used to eat lunch in the cafeteria at our school in Suzhou. In fact, this is my first time ever having a packed lunch. It's kind of a novelty.

"Come on. Let's go!" Beck calls again and then starts clapping his hands to hurry us.

I clomp down the stairs and take in his overalls. He must have rushed up from milking in order to see us off. That's kind of sweet.

"We have one bathroom, Beck!" Stacey trots down the stairs behind me. "How are we supposed to make this work?"

"We'll figure it out." Tane smiles helpfully, passing her school bag to her.

She snatches it off him and mumbles, "Whatever."

Tane pulls a face behind her back, which makes me grin. I really like Tane. He's a good guy. I share a quick look with Willow, who is biting the edge of her lip, before trailing Stacey out to the car.

Harper and Oscar are heading for the Honda Jazz while we're taking the station wagon to school today. Technically, Oscar starts school like half an hour after us, but Harper probably wants to get him there early so they have time to look around and settle in.

"See ya later, Will." Harper runs back to give her sister a sideways hug. "Good luck. I know you're going to do great."

Willow gives her a half-hearted smile and nods before shrugging her sister off and heading for the back seat. Harper watches her go with this slightly pained look on her face.

Poor Harper.

Poor Willow.

This whole situation sucks.

We shouldn't be starting school saying goodbye to each other. I want my mum and dad standing out here, waving us off with proud smiles on their faces.

"Good luck, you lot." Beck raises his hand in a wave that encompasses us all.

I wave back and shuffle to the car.

Tane's watching Harper. She's rubbing her forehead as Willow pulls the car door shut.

"Hey," Tane calls, making Harper look at him. He grins at her and then winks. "Don't work too hard."

With a little snort, she shakes her head and ushers Oscar to the passenger seat. He's looking pretty morose about the whole going to school thing.

I get it.

I'm feeling the same way.

"Let's go, Bee! You can have shotgun." Stacey opens the door with a bright smile, and I'm surprised by the sweet gesture. She really is going out of her way to look out for me.

Maybe I'm worried about nothing.

Clutching my bag strap, I walk around to the front of the car and slip in as Tane starts the engine. He waits to watch Harper drive past first, his expression one of tenderness.

Aw, does he have a thing for Harper?

That's kind of sweet.

He senses me watching him and gives me a flustered smile before pumping up the volume on the radio.

I don't say anything, just turn to look out the window and focus on the music rather than the squirming worms in my stomach.

9

TANE

The Hughes family wagon is super lush compared to Beck's old ute. It feels weird driving it. I don't actually think Harper wanted me to take it today, but when we were hashing out details around the dinner table, it soon became clear that it was more practical for me to take the wagon and for her to use the runaround.

She compromised with a tight smile, but I still felt kind of bad.

After she rejected my lame advances at the cafe, I spent the drive home trying to figure out how to play this. She didn't reject me in a mean way. She didn't even outright say no. She just said she wouldn't be good for me right now. That's where I need to convince her she's wrong.

So, I'm not giving up.

I won't push. I'll be subtle about it. I'll just be the guy

who's there for her around each corner. The one that can give her a hug when she needs it, tell her she's doing great. Eventually she'll start to believe me. Eventually she'll start to see that we'd be good together. I can tell she likes me. That blush she sometimes gets when she catches me looking at her. Oh yeah, it's on. I just have to convince her that it is.

Whatever reasons are holding her back can't be as strong as my determination. The feelings I've got going on are powerful, and I have to believe they're powerful for a reason. Like we're meant to be together.

I glance into the rearview mirror and check on Willow. She's sickly pale, but I've already asked twice if she's feeling okay and she nodded both times. The second time she even threw in a smile.

She's probably just nervous. Like Bianca, who is staring out the window and munching on her lip. She occasionally stops to hum with the radio, but it never lasts long.

"You need to chill." Stacey grips the back of my seat and pats Bianca on the shoulder. "It's going to be fine. Jonas and his friends will show us around. You'll see."

She moves back in her seat, obviously feeling like she's doing her sisterly duty.

But what about Willow?

I guess that's my responsibility.

Flicking the blinker, I turn left onto North Ridge Road

and head down the hill. You can see the school sprawled to the right. It actually started out as a little country school, but due to the growth in north Hamilton, it's expanded over the years. I can't remember what it used to be called, but about eight years ago, it changed to North Ridge High School and was repainted pale blue with orange trim. All the signage has been redone, and it makes this patchwork school a little more uniform. The main block will always stand strong and sure in the center, but over the years, it's been surrounded by prefabs and other blocks so it's now this mishmash of buildings with lots of mini corridors and hidden alcoves which I know for a fact the student body don't mind.

Even I've stolen a kiss or two in those alcoves.

My lips twitch and I wish for just a second that Harper was at school this year too. It'd be awesome to have her here with us.

Turning into the parking lot, I find a space near the bike racks and check that everyone's got everything before locking up the car.

"There's Jonas!" Stacey squeals, grabbing Bianca's hand and taking off without so much as a goodbye.

"Later!" I shout after her, but she doesn't hear me as they disappear around the corner.

Glancing over my shoulder, I see Willow hovering on the other side of the car.

"You right?"

She nods.

"Want me to walk you in?"

She shakes her head.

"You know where to go, though?"

She nods again. I arranged for a tour before I left for Upper Hutt. The teachers had already started for the year, and they were cool with me showing the "family" around. I figured it would make today easier on them.

Sliding my hands into my pockets, I can't help a small snicker. "You know you're going to have to talk when you get in there, right?"

She pulls in a breath and softly replies, "Yes."

That'll have to do.

"Come on, then." I tip my head toward the main entrance and she glides around the car, walking in step with me.

The sky is overcast this morning, but there's a vibrant heat in the air. It's going to be muggy, all right. Hopefully the clouds will clear and we'll see a little sunshine before the end of the day. Assembly is going to be a sweat-fest. Glad I'll be up front is all I can say. They're introducing the prefects to the school this morning.

I run a hand down my shirt, wondering if I should have

ironed it rather than doing a couple of minutes in the dryer to get rid of the wrinkles.

Oh well, too late now.

Once we reach the sliding glass doors, Willow raises her hand. "See ya later."

"You've got my number if you need me." I wink at her, then grin when she gives me a miniscule smile. "Good luck today, and I'll see you by the car after school."

"Okay," she whispers, letting out a shaky breath before heading toward the Year 11 block where her homeroom is.

"Brave girl," I whisper under my breath.

She may be quiet, but she's walking into the ocean of North Ridge High with a hell of a lot of class.

It must be a Hughes thing, classiness.

Both Willow and Harper move with such grace. I can't remember their mother very well. I only met her once at that picnic, but I can imagine they get those gliding, smooth movements from her.

"'Sup, Tane!"

Manu struts up to me, holding out his hand for the high five/shake we always do.

"Hey, Moo, what are you doing here?" I hassle him.

"The late bell isn't due to ring for another fifteen minutes."

He laughs, which always makes me smile. He's got one of those high, pitchy kind of giggles that rises up like a musical scale. "I'm not on Moo-Time this morning. It's the first day, bro. Gots to be on time."

"Manu Taylor, tuck in your shirt." Mrs. Bright breezes past us.

"Aw, sorry, miss!" Manu shouts after her.

I roll my eyes and head for my locker. I got to keep the same one from last year, as the Year Twelve and Thirteen homerooms are in the same section of the school.

Manu tucks in his shirt and then sprints after me. "So, where's your tribe?"

"They've dispersed."

"Aw," Manu whines. "I want to meet your cuzzies, bro. Any of them hot?"

"Don't even think about it." I give him a sideways glance.

He just laughs his silly laugh, and I can't fight my smile. He's such a loony tune, and it's impossible to stay mad with the guy.

"Tane." I glance up and see Cam raise his hand to grab my attention.

"Later, Moo." I slap him on the shoulder, and he lopes off to greet Adonis and Killian.

Running my hands through my hair, I stop by Cam's locker and lift my chin instead of saying hello.

"Sucky morning?" He snickers.

I raise my eyebrows at him. "Do I really look that bad?"

He laughs and zips his bag up. "They'll get easier, mate. You're in the adjustment period right now."

"The kitchen was chaos." I move past him to get to my locker. I want to dump some of this weight before the morning assembly. "Hey, we don't have to speak this morning, do we?"

"Nah, just stand there and look pretty. Mr. Kingsley wants to meet all the prefects after school tomorrow, though, and I'm pretty sure we'll have to do something on Friday to get people geared up for Athletics Day. It's in week four, which will be here before we know it."

"Yeah, good call," I mumble, trying to figure out which books I'll need for my first two periods.

"I thought maybe we could get together and…" Cam's voice trails off and I glance up, following his line of sight and trying to figure out what he's staring at.

All I can see are students milling around.

Oh, there's Stace and Bianca. They're probably looking for their lockers. My eyes narrow at the way Jonas has his arm draped over Stacey's shoulders like she's a bloody coat hanger. He says something to make her grin while Bianca stands there fiddling with the strap of her bag. Poor thing. She looks kind of lost right now.

Come on, Stacey. Stop making goo-goo eyes at your boyfriend and check on your sister.

Maybe I shouldn't have helped Stacey have that first date with Jonas. Manu said he's an okay guy, but I don't know. There's something about his strut and the way he's chewing on a toothpick like he thinks he's hot shit that's bugging the hell out of me.

Who chews on a toothpick?

I turn to say that to Cam, but he's still staring at something like he's been hypnotized.

"You right?" I nudge him with my elbow.

"Who's that?" he whispers, pointing straight at Stacey, but he already knows who she is, so he must be talking about…

"Oh, that's Bian…ca." I catch the way Cam's eyes track my cherry blossom cousin, the way his lips part in wonder. I lightly smack him in the chest. "What are you doing? What is that look on your face?"

"Nothing." He blinks and tries to hide the fact that he was full-on drooling.

Spinning back around, he smooths down his shirt and

scowls at me. "What?" He shrugs but can't help glancing over his shoulder.

Bianca's moving on, out of sight, and his eyebrows wrinkle like that's the worst thing in the world.

I narrow my gaze, crossing my arms and clearing my throat so he'll look at me again.

Oh yeah, I see you, Cameron Jones. I see the way you're checking out my family.

Cam clears his throat, brushing a hand back through his hair and trying to look like he's not fallen into a deep hole of instant crush. "So she arrived safely, then?"

I don't let up with my glare until his cheeks flame red, and then I can't help my bemused smirk.

Cam shoves my shoulder. "Shut up. She's gorgeous!"

Interesting.

Looks like Jonas isn't the only guy I'm gunna have to watch this year.

I start to laugh in spite of myself. Of all the people in the school, Cam is the least of my worries. If anything, Bianca is one lucky lady. Not many girls catch Cam's attention. The fact that she made him blush, well... that says it all.

He's gunna have his work cut out for him, though. If Willow's the quietest person I've ever met, Bianca would rate pretty damn high on the shy scale.

10

HARPER

The house is still and empty when I return.

As I dump the keys in the bowl near the kitchen, the only noise to keep me company is that steady grandfather clock that just refuses to quit.

I turn to scowl at it, crossing my arms and trying to dodge images of Oscar's pale face. He was pretty quiet on the drive, but I managed to get a few words out of him, like he's keen to play club rugby. Beck has been telling him all about it, and he'll sign up in April when the season starts.

I'm pleased about that. Dad would be stoked.

Dad should be here.

I grip my biceps, my short nails digging into the skin. Even though it hurts, I don't let up. How can I, when

I'm standing safely inside this empty house and Oscar is out there dealing with a brand-new school all on his own?

When I parked the car next to the small country school, I swear Oscar went from pale to translucent.

"It's going to be okay." I tried to smile. "First days are always the hardest, but you're a tough kid. You can totally handle this."

He just looked at me like I was stupid.

I didn't ask if he wanted me to walk him in. I made the executive decision and we walked into the school hall together. It's a full primary school—Years 1 to 8—so I wasn't the only "parent" milling around.

Oscar hung at the back with me while a bunch of what I can only assume were Year 8 boys eyed him up. A couple looked friendly enough. I've already started praying that they play nice and let Oscar into their circle.

After the principal gave a brief, welcoming message, she sent the students off to different areas of the school. The intermediate area is near the field, and by the time we arrived by the block of four classrooms, I was the only "parent" left.

"You can go now," Oscar mumbled.

"Are you sure?"

"Yes." He bulged his eyes at me, and I read the message loud and clear—*you are embarrassing me. Please vanish!*

As much as I wanted to hug him and tell him he was gunna be great, I resisted the urge and walked back to the car, feeling hollow and unsettled.

And now I'm back in the farmhouse.

Beck's no doubt somewhere with Lincoln, and I have an entire day stretching out before me.

Spinning slowly on my heel, I survey the disarray left over from this morning. Dirty dishes are scattered from the dining room table to the kitchen sink. A newspaper is haphazardly piled up on the arm of the couch, along with a smattering of discarded clothing and shoes.

The house is a tip.

It kind of makes my skin crawl, so I race up the stairs to get changed.

Folding up my clothes, I leave them on the end of my bed for later and pull out my "work" clothes. The dungy pair of shorts with the fraying seams and my T-shirt with the hole in the armpit are what I go for. As I yank them out, the dresser rattles and the picture of Mum and Dad flops over.

I go still, my heart hammering as I work up the courage to reach for it. When I was unpacking boxes yesterday, I felt compelled to display it proudly. It's always been one of my favorite photos—Mum and Dad in their finery at a gala event at the Te Papa museum. Mum looked so beautiful and Dad so proud.

My fingers shake as I lift the frame and see them smiling at me. Tears burn my eyes, my throat, my nose. If I open my mouth, is fire going to spurt out—a raging inferno I can't control?

Slamming the photo back down, I open my top drawer and put the picture away.

I love them. I love them so much it hurts like a hot blade through my heart.

It shouldn't have been me dropping Oscar at school this morning.

It should have been them.

With a thick swallow, I race down to the laundry and unearth the cleaning products. I need to keep busy today. That's the only way I'll get through this.

Armed with a bucket and rags, I head up to the bathroom and figure I'll start there and work my way through the house.

Within minutes, country music is blasting from my portable speaker and I'm on my knees scrubbing out the bath. It doesn't take long to work up a sweat, but my arms move on autopilot. I wish my brain could do the same, but the menial task is driving me to think. To worry.

I can't get Oscar and Willow out of my head. Their lost expressions this morning tore at me. And then there was Tane's sweet smile.

Dammit, he looked so freaking hot in his uniform.

That pinstripe shirt and his new haircut, all short and trim on the side with those reckless curls on top.

He's a prefect. He'll be so good too. If I were a student at North Ridge High, I'd follow him. I'd listen to anything he had to say, because he's a really nice guy with a good heart.

And so freaking gorgeous.

Squeezing my eyes shut, I will my thrumming heart to calm the hell down.

The way he spoke to me in the cafe yesterday. His tender brown gaze. The huskiness in his voice when he told me we'd be good for each other.

How easy would it be to fall for those words?

To sink right into them and let them carry me.

But that won't work.

I can't bend right now. I can't get soft and mushy.

Clearing my throat, I open my eyes and mutter, "I used to be a prefect."

Adding some extra Jif scouring cream around the plughole, I go to town with the Stello pad, determined to have this porcelain tub gleaming again.

I loved being a prefect, that responsibility. The way other students looked up to me, came to me for advice, treated me like I was important.

Mum and Dad were so proud of me.

I lived off that pride. Thrived off it.

"And now it's gone," I squeak.

Flopping onto my butt, I ignore the water soaking into my shorts and press the back of my hand against my mouth. I'm shaking again. I hate it when my body does that. It never used to.

I can't do this.

The thought haunts me.

I'm going to fail them.

Breaths punch out of my chest, fast and rapid, as the weight of this new role presses down on me.

Closing my eyes, I try to ward off the rocket exploding inside of me. I can't breathe. My ears start to ring, sweat beading my skin as I grit my teeth and suck in these insufficient micro-breaths.

"Breathe," I pant. "Breathe."

I manage a few more short gasps, gripping the side of the tub until my fingers hurt.

"Breathe," I squeak.

Sucking in a full breath, I hold it and an image of Tane pops into my mind. He's standing in the kitchen, his finger moving in a circle as he gets me to breathe and release, breathe and release, until the ringing in my ears stopped.

I twirl my finger through the air, repeating that process until I can hear my country music again. I let it wash over me, focusing on the lyrics until my heart settles back into my rib cage.

"You can do this," I whisper. "You have to do this. They need you to do it." The reminder forces me back up onto my knees.

I can't let my parents down.

They need me to look after Oscar and Willow.

Mum would want them bathing in a clean bathroom.

And so I scrub.

I scrub and I wipe and I spray and I clean until the bathroom reeks of Apple Blossom Ajax. And then I move on to the kitchen until that's sparkling. After that comes Beck's downstairs bathroom, which is the size of a closet. I bet it used to be. I bet it was once a huge closet that they converted into a shower and basin. The toilet next door is a damn sight cleaner than the one upstairs, and by the time I'm finished in there, I'm starting to feel just a touch better.

"Let's get dusting, then." I move back upstairs, my cleaning frenzy only just getting started as I attack every corner of the house until it's as spotless and shiny as my mother would want it to be.

11

TANE

The sun's come out to play, and lunchtime chaos reigns on the field. A few games of touch rugby intersect an intense game of soccer. I watch the scowls and silent power plays, monitoring faces and the potential fight that might be brewing.

That's why Cam and I chose this spot to eat our lunch and hang out. It has a great vantage point of the field, as well as the slope where a bunch of girls like to work on their tans. That's why Manu and Junior joined us—to babe watch—and a few minutes later, Killian and Adonis strolled up. The Kenyan brothers are only a year apart, but they move like twins. Funnily enough, they're more alike than Stacey and Bianca, who *are* actually twins. They sat on the wooden bench seats beside me, and by the time I'd finished eating, I was surrounded by all my usual mates. Logan brought his rugby ball along, and Cam and I have been passing it to each other while the rest of our crew finish up their lunch.

"Just half your sandwich, TimTam. Come on, please." Manu presses his hands together and bats his eyelashes at Tameka.

Logan scowls at him. "Stop being such a hungus, Moo. Bring your own frickin' lunch."

Manu just grins in triumph as Tameka hands over her chicken salad sandwich with an eye roll. "I don't need to bring food when I've got yous guys."

Logan keeps glaring until Tameka nudges him in the stomach with her elbow. "Don't worry about it, babe. I was done anyway."

Kissing his lips, she rests back on her arm and starts chatting with Kim and Melina. Logan threads his fingers between hers and brushes his mouth over her knuckles.

I spiral the rugby ball back to Cam, trying to dodge thoughts of Harper's delicate hands and how much I'd love to skim my lips over them. Man, I wish our conversation at the cafe had gone better, but what did I really expect? That she'd jump onto my knee and cry, "Oh, baby, what took you so long?"

The thought of Harper ever doing something like that is so ridiculous I actually snicker.

"What's so funny?" Manu asks around his mouthful of food.

I dodge the question with a quick topic change. "You playing touch this year?"

"Yeah, bro. As long as I don't have work that day, I'll be there."

"My dad will let you off work for touch," Tameka pipes up. "He's already said we can play this year."

"Great. So you're in." I start counting in my head. "I reckon we need at least ten on the team. That'll give us three subs, and no one can make it every single week, so it'll guarantee a full team most weeks."

I look to Killian and Adonis. They both shake their heads.

"Sorry, we work every Wednesday," Killian says. "We'd be there if we could."

"That's cool." I smile at them and look to Eddie.

"Yeah. I'm there, and Sione will be too."

"Junior, you're up for it, aye, mate?" A few crumbs fly out of Manu's mouth as he talks around his food.

"Ew." Tameka picks a speck off her shirt and scowls at him.

"I'm in!" Kim raises her hand. "But we need another girl. It has to be a minimum of three, right?"

"Such a bummer that Luka dropped out," Tameka mumbles, her lips turning down at the corners. "I don't know what is up with that girl."

She and Luka used to be great mates, until Luka hooked up with this new guy.

"What's her boyfriend's name again?" My eyebrows bunch together as I catch the rugby ball and flick it to Killian.

"Leon?" Cam looks to Manu.

"Yeah. Good mates with Jonas."

"What?" I catch the ball and rest it against my hip so I can turn to look at Manu properly.

"What?" Manu shrugs.

"Luka's boyfriend is mates with Jonas Kerrigan?"

"Jonas lives on my street," Eddie mutters. "What about him?"

I huff, not sure why I'm so irritated. "He's kind of dating Stacey."

Manu's black eyebrows rise, and he lets out his high-pitched cackle. "The blonde? *Tu meke*, bro."

I give him a warning glare.

He raises his hands but doesn't stop laughing.

"What's so funny?" Cam steps up beside me until we're

both glaring down at him like a couple of parents about to lecture their kid.

"I saw them this morning, practically dry humping each other outside Mr. Attley's class."

I rocket the ball at him. "You told me he was all right!"

Manu catches the bullet against his chest and slings it straight back. "I said he wasn't trouble. I don't know him that well. He's probably just handsy. I would be too with a girl like that. She is—"

"My cousin," I cut him off.

"She's not really your cuz."

"She basically is!"

Manu wipes the sandwich crumbs off his mouth and does another shrug. That's always his first line of defense, a silent shrug like he doesn't give a shit.

Problem is, he does. And I don't want to be the one who makes him feel like crap. He has enough to deal with. That's why we're all so lenient on the guy. That's why Tameka always gives up her lunch so easily and none of us say anything when he shows up with no money.

Every dollar he earns goes straight into his mother's pocket. Manu's mum already works two jobs, sometimes three, and his meager earnings help pay the rent some months.

I press my lips together and silently forgive him with a flick of my fingers.

He runs a hand through his hair and musses up the back.

"I just don't want her getting hurt." I throw the ball up and catch it again. "They've been through enough shit, you know?"

"Yeah, I get it." Manu nods. "I just haven't heard anything bad about Jonas."

"We never hear anything bad about Leon either, but…" Tameka cringes. "Luka's become a different person."

I glance at her, irritation pulsing through me. Or maybe it's worry.

I'm still getting to know Stacey, but I can already tell she has an impulsive streak. I can sense it in her. With all the grief she's no doubt trying to dodge, she could end up doing something reckless.

"Come on." Cam lightly kicks my foot.

"Where are we going?"

He looks around him, squinting in the sunshine and casually shrugging. "Just doing a walk by."

A smile stretches across my face as I hand Logan's rugby ball back to him. "Let's just hope we catch them doing something dumb."

Cam laughs. "Being a prefect has to be good for something, right?"

With a "see ya" to our mates, we saunter off together, scanning the school for trouble and hoping like hell that we'll catch some of it.

12

BIANCA

The quiet spot I've found is sunny and hidden. I stretch my white legs into the ray of light and then quickly tuck them back under the seat. That's a blinding glow right there.

Nibbling on the corner of my honey sandwich, I lean my head back against the classroom wall and just enjoy the solitude for a minute.

I was supposed to be meeting Stacey for lunch, but when I reached our agreed spot, all I could see was Jonas's hand on my sister's back and his tongue inside her mouth. It kind of put me off, so I did an about-face and searched the school for a hiding place.

And I found one.

My smile starts to fade as thoughts of Stacey invade my brain again.

When she first spotted Jonas this morning, I thought she was going to wrench my arm off. I had to run to keep up with her.

"Jonas!" she shouted, dropping my wrist and jumping into his arms with a squeal.

He tongue-kissed her like they were in a darkened room, his hands pawing her.

It was actually kind of gross.

I love romance. I swoon at movies, I happy-sigh reading novels, but that slobbery kind of kiss where their tongues are already out of their mouths before they even connect... well, it's... it was icky to watch.

After they'd finished pashing, Jonas finally noticed me and said hi.

Sort of.

Stacey had reclaimed full use of her mouth, so she introduced us and he raised his eyebrows at me. "Hey."

"Hi." I gave him a closed-mouth smile and tried to think of something polite to say, but then he turned and started walking, dragging my sister along with him.

I trotted behind them, feeling like every eye in the entire school was on me.

You know how they say the camera adds ten pounds? Yeah, well, the eyes of curious students add more than a hundred, maybe even a full ton.

I was a fat, clunking elephant trying to keep up with a fairy king and queen as they floated across the speckled lino. Their narrow bodies found spaces that didn't exist, brushing past people rather than banging into them.

"Sorry... Oh gosh, sorry... My bad." I have no idea what else I murmured before we finally stopped by a small clump of people.

"Hey, guys." Stacey had her perky, upbeat voice on, whereas I could barely form two words.

"This is Leon, Luka, Dee and Nico." Stacey pointed them out for me while Jonas eyed me up and Leon gave me this smirk that made me feel like my uniform was made of see-through material.

"How was Aussie?" he asked.

"Oh yeah, um..." I nodded.

"She hated it." Stacey winked at me. "But I saved her."

I don't know why that hurt so much. I mean, she kind of did save me, but she also drove me there in the first place.

Didn't she?

Yes.

But maybe it was more than that.

I ignored the thought and forced a smile when everyone

started laughing at something Stacey said. I didn't hear it, but I wasn't going to be the only one not smiling.

Thankfully, I've managed to escape this lunchtime. I just couldn't face another session of playing pretend, so I texted Stacey to say I wanted to get a head start on my homework.

Yes, it's day one and we already have homework. I mean, the teacher did say it wasn't compulsory, but it would be useful, so...

I catch a movement out of the corner of my eye and lean forward as Tane and his tall friend walk past my private spot. They don't see me, but I watch them walk all the way to the end of the path before veering right.

A bunch of girls come running up to talk to them, smiling all flirty-like. I've grown up with a sister who has perfected the look over the years and I can always spot it, even from this distance.

Tane and his friend are obviously popular guys.

I can see why. They're good-looking, sporty, charismatic. I mean, Tane is; I'm just assuming his friend is too. He's got a really big smile. As they walk off, the girls kind of lean against each other and giggle.

It's a little ridiculous. They remind me of those triplets from *Beauty and the Beast*, the ones who can't stop drooling over Gaston.

I wonder what it must be like to be admired that way. No one ever swoons over me.

Not even Riku.

Closing my eyes, I drop my unfinished sandwich into my lunchbox and snap the lid shut. I thought he was into me. I honestly thought we'd made a connection, but it was just a big game of BS. He was probably only being nice to me in order to get to Stacey. And he did get to her—at the Christmas party, after Stefan cheated on her and she'd been antsy and vulnerable.

"Asshole," I mutter under my breath.

All the flirting we'd been doing in class meant nothing after all. I guess I shouldn't be that surprised. When you're related to one of the hottest girls in school, it's inevitable that guys will use you to get to her.

I shove my lunchbox back into my bag and wish I'd brought a book with me. I check my watch. There's probably enough time to whip to the library, but I don't want to leave my hiding spot. I feel safe here. Unexposed.

I'm not bumping into anybody. No one's noticing my red hair or wondering how on earth I can possibly be related to Stacey Freeman.

I check my phone. Neither Ellen nor Greta has replied to my latest message. They are five hours behind me, so they're probably only just getting out of bed right now, but… I don't know. It's getting harder and harder to keep the communication going. Maybe I should just give up.

Checking the time, I figure I could probably read an ebook until the bell rings, but we're not really supposed to use our phones until after three thirty. It's a school rule.

That's why I texted Stacey from the bathroom. She hasn't replied to my text either. She probably hasn't even noticed that I didn't show up. With a sigh, I tuck my phone away and eye my history folder. There's going to be a lot of reading involved in the assignment we were given today. I should spend some time going over the brief, making sure I fully understand it before selecting which historical event in New Zealand history I want to focus on.

I should get ahead of the game. There's nothing more stressful than chasing a deadline. I don't work well under pressure. Pulling out the folder, I open it up and start humming to myself as I read through the first paragraph of the brief. But my tune is cut short when a shadow passes over the white page in front of me. I glance up to see what's blocking the light and jolt back when I find Tane's friend towering above me.

He's the tall one with the big smile and the dark hair.

"Hey." He grins. "Mind if I sit down?"

"I'm sorry?"

He points at the bench seat. "Next to you. Can I sit next to you?"

"Um…" I shuffle to the side and give him an awkward glance.

What is he doing here?

Why does he want to sit next to me?

"Cam." He points at his chest after squishing into the space beside me. He has a very broad chest. I can sense the power and strength beneath his school shirt, the way it strains just a little across his shoulders.

It makes me feel kind of tiny…and very short. If we stood up, I'm guessing the top of my head would reach his shoulder, maybe.

Tucking my fringe behind my ear, I softly murmur, "Bianca."

"Yeah, Tane told me." He's grinning again, his straight white teeth so perfect he must have had braces.

I run my tongue over my teeth, still loving the smoothness of my pearly whites after getting my braces off last year.

"Sorry for surprising you. I thought you might have heard me approaching."

"No." I shake my head, thinking about the tune I'd been humming. "I was in *La La Land*."

"Good movie." He bobs his head, and I blink at him in surprise.

"You've seen *La La Land*?"

"Yeah, it's awesome. Did you know Ryan Gosling literally played the piano for the whole movie? I read that it took him months of practice to get that good."

It's an effort not to gape. I know I'm being totally judgy right now and doing some major stereotyping, but I did not expect a guy who looks like Cam to be into musicals.

"Uh, yeah, I did hear that. You like musicals?" My heart has taken off for some reason. It's galloping inside of my chest. I *love* musicals. I think I've seen every musical movie that exists, and Mum used to take me to some kind of stage show every year. It was our thing.

A shard of glass wedges between my ribs and I rub at the ache, trying not to think about who will take me to a production this year. Probably no one.

Cam distracts me with his chipper voice. "I'm a movie buff. I'll watch anything."

"Me too." I nod. "Except horror." My spine shudders, and I grip my binder to my chest while Cam chuckles beside me.

"I don't mind horror. It's fun to be scared."

"Not for me." I shake my head and wince. "My sister and I watched *It* once. Our parents were out and she dared me to do it, and she can be…persuasive when she wants to be." I wrinkle my nose. "I was terrified and haunted by nightmares for about a week. In fact, I can still see images of that freaking clown in the back of my mind." I shiver like the air around me is icy rather than the sticky heat I've been wrestling with today. "Stacey was, of course, completely unaffected. At least that's what she said," I finish with a mumble, suddenly aware of how much I'm talking. He probably doesn't want to know all those silly details.

I steal a glance at his face, surprised by his gaze. His eyes, a light gunmetal blue, study me like he thinks I'm cute or something.

That can't be right.

Guys like Cam do not like girls like me.

It's kind of unnerving, so I stand like a crab has just pinched my butt and start gathering up my stuff. "Well, thanks for being nice to me. The new kid and everything. I'm gunna…" I hitch the bag onto my shoulder and check my watch.

The bell is due to ring in about two minutes, so it's not completely lame if I start heading to class now.

"What have you got this afternoon?"

"Um…" I bite my lip and pull the timetable from my pocket, even though I've already memorized it. It gives me an excuse to look at something other than his blue eyes. "Music, then English."

"Nice." Cam stands, and I'm totally right about the height thing. He's freaking huge. "Who have you got for English?"

I look up at him but then glance at my piece of paper, which for some reason is trembling slightly. I snatch it with my other hand and pull the paper tight. "Initials are KD."

"Ms. Dixon. She's cool. I had her last year."

"Oh. Okay." I shove the timetable away and re-zip my skirt pocket.

"Can I walk you to music?"

"What?" I blink, thrown by the question. "No. I'm good." I'm already backing away and waving at him.

He gives me a slightly confused frown before waving back.

The bell trills loudly as I duck around the corner and power-walk to the other end of the school.

Well, that was completely bizarre.

Why was he even talking to me?

Did Tane ask him to?

Maybe they *did* spot me hiding alone in my little alcove and that's why Cam wandered back to check on me. That's kind of sweet.

But so unrealistic.

He's probably using me as an easy in for Stacey. That makes way more sense. He's obviously a sporty, popular guy. He would be attracted to my sister. Basically *all* guys are.

Irritation fires through me as I enter the music department and storm down to the right classroom. I actually pass it and have to backtrack, which is totally embarrassing, but I'm too riled up to really care.

Finding a space in the back of the room, next to the tired-looking timpani drums, I plunk into my chair and cross my arms.

What's the bet Cam's going to try talking to me again and then slip in some easy line about hanging out sometime?

"You could invite your sister as well, if you like?"

Oh, so subtle!

Well, I'm not doing that, even for a guy who likes *La La Land*.

Especially for a guy who likes *La La Land*. He'd be wasted on Stacey. Sure, she watches movies, but she doesn't love them the way I do. She's not a buff. Not like me.

And not like Cam.

13

TANE

I skim Mum's text asking me about my first day back, but I shouldn't be trying to read and drive, so I shove the phone into the cupholder to concentrate on the road. I'll reply later with an "Awesome, life is good" type text. That'll make her smile, and it's mostly true. The first day back went pretty well.

Glancing in the rearview mirror and to my right, I wonder if that's the case for my three passengers. The girls aren't giving me much. Willow's thumbing through something on her phone with this glazed expression, Bianca's nibbling her thumbnail while staring out the window, and Stacey's twirling the end of her ponytail around her finger.

"So, everyone have a good first day?" I try to keep my tone light and conversational as we head back to the farm.

"It was great," Stacey chirps from the back. "English sucked, but photography was interesting enough."

"You don't like Ms. Dixon?" Bianca turns to face her sister. "I thought she was nice."

"She's making us write an essay on a full-length novel for our first assignment. That's not nice."

"At least we get to choose the novel and aren't being forced to read some boring book chosen by the teacher." Bianca shrugs. "I think that's cool."

Stacey tips her head back with a groan. "Why did I choose to take English? I'm finally old enough that it's not compulsory anymore, but stupid me picks it anyway!"

"Dad always said it's good to take a variety of subjects. It gives you options when you leave school." Bianca's quiet statement shuts Stacey up.

No, more than that, it shuts her down for a minute. I glance into the rearview mirror and watch the muscle in Stacey's jaw clench and unclench a couple of times. The sudden silence in the car is kind of overpowering. You can sense it with more than just your ears.

I can't see Bianca's face unless I turn, but I spot her fingers brush lightly down Stacey's arm as she quietly checks on her sister. Forcing my eyes back to the road, I soon can't help darting another glance in the rearview mirror.

Stacey sniffs and shrugs Bianca's hand off. "Anyway, at least I had a good lunchtime. Better than your dumbass one in the library."

My forehead wrinkles. I thought Cam said he spotted Bianca sitting outside the science block.

"You should have come sit with us. Nico was on fire today. He was so funny. You should have been there. It's going to be pretty hard for you to make friends if you sneak off to read books all the time."

Bianca doesn't say anything, and I get the inkling that maybe she lied to get out of having to sit with hilarious Nico and no doubt Jonas and Leon.

I don't know this Nico guy. Cam and I didn't spot Jonas and his mates when we did our lunchtime walk around, and then Cam wanted to split before the bell rang, so I just wandered back to my crew and talked rugby with Logan until we had to go to class.

As we cruise through Gordonton, past the graveyard and orange-brick church, an idea hits me and I spit it out before I forget.

"Hey, Stace. A bunch of us are going to be playing touch rugby this term. It's on a Wednesday after school. Just a social league. No huge pressure or anything, but I know you love sport, and we need an extra girl on the team. You interested?"

"No." Blonde curls bounce around her shoulder as she shakes her head. "I don't want to play sport this year."

"What?" Bianca grabs her wrist. "What are you talking about? You're not playing sport? What about netball?"

Stacey shrugs. "I don't want to."

"But you're so good at it. It's your thing. You always play."

"So?" Stacey frowns, her tone tightening with each syllable. "Just because you're good at something doesn't mean you have to do it for the rest of your life."

"I know, but…"

I adjust the rearview mirror so I can see Bianca for a second. She's chewing her lip, her eyes darting from Stacey to her lap and back up again.

"But what?" Stacey snaps. "I hate it when you do that—start a sentence and don't finish it. So, what?"

"Well…I think Mum would want you to keep playing. I mean, she coached you all through school, and she always talked about how talented and athletic you are. You love playing sport, and I think she'd be really sad if—"

"I don't want to do it!" Stacey explodes. "And it's not like she's here to have an opinion! Just drop it, Bianca!"

Bianca lets her sister go, retreating so far into the corner of her seat that I can't even see her arm in the rearview mirror anymore.

Willow sits beside me, gripping her phone and looking like she wants to jump out the window.

I don't say anything.

I don't know what to say. The tension in the car is so thick I don't even think a machete could hack through it.

Turning off the main road, I'm grateful the farm is only fifteen minutes away. It will be a pretty freaking icy drive if I don't think of something.

Maybe music?

I reach for the stereo but am stopped by Stacey's huff.

Her lips purse before she quietly explains herself. "I just want a year off. I've played sport all my life, and I want a rest. It's not a big deal." She glances at me, catching my eye in the mirror before looking at Bianca. "Seriously, Bee. Don't get all emotional or psychoanalyze it. It's no biggie."

"Yeah," Bianca murmurs so softly I wonder if I imagined it.

Clearing my throat, I glance at Willow. She looks at me, then reaches for the control button on the console. Within seconds the radio is blasting.

I tap my fingers to the beat, grateful when I hear Bianca softly singing in the back.

Shit, what a ride.

I hope Harper's pickup with Oscar has gone more smoothly than this.

14

HARPER

By the time I leave to pick up Oscar, I'm exhausted. My fingers are raw and dry from too much scrubbing and water. My shoulder muscles are aching from the archaic, stubborn vacuum cleaner that refused to play fair. We need a new one, and I'm annoyed that I didn't bring ours up from Wellington. If only I'd known.

The only thing to make me feel better as I swing into Oscar's new school is the fact that the house smells fresh and clean, the floors are sparkling, and everything has been put in its rightful place.

Walking in when I get home will be a pleasure. I finally understand what Mum meant when she used to say that there's nothing quite as satisfying as a clean home.

Even if no one else appreciates it, I will.

Although, I'm sure they will too. Who wants to live in

filth and mess? Honestly.

I spot Oscar in the pickup zone and brake behind the red Holden in front of me. Giving my brother a little wave to grab his attention, I smile as he stomps toward the car.

He slams the door shut behind him and wrestles his seatbelt on.

"Are you okay?"

"Just drive." He thumps his feet onto the dashboard and slouches down in his seat.

Waiting my turn, I follow the Holden away from the school and scramble to think of something to brighten Oscar's mood.

"So, a shit day, then?" I cringe, wondering if I should have sworn.

My parents never swore, but I'm hoping it'll make Oscar grin.

His lips twitch but then dip again as he turns to look out the window.

"Do you want to talk about it?"

"No! Isn't that obvious?"

I sigh, riled by his rudeness but also too weary to make a big deal of it.

If he doesn't want to talk, fine. Flicking the dial, I turn

the radio on, and we don't say another word to each other until we pull up next to the house. Oscar jumps out of the car before I've even pulled the handbrake up.

"I'm going to find Beck!" he hollers over his shoulder, breaking into a run the moment he reaches the fence line.

I watch him go, worry and doubt gnawing at me as I gather his school bag and carry it toward the house.

Our family wagon turns into the drive, and for just a moment, my heart hitches. For just a split second, I think Dad's turning into the drive and everything is going to be okay. He'll find Oscar and talk to him, get to the bottom of everything, and I'll be let off the hook.

But then I remember that he will never do that again. Ever. He won't be here at the end of Oscar's shitty day to listen and then make some lame dad joke that Ozzy can't resist.

Pain washes through me in a sick wave. My head starts to spin, but I can't let it show.

Pasting on a smile, I approach Willow and wrap my arms around her. "Hey, sis. How was your day?"

She steps back from me so I can see her, so she can just nod and not actually use words.

It's an effort not to squeeze her shoulders and shake her. "Talk to me!" I want to scream in her face, but instead I go for mature and quietly say, "Well, a nod is a good sign. There's fruit and veggie sticks in the fridge if you're hungry."

She smiles her thanks and then walks into the house after Stacey and Bianca.

"You okay?" Tane's smooth voice glides over me, through me, like a cool, blissful breeze against hot skin.

I want to bask in it, lean against him, let his easy way soothe me into a place of peace.

But it doesn't work that way. His arms won't take away Oscar's foul mood or Willow's silence. His kisses won't fix anything.

"I'm fine." I sniff, clutching Oscar's bag and juggling my keys.

"Do you want me to take that?" He holds out his hand, but I shake my head.

"I've got it."

He smiles at me. It's a soft, gentle one that is so freaking gorgeous it's hard to breathe for a second. He looks so good right now. His uniform, just a little disheveled after his day, gives him this sexy edge that I don't have the luxury of drooling over.

"So, how was your first day?" I turn for the house so I don't have to look at him, but he steps in time with me.

"Pretty good." He lightly nudges me with his shoulder. "You work too hard?"

It's impossible not to smile, and I can't help a grin as we walk into the house. I can't wait for him to admire all my hard work, to be awestruck by how nice the house smells, how tidy it is.

"You knew I would." I tip back on my heels as we step into the lounge, my smile disintegrating when I notice the pile of bags at the foot of the stairs, the pair of sandals that have haphazardly been thrown off next to the kitchen.

Willow's standing in front of the open fridge, munching on an apple, while Stacey glugs down a glass of water and then just leaves it on the bench before taking off up the stairs.

I should yell out for her to take her bag, but I'm not her mother.

Can no one see the massive difference in here?

"Something smells good," Tane murmurs.

Finally!

"You cooking dinner tonight?" He gives me a hopeful smile, and all I can do is hitch my shoulder.

What I want to yell is *Who the hell else is going to do it?*

But I don't want to act like a bitch, so I just give him a demure smile as he kicks off his sandals and shunts them toward the front door, *next* to the shoebox I specifically moved there.

Is he blind?

Can he not see the other shoes in there?

"I'm just gunna get changed and see if Beck needs a hand with the milking." He's already untucking his shirt, flashing me a shot of his toned abs while he wanders toward the stairs.

Curse the desire pulsing through me!

I don't want to like this messy slob who can't even put shoes away properly!

As soon as he's gone, I snatch his sandals and dump them in the box, then thump over to the pile of school bags and unzip each one, pulling out the drink bottles and lunchboxes that I'll no doubt be expected to clean and refill for the morning.

"Everything okay?" Willow asks me.

I nearly snap, "No!" but am so relieved to hear her actually speaking that I beam her a hopeful smile. "Tell me one thing about your day. Just one."

The corner of her mouth rises in a sort of half grin before she softly says, *"Mon prof de francais est une bite."*

"What does that mean?"

She just smiles and floats past me, the little French-speaking toad.

"Willow?"

She ascends the stairs and I can't help myself—I flip her the bird just as Tane pops into view.

He gives me a surprised blink before snickering. "That for me?"

"No," I mutter, turning my back on him.

I hear his footsteps approaching and dump the lunchboxes into the sink. The plastic containers clatter against each other, and I actually jump when Tane's hand snakes around my shoulders.

"It's gunna be okay."

I wish he'd stop saying that, but I know he's only trying to be nice.

I flash him a tight smile and he kisses me lightly on the forehead. My heart goes nuts while my body stiffens. I gently shrug him off me, and he walks out the laundry door.

Flicking on the tap, I start throwing away sandwich crusts and rinsing out the lunchboxes.

"Wow, the house looks so amazing, Harper. You've worked so hard," I murmur, then put on a different voice. "Thank you for noticing, everyone. It's so nice to be appreciated."

I slam the rinsed lunchbox onto the drying rack with a growl.

15

BIANCA

I sit on the bed, thumbing through my binder and figuring out what I'll knock off for homework first.

"Are you seriously starting homework on day one?" Stacey whips off her shirt and dumps it on the end of the bed.

Mine's hanging in the closet so I can reuse it tomorrow, wrinkle-free.

I don't say anything as a cloud of deodorant billows into the air. I wave my hand in front of my face, a little jealous of the cute pink and yellow bra Stacey's wearing. They never do fun patterns like that for bigger cup sizes. It's like the designers thought, *"As punishment for having big boobs, we're going to make you wear industrial-style beige and white bras. We'll give you a touch of lace if you really need it, but tartan patterns and cute little flowers... you don't deserve them."*

Forcing my eyes back to my binder, I'm distracted by a cute chirp outside my window. A smile tugs at my lips when a red-faced finch stops on the sill, tipping its head and letting out a beautiful song before flitting off again.

I watch it go, wishing my sister's chirp was half as pleasant.

She's still talking, although I've lost track of what she's saying.

"So?" She lightly nudges my knee with her big toe. "Where were you?"

"What do you mean?" I brush the hair off my face.

"I know you were lying about the library. It was so obvious in the car."

I swallow and look down. "I didn't want to offend you."

"Gimme a break, Bee. Just tell me where you went."

"I found a quiet little space to hide in."

"Oh my gawd." She rolls her eyes. "You are so pathetic. I am hand-feeding you friends on a silver platter. You don't need to go hide."

"I just needed a quiet space. Come on, you know I'm an introvert. I can't be around people all the time the way you can."

Stacey gives in with a sigh, jumping onto her bed and

crossing her legs. "So, you just…sat by yourself? *All* of lunch?"

I shrug. "I liked it."

Thoughts of Cam barge into the forefront of my mind, and for some stupid reason my heart trills, like I was happy about his interruption or something. I frown, snatching a pen out of my pencil case and doodling a line down the edge of my assignment brief.

Why am I even thinking about that jerk?

He's only being nice to me so he can get to Stacey. Does he not know she has a boyfriend? Or maybe he thinks he can outclass the guy.

That wouldn't be too hard.

Jonas doesn't exactly strike me as quality.

That's mean, but compared to the sweet smile on Cam's face when he talked to me today…

It wasn't sweet! He was playing you!

My eyebrows bunch together, and I nip my bottom lip.

"You don't like my friends, do you?" Stacey pulls the tie out of her hair and starts running a wide-tooth comb through it.

"It's not that," I lie, trying to erase the hurt look on her face. "I just don't know them."

"So you spend time with them. That's how you get to know people."

I shrug. I have nothing to counter that argument.

"Just give them a chance." Stacey puts her comb down and kneels next to my bed. "I want to hang out with you this year. We're sisters. We're a team. We have to stick together."

I take Stacey's hand when she offers it to me, and we squeeze each other for a moment. I know she's right. Now that it's just the two of us, we really do have to look after each other. I just wish I didn't feel so out of place around her friends.

"Promise you'll try." Stacey puts on her pleading face, the one that makes her blue eyes big and compelling.

With a little sigh, I give in. "Of course I'll try."

"Yes!" Stacey launches to her feet with a little squeal, wrapping me in a hug and tipping us backward so we're both lying on my bed.

"Get off me." I laugh.

She gives me a smoochy big kiss on the cheek. "Love you, sis."

"Love you too." I pat her back and inhale a full breath when she jumps off me and skips out of the room.

I sit up, straightening my T-shirt and feeling kind of stink. I don't want to hang out with her friends tomorrow, but it looks like there's no way around it. I don't want to hurt Stacey's feelings.

Even so, I snatch the novel off my nightstand and shove it into my bag. It'll give me something to do if I get lucky and manage to sneak away for a few minutes of peace.

16

TANE

The rugby fields are dotted with players in different-colored shirts. With the crystal blue sky for a backdrop and the vibrant grass beneath our feet, it's a pretty awesome view.

Week one of the Wednesday night touch tournament began about twenty minutes ago. I tried to convince Stacey to join us, but after nearly a week of pestering her, she got feral on me and I backed right off. I can't believe we've been at school for nearly two weeks. It's gone so fast yet feels like forever at the same time.

I pull my bright orange game shirt on. We're just using the same ones from last year. There's a big Four Square logo on the back. Tameka's mum convinced her tight-ass husband to sponsor the team. He eventually gave in, but he wasn't about to upgrade our uniform from last year.

"It will be fine." He brushed his hand through the air. "A little mud stain is not bad. You can still see the logo, so it is okay."

Tameka had rolled her eyes but smiled. Her dad drives her crazy, but underneath it all, he's a solid dude. He'd do anything for his daughter. He'll just never admit that he will. It's probably the reason he lets her keep dating Logan, although he probably couldn't stop her. Those two are in love.

I spiral the ball to Logan, who catches it and does a quick pass to Cam. The rest of the team is dribbling in for our five thirty kickoff. Hopefully Manu won't be too late. He told Tameka he was coming. Let's hope he's good for it.

Junior fires the ball at me, and I lob it to Kim. She does a little spin and passes it off to Logan again. He laughs at her dance moves and shakes his head. Having girls on the touch team is kind of fun. The full-tackle rugby season is just around the corner, and that's intense. The fifteen blokes who run onto that field are ready to fight like warriors and come away with a victory.

But this touch tournament—it's just a bit of fun. I like the light casualness of it. There's no pressure out on these fields this afternoon. Unless, of course, we end up playing a team of douchebags. It happens.

"Who are we playing today?" I ask the warm-up circle.

"The Dopey Buggers. I just checked." Tameka runs into

the circle with Melina in tow. She doesn't look that stoked to be here, but we needed three girls.

"The what?" Logan laughs. "That's their name?"

"Yep. I think they're new this year."

Cam and I share a quick grin. It'll hopefully be an easy win against some newbies. Not that winning's the point, but still... Pressure or not, there's something so satisfying about walking off the field as champions.

"We're gunna cream 'em." Kim punches her arms in the air and does a whoop. "Mooloo Warriors, baby!"

I don't know how we came up with the name Mooloo Warriors. Manu must have chosen it. Only he would put his nickname into our team name. It's got to be better than the Four Square Fighters, which is what Tameka's dad was gunning for.

I check my watch, nearly missing the ball Cam fires at me. My quick reflexes snatch it, but it stings my hands.

"Nearly dropped it," he hassles me.

"Shut up," I mutter, throwing the ball back with just as much force and speed.

He dramatically catches it into his stomach as the team disperses to grab a drink and head to our designated field.

"Why do you keep checking your watch this after-noon?" Cam hands me his water bottle.

I open my mouth and squirt the water in, catching the drips with the back of my hand.

"I'm not."

"Yeah you are. Got some place better to be?"

I try for a scoffing grunt, but he knows me too well. "Just don't want to be late home."

Grabbing my shoulder, he gives me a friendly shake and pulls me toward our field. "You are so gone, bro."

"I don't know what you're talking about."

"Yeah you do." He snickers. "You're definitely not focused on rugby. You're thinking about getting home to a leggy brunette."

I shoot him a quick glare. Not once have I said how I feel about Harper. Where the hell is this coming from?

"You talk about her all the time, man. You probably don't even notice it. And I saw the way you were looking at her when you first introduced me. Tane's got a serious case of jelly heart."

I scrub a hand down my face, figuring there's no point lying to my best mate about it.

Cam just laughs and pats my back. "We can talk about it later. For now, get your head in the game. We need ya."

I nod and jog onto the field, huddling with the six other

players as we wait for the whistle to blow. As usual, everyone looks to me to take point, so I give them a very short speech on tactics, and then we break and set for the game.

It's fifteen minutes each side and we don't have any subs today, so it's an intense half hour. Manu shows up for the second half to relieve Junior, and we end up scoring three extra tries in the last five minutes. The guy is freaking lightning on the field.

The Dopey Buggers come away with only two tries to our eight. I'm pretty damn happy about that.

"Good game, guys." I muss up Manu's hair. "Glad you showed up finally."

"Thanks, bro." He lightly punches me in the arm, then starts jogging away.

"Where you going?"

"Pick up Mum from work. She let me borrow the car to get here."

"Sweet. See ya."

He raises his hand in farewell while the other guys form a plan. Most of them have to split. It is a school night, and even though we're only into our second week of school, it's going to be an intense year.

Cam invites me out for takeaways, but I shake my head. "Want to get home, remember?"

"You sure?" Cam asks. "I was gunna grab a little BK and eat it down by the river."

I pause by the car and turn to look at him properly.

His eyes are saying more than his mouth is, and I cringe in sympathy. "Anything to delay going home, right?"

Cam scratches between his eyebrows. "Dad's having a bad week at work."

"Your mum hidden the juice?"

"I think she's locked the cabinet, but if he wants a drink, he's gunna have one." He shrugs and holds his rugby ball like a teddy bear.

"You know you can always stay at my place."

"Your place is kind of full right now."

"There's that foldout couch in the garage, or you can sleep on my bedroom floor."

"Yeah, thanks." Cam nods. "Don't really want to leave Mum to it, though, you know? I'll just stay quiet and creep up to my room. If he doesn't know I'm there, he can't get pissed at me."

I hate this. Cam's the nicest guy in the world, and his dad's an absolute asshole that his mother refuses to leave. She's got this weird kind of loyalty toward the guy. I'm glad my mother didn't feel the same way about her husband, although Cam's dad has never tried to beat him to death. As far as Cam's told me, he yells a lot, but he stopped hitting my mate a couple of years back when Cam overtook him in height and strength.

"How are things in *your* house this week?" Cam kicks the front tire of the little runaround. "Haven't really had a chance to ask."

"They're... you know." I shrug. Cam's eyes narrow and I sigh. "I don't know what they are. Harper's working herself to the bone. The house is freaking spotless, which is great and all, but you put one sock out of line and she's right behind you, clearing it away. I swear she's lost weight, and she's already skinny. She just can't sit still for a microsecond." My voice pitches in frustration. "Stacey's dating this dickhead. Oscar's hating school. He comes home feral every afternoon, and he always takes it out on Harper. I hate it so much."

My fist hits the roof of the car before I can stop it. Gazing down at my hand, I stretch it out and run it through my hair instead, my voice sagging with fatigue. "She won't let me help. Beck will step in. He's the best with Ozzy, knows how to calm the kid, but that still leaves Harper shaken. I try to support her, but she just keeps pushing me away. I'll go to squeeze her shoulder, to let her know I'm on her side, but she just shrugs me off and walks away like I'm infected." I huff and pinch the back of my neck. "I wish I didn't like her so much. It'd be so much easier."

"Yeah, the heart can be one stubborn bitch." Cam raises his eyebrows at me and then starts smiling.

It pulls a soft laugh out of my throat.

"You gunna do anything about Stacey and Jonas?"

"What can I do except keep an eye on them? If he steps out of line, I'll be the first there with my fists ready, but I can't make Stacey break up with the guy. Even suggesting it will probably drive her closer to him."

"Yeah, good point." Cam cringes. "I just hate the way Bianca's forced to hang with them too."

Now it's my turn to snicker at *him*. Crossing my arms, I stare him down and can't help cracking a grin. "You mean, you hate the way you can't get her alone to put on a little Cameron Jones charm."

Oh shit, is he blushing?

I start to laugh.

"Shut up, man. It's not like that. She's…" He shakes his head and rubs a hand over his day-old stubble. "She's different."

"Never seen you like this, mate. You got some kind of love at first sight thing going on?"

"I don't know." He starts gripping the rugby ball, his fingers tight enough to pop that thing, but he doesn't seem to notice. "She's not like all the other girls, and I want to get to know her better. If she'll let me," he mumbles, then clears his throat and looks at me. "I want to figure out what makes her different."

"Yeah, I guess she's not like those girls who seem to trail you, slipping their numbers into your pockets."

"I hate it," Cam spits. "I wish they'd all just leave me alone. I don't want some brazen flirt. I want a girl with soul. Someone real."

I know what he means, and it turns my smile from teasing to genuine.

"I know I don't really know her at all, but Bianca's got this...sweet aura or something about her. It makes her beautiful... to me. It makes her stand out from all the rest. And that red hair is..." He blushes. "It's somethin' else. I love it."

I have never seen Cam like this before.

And he thinks *I'm* gone.

Resting my elbow on the roof of the car, I raise my eyebrows at him. "I guess you better do something about it, then."

He grins, silently asking for my permission.

"You don't have to ask, mate."

"Well, she's kind of your cuz."

"And you're my brother. I don't have to worry about you."

17

BIANCA

S tacey and I have been at North Ridge High for two weeks now.

I still don't feel like I fit in, but I guess it took me ages to feel comfortable in China, so why should this be any different?

It's Valentine's Day today, and unlike our American-based international school, North Ridge High doesn't do anything special to acknowledge it. There are no love hearts floating around, no posters or sweet treats secretly left in lockers. Not that I ever got one anyway.

All I did get was an invitation to join Stacey after school —so I could sit here watching her snuggle with Jonas and listening to all of his annoying friends talk about how horrible families are and how *cool* they are.

I can't stand it.

Shuffling on the picnic rug, I tuck my white legs out of the sun and under my butt. The sun catches the river water, sending diamonds of light rushing past our spot on the grassy bank. The Waikato River always moves so quickly. We drove to this massive grass area that slopes down toward the river. It's actually a dog park, according to Leon, but not many dogs come at this time of day. At the bottom of the slope is a paved walkway that stretches a huge length of the river. Over ten kilometers, apparently. It's a place people can bike, skate and stroll. I get why. It's really pretty, and it's kind of awesome that we have this available to us, free of charge.

The sun is bathing our spot as we sit in a circle. Leon's music blasts from his Bose speaker at an irritatingly loud volume. It's so disrespectful for the people who live in the houses that border this park, not to mention the people who just want a nice Friday afternoon walk along the quiet, peaceful river.

Nico tries again to hand me a bottle of Coke. Stacey warned me in advance that they were special, because she knows I can't stand the taste of alcohol. I've tried a few different kinds, but I think they're all gross.

I shake my head at him.

"Go on, Bee. Just have one." Nico shakes the bottle in front of me.

I kind of hate that he calls me Bee. That name is

reserved for my friends, which he is most definitely not. Although I have been suffering his company a lot lately, so maybe he thinks differently.

Even so, I give him a stiff smile and say, "No thanks. Not a big rum fan."

"So lame," Nico mutters.

"Hey!" Stacey snaps. "If she doesn't want to drink, she doesn't have to. Don't push some peer pressure bullshit on her!"

Nico rolls his eyes. "Sorry. I just want her to loosen up and have some fun."

Desperate to stave off an argument, I force my smile to relax and show a few teeth. "I am having fun."

Nico gives me a skeptical frown, his right eyebrow arching as he swigs down his cola. Leon snickers and shakes his head, while Luka gives me a sympathetic smile.

"It takes time to adjust to a new school. I've only been at North Ridge for eighteen months, and I still feel new sometimes." She licks the sheen of sugary Coca Cola off her lips.

I appreciate her sweetness. Out of this whole group, Luka is by far the nicest.

"Yeah." I nod. "You'd think I'd be used to it, but fitting into an international school is kind of easier. There are a lot of students in the same boat, and they're set up to welcome new people all the time. Hamilton feels more... *settled*."

"Stuck in our ways, you mean?" Leon challenges me, his eyes glinting hard in contrast to his soft voice.

I look down with a shrug and start picking blades of grass. "Maybe." My voice always goes so small and tiny around Leon. I wish it wouldn't, but the guy has a dangerous edge that creeps me out.

An image of Cam bursts into my mind, and for a moment, I wish he was here. Even if he doesn't like me that way, he'd still make me feel safe. I'm sure of it. He's so tall and strong. I watch him sometimes, without meaning to. The way he moves with so much confidence and always has this happy grin on his face. No wonder all the girls like him.

Tane and his mates are super popular and cool, but they're not mean or snobby about it. I kind of wish I could hang with them, but I don't fit into their crowd either. I'm not sporty, and they're always throwing a rugby ball between them while they talk. They're always sharing loud laughs and joshing each other. I'm too quiet and shy. Besides, they're too tightly bonded already. There's no room for me.

The sound of kissing lips makes me glance up from the grass.

Leon is making out with Luka—the heavy tongue stuff

that makes my nose wrinkle. Stacey and Jonas are no better. She giggles into his mouth after he licks her bottom lip.

Gross.

I look to Nico, who is nursing his cola, and we share an awkward glance. I wish that Dee girl was here to distract him. I don't like how he looks at me. His eyebrows rise while mine bunch at the suggestive look on his face.

I go back to picking the grass blades, focusing on the vibrant green color and the softness yet strength of each blade.

Nico scoffs and mutters, "As if."

Humiliation scorches me, hot tears burning my nose and throat. I will not cry in front of this dickwad. So he doesn't think I'm pretty; what else is new?

I carefully select a grass blade and wrap it around the knuckle of my index finger, seeing how tight I can make it before it snaps.

"Leon, stop it." Luka leans away from her boyfriend, her cheeks flaming as she tries to remove his groping hand from her breast.

"What's your problem?" he murmurs against her cheek, giving her another squeeze and then sucking her earlobe.

"It's…" She indicates with her eyes toward me.

I feel like my face is going to catch fire, so I quickly look away from them, my eyes bulging when they start talking about me.

"She won't care. She might enjoy the show." Leon snickers, and I whip back to give him a disgusted frown.

He ignores me, grabbing Luka's thigh and gliding his hand right up and under her skirt.

Luka gasps and shoves his hand away. "Don't be a dick."

"I had you naked in my bed yesterday afternoon," he snaps. "Everyone knows we're doing it. Why are you acting like a stuck-up bitch right now?"

Luka's olive skin flushes red as she bites her lips together, folding her arms across her waist when Leon starts muttering curse words under his breath.

"Hey." Stacey snaps her fingers to get Leon's attention. "You shouldn't talk to her that way, or she'll never be naked in your bed again."

Leon cackles, a harsh, ugly laugh that tells us he thinks Stacey's full of shit. Luka closes her eyes and looks almost defeated, which makes my guts swirl with unrest.

"You want to keep a woman, you treat her with respect."

Go Stacey!

I wish I had the courage to talk to assholes like that.

Leon's eyes glint. They look darker somehow, and a chill whips down my spine, but Stacey doesn't seem to care. She just keeps going.

"If I was Luka right now, I'd be dumping your ass for talking to me that way."

"Well, you're not her, and she's not dumping me because she knows I was kidding." Leon squeezes her knee, and Luka forces out a lame laugh.

Nico sits up and punches out a laugh of his own, pointing his bottle between Stacey and Jonas. "You better watch your back, Jo. You've got yourself a feisty female."

Jonas grins and wraps his arm around Stacey's neck, bringing her in for a kiss. "She's not going to dump me. I'm way too sexy and irresistible."

Stacey giggles and lets him kiss her like the biting tension from moments before didn't even exist.

But it did.

My surging stomach tells me so.

I want to get out of here. I *need* to get out of here.

"Hey, Stace, we should probably get going." Glancing at my watch, I'm disappointed that it's only four fifteen. It feels way later than that. Have we seriously only been here for twenty-five minutes?

"I'm not ready," she murmurs between kisses.

"Well…" I bite my lip, trying to think of a good excuse to leave. "I want to get my homework out of the way so I can have the weekend off."

Nico groans. "Could you be more boring!"

Stacey kicks his foot, her eyes blazing a blue fire warning.

He shuts up and dips his head.

"Why don't you just go?" Stacey smiles at me. "I'll get Jonas to drop me home."

"Is he allowed to?" I ask, doing nothing to shed my geek status.

Nico groans again like I'm a lost cause, and Leon smirks at me. "We'll get her home safe. Don't worry about it. Off you go." He wriggles his fingers in the air. "Go study."

I stand up with a sigh and check the keys are still in my pocket.

"Okay, well…" I give Stacey an uncertain smile, but she just winks at me.

"See you later, sis."

"Bye." I wave and walk up the grassy hill, feeling like

all eyes are on my whale butt. They're probably talking about what a lame waste of space I am or how this blue school uniform accentuates all of my lumps.

I wonder if Stacey will stand up for me when I'm not there.

The way she stood up for Luka was pretty awesome, so I have to trust she's got my back too.

Slamming the car door shut behind me, I grip the wheel for a moment, still feeling sick and unsettled.

Should I have left Stacey there?

She's trying so hard to include me, but maybe I should be doing more to protect *her*.

But how?

I can't make her leave her boyfriend.

She does things on her own terms. She always has.

With a helpless sigh, I start the car and head for the safety of the farmhouse. There's something about driving down that long driveway that eases the badness. Even though Mum and Dad aren't there, the farm makes me feel just a touch better about life. If I could have my way, I'd spend every day there and never have to go to school or hang out by the river with people who don't even want me there in the first place.

18

HARPER

I run up the stairs, feeling pretty pleased with myself as I burst into my bedroom and sit on the edge of Willow's bed. I managed to unpack our last box yesterday, so now everything has a place either in the house or stored in the attic. I've managed to stay on top of the housework and the plethora of tasks involved with running a home and looking after five teenagers, plus a grateful farmer. Beck took the time to thank me the other day for all my hard work, and it meant a lot.

Perching the laptop on my knee, I wait for Willow to pull out her earbuds so I can tell her what I've spent a few hours of my afternoon doing. I wanted to tell her the second she walked in the door, but I was dealing with Ozzy shouting at me and Tane trying to step in and calm him down.

They ended up getting super riled at each other, and I

had to send them in opposite directions. Ozzy stormed off to go find Beck, and Tane stalked up to his room.

"What's up?" Willow rests her iPad on her lap.

"Well, I've been doing some research, and I think I've found you two options for ballet." I spin my computer around. "These two are probably your best bet. Hamilton doesn't have the same selection as Wellington, but I think one of these will do. I don't know anyone around here that I can ask for a personal recommendation, but if you like, you could check them both out and go with the better feel, you know? I've already called and spoken to both the head dance teachers. They're really impressed with your history and exam results. They're both keen to meet you."

Willow gives me a deadpan stare, and then her eyebrows dip in the middle. Her hazel eyes, so like mine, are stormy and irritated.

"What?" I turn my laptop back around to double-check I have it on the right screen.

"I don't want to dance anymore."

"What?" My voice pitches to a high squeak, and then my mouth just drops open.

What did she just say?

She keeps staring at me, silently telling me that I didn't just imagine her response.

"But…" My mouth opens and shuts a few times as the stale air in my lungs struggles to circulate. "You have to. I mean, it's your dream. You're too good to quit. You *love* it."

Willow shrugs. "No."

"Willow," I reprimand her. "Don't do this to me, okay? Mum and Dad want you to keep dancing."

"How would you know?" she snaps. "Are you talking to the dead now?" Her voice is sharp and tacky, like she's flinging darts rather than words.

Closing my laptop with as much dignity as I can muster, I smooth my hand over the gunmetal surface and try to keep my voice calm. "I know they'd want you to keep dancing. They loved watching you, because you were always so happy when you did it. You're a natural. Dad always said you were born to dance, remember?"

Willow's eyes glass with tears and she quietly repeats, "No."

"You don't remember?"

"I remember," she grits out. "But my answer is still no."

My stomach clenches painfully. How can this be happening?

And what the hell am I supposed to do about it?

"Well…" My fingers curl around the edge of the laptop

as I fight the urge to chuck it across the room. "Can you at least tell me why?"

Willow bites her lips together and shakes her head.

No! Don't go silent on me again, dammit!

"Please, Will, just talk to me. Maybe we can figure this out together."

She sniffs and ignores the soft tears trailing down her cheeks, reaching for her earbuds instead.

"Is it because they're not here to watch you anymore?" I rush out. "Because I'll watch you. I'll come to every recital."

Willow goes still but doesn't say anything.

After a painful beat, she shoves her earbuds back in. I go to reach for them, but she knocks my hand away, glaring at me with a dark warning that actually makes me listen.

I raise my hands in surrender. They're shaking, along with my voice. "Just promise you'll talk to me about it when you're ready."

Willow stares at me and then finally gives me one short nod.

I have no choice but to accept it.

Getting off the bed with a heavy sigh, I dump my laptop on my nightstand and trudge out of the room.

I'm failing my parents big-time.

The girl who was born half-fairy is refusing to fulfill her amazing potential! Mum and Dad would be gutted.

But I can't make her do it. I don't even know how! I don't know what to say to make her change her mind, and it's not like I can physically wrestle her into a dance studio.

Agony rips through me, making my stomach shudder, and those short breaths punch out of my lungs again. I try to sniff them back, to get air into my body, but my heart is racing.

I rub my forehead and don't even notice Tane on the stairs until I bump straight into him. He doesn't say anything, just gives me one worried look before pulling me into his arms. Unable to resist him, I sag against his chest and nearly sigh with relief when his large hand cups the back of my head and holds me to his shoulder. I wrap my arms around his waist, clinging to the back of his shirt.

I could wilt in his embrace right now. He's like a solid kauri tree, holding me up. All I want to do is fold against him so I don't have to deal with my failures.

Tears start to burn again, and I pull back before any can fall.

"Sorry," I whisper, sucking in a deep breath.

He just smiles at me—his gentle, kind one that is doing

nothing to kill my tears. "You never have to apologize for that."

I swallow and brush past him, needing space and air to breathe. Although, to my surprise, I am breathing normally. I suck in another lungful of air just to reassure myself.

"I was coming to find you." He follows me, so I make myself busy in the kitchen. I need to think about dinner prep. "I just wanted to apologize for yelling at Ozzy. I didn't help the situation."

"Don't worry about it." I pull a recipe book out from the cupboard and try to find the page I marked for tonight.

"You want to talk about what's bothering you?"

"I'm fine." I shake my head, hating the way my fingers are trembling as I open the book. Slapping it onto the counter, I press my palms against the pages and try to read the blurry, black text.

It's so small and fuzzy.

I squeeze my eyes shut, hoping to clear my vision.

"Hey, I'm here if you need me."

"I know." My voice is clipped as I pop my eyes open and resist the urge to run back into his arms. I want his hand on my head again. I want his strength holding me up.

But I can't ask for that.

Cuddles don't solve anything. They only weaken me. And I can't be weak right now.

I have to do this on my own, for my parents.

Willow is not Tane's responsibility. He shouldn't have to carry this burden as well, so I softly tell him, "I don't need you. I'm okay."

He frowns, his expression kind of injured as he nods and quietly walks out of the kitchen.

Drooping my head, I brace my hands on the kitchen counter and try to rally myself to cook a meal.

My phone dings and I reach for it, quickly opening Dylan's message.

Dylan: Happy Valentine's Day! Glad I remembered the different time zone. I didn't want to be a day late on this one.

His words are followed by a couple of love heart and smiley face emojis.

I scowl at the message from my ex-boyfriend. Why is he sending me this? We're not together anymore, and I don't know how to respond.

How the hell can anything be happy today when my

sister won't dance, my brother is an angry hulk, and I just hurt Tane's feelings?

I want to reply with the truth, but Dylan's too far away and he probably won't even get it. I'm falling for another guy while he's still sending me Valentine's texts.

You're not falling for Tane. Stop it!

With a huff, I send back one smiley face and a polite *Thank you*.

Sliding my phone away from me, I focus back on the recipe book, determined to cook the best damn dinner I've ever made in my life. I have to get at least one thing right today.

19

BIANCA

I crank up the volume on my phone and try to drown out the buzzing worries in my head. Belting out the lines to "I'm Not That Girl" from *Wicked*, I really try to feel the lyrics the way I usually do, but all I can think about is my sister and her tongue in stupid Jonas's mouth.

I don't mind her having a boyfriend. I want her to be happy. I just don't know if Jonas is that good for her. But trying to talk about it with Stacey will be a waste of breath. She's not going to listen to me. She'll just end up being all offended that I don't like her friends.

Gripping the wheel, I let the music wash over me as I drive without singing. It's so unlike me. Music is always my salvation. But not today. Today, it's doing nothing to ease my surging stomach or relax my aching shoulders.

I rub my thumb over the hard plastic steering wheel and check my rearview mirror. I'm the only car on this country road right now. There's something kind of nice about the solitude.

It's kind of like—

Pop!

The wheel jerks in my hands and I gasp, gripping ten and two as the car swerves slightly. I pull it back into line, but the controls are kind of sluggish, and my brain sizzles with panic as I try to figure out what I've hit.

Screeching tires and terrified screams echo in my brain and I squeeze my eyes shut, trying to block out the noise of my parents dying. I've imagined it too many times before.

Open your eyes, you idiot! You're driving!

I gasp and snap my lids open, becoming aware of the rhythmic thumping noise happening underneath the car.

Is that me?

Slowing down, I search for a safe place to pull over. I find it a few hundred meters along the road and pull Beck's little runaround right up to the fence line.

My heart is racing so hard and fast that I'm worried it'll punch its way out of my rib cage. Pressing the heel of my hand between my breasts, I try to calm myself down.

"It's okay," I whisper. "You probably just hit something."

Letting out a shaky breath, I check my wing mirror for traffic, then ease my door open.

I have no idea what I'm really looking for, but I figure the tires are a good place to start. Wandering around the car, I crouch down by the back tire and don't notice anything weird, so I work my way around to the other side.

I spot it immediately. The front left tire is flat on the bottom.

"Crap," I mutter, opening the passenger door and grabbing my phone.

I'll call Beck and he can come fix it for me.

My thumb hovers over the screen as I hesitate, then check the time. He's probably milking cows right now, and Tane's no doubt with him. I can't ask either of them to leave that just for a flat tire.

"Come on, Bee. You can do this." I hear Dad's chipper voice in my brain, see his cheerful smile egging me on. "I've shown you how to do it once. You know what you're doing. You're a tough chick."

Huffing out a breath, I ignore the yearning sadness

thrumming through my chest. I wish Dad was here right now. I wish for that so freaking badly it hurts.

Fighting tears, I shuffle around to the boot of the car and find the interior panel. I lift it away, unearthing all the tools I'll need, plus the spare tire.

With a sniff, I slash the few tears that have escaped and try to pull myself together.

"Right. Okay. Um…" I grab out the jack first and walk around to the front of the car, setting it down where I think I remember it should go.

I then head back and get out the spare tire, ensuring I lay it flat on the ground behind me rather than resting it upright against the car like instinct is telling me to. I can't have it rolling away.

"Flat ground," I murmur to myself, crouching down and picking up the wrench socket. "Do I loosen the nuts before I jack the car or after?"

I bite my lip, scrambling to remember the order, but with zero confidence, I have to end up Googling the answer. I find a great page on Supercheap Auto telling me exactly what to do, and I start working through the steps easily enough until I hit a really big snag.

No matter how hard I push, grunt or strain, I can*not* loosen the second nut on this bloody tire.

Frustration and maybe just a little desperation course

through me as I struggle with the stupid, stubborn asshole of a nut.

I'm going to have to call for help soon, which sucks, because I kind of loved the idea of arriving home and being able to say, "I did it!"

A few cars have passed me while I've been working, but none have stopped. Maybe they don't realize what I'm trying to do, or maybe they're running late, or maybe they're all just selfish bastards!

Tears blur my vision again, but dammit, I don't want to cry!

My internal tantrum is just kicking into full swing when a black ute pulls up behind my car. My eyes bulge when I see who the driver is, and I quickly turn my head away, wiping my finger under my eyes and sniffing wildly to hold the tears at bay.

It's Cam.

"You right?" He smiles at me, walking around the front of his ute and coming to see what the problem is.

I'm suddenly aware of the sheen of sweat on my forehead, and the no doubt sweat patches under my arms. Oh no! How big are they?

Panic seizes me, and all I manage is a little squeak.

He looks like he's trying not to laugh at me. I dip my head with a frown.

"I recognized the car and thought I'd pull over and check that everything was okay." He stops beside me and I focus on his giant shoes. They're like boats—long black sneakers that are probably twice the length of mine. Crouching down, he eyes the socket wrench in my hand, then glances at my failing operation. "Aw, bugger. A flatty is always so annoying. Do you need a hand?"

With a resigned sigh, I relinquish my chance at an independent victory and hand over the tool. I know a lost cause when I see one.

"I can't loosen that top nut." I point at it.

"Cool." Cam takes the wrench and shuffles around for a better angle. With barely a grunt, his arm muscles give a little strain and he pops it loose easily.

I can't help an annoyed scoff. "I've been working on that for ages."

He looks up with a grin and winks. "You loosened it for me."

"Yeah right." I roll my eyes, but my lips want to pull into a smile. I fight the twitch by biting them together.

"Do you have a jack handle?" He lines up the jack pretty much where I was planning on putting it, and I hand over the tool. "Unless you want to do it."

"No, I'm good. Thanks for your help."

"No worries."

I stand back and watch him work, kind of stoked that he actually asked if I wanted to help. Most guys would just barge in all heroic and promptly take over.

Crouching down, I watch him work in silence. It's pretty impossible not to admire the way his muscles flex and shift. For someone so big, he moves with grace. I like the curve his bicep makes and the slightly olive tone of his skin.

Even though I'm not a massive fan of the undercut, I like the way his hair flops down and he has to tuck it behind his ears. It's kind of sexy.

Sexy? Bianca! Stop it! You'll only get yourself hurt.

Standing up, I move toward the spare tire, ready to lift it for him once he's finished jacking the car. It doesn't take him long and he's soon wriggling the flat tire off.

"Nail." He points to the offending metal circle wedged into the tire before placing it down and reaching for the spare.

I roll it toward him and he smiles at me again.

He has a really nice smile. It's so warm and friendly, lighting up his entire face.

I avert my gaze and focus on his black shirt, which I've just noticed has a logo on the sleeve. I squint to read it: Morley's Garage.

"You off to work?" I ask.

"Yeah." He slides the spare on and starts picking up the nuts.

He hands one to me and points to where it should go.

My stomach jitters as I shuffle up next to him. I'm suddenly aware of how close he is. I can hear his steady breathing, feel the warmth of air brushing between us.

I start winding the nut on, noting how small and short my fingers are compared to his long ones.

"I work two afternoons a week and the odd weekend. It's a private garage, and he also has a couple of gas pumps. It doesn't do thriving business, but it keeps me busy enough."

"That's cool. It must be nice to earn your own money."

"Yep. Got to have some money to pay for movies and popcorn. You know, stuff like that."

I laugh. "Nice."

He tightens the nuts with the wrench socket and I don't say anything, instead listening to his very soft grunt as he makes sure the tire is secure. Once he's done, he flashes me another one of those friendly grins and looks like he's fighting laughter again.

I frown and brush my hand over my forehead.

Then he reaches for my face. I freeze, my heart thrumming wildly. "You've got a little…"

The pad of his finger just skims the top of my cheek.

My skin flushes neon, I'm sure of it, and I scramble in my pocket for a tissue while he lets out a very soft chuckle.

"I didn't know if you wanted me to say anything," he murmurs as I swipe the tissue across my face and pull it back to check. Yep, it's totally black. I must have smeared dirt all over me when I was trying to hide the fact that I was crying.

Oh, Earth, swallow me whole!

"You got it." Cam's eyes sparkle like God inserted fairy lights behind his retinas or something. They're so warm and friendly. I've never met a guy like Cam. Tane's close. He's kind and stuff, but I don't know. There's something so nice about Cam.

Unless it's all an act and he's just buttering me up so he can find an easy in with Stace.

I scrunch the tissue in my hand, creating a tight fist around it as I follow Cam around to the boot. He returns the tools and then pops the flat tire in the back. His hands are all dirty and black now. I glance at mine, rubbing them together as I'm scorched once more by humiliation. I must have looked like such an idiot with black smudges under my eyes.

The boot lid snaps shut and I remember my manners, offering a grateful smile. "Thank you so much for stopping."

"I might not have if I hadn't recognized the car. If this ever happens again, remember to flick your hazard lights on."

"Oh yeah." I rub my cheek, and the change in his smile warns me that I probably have a nice black smear running from my ear to my chin.

Great. Will I never learn?

Black smears and sweat patches. This is just getting better and better.

I pull a fresh tissue from my pocket and wonder how red my cheeks are as I make a self-deprecating face and wipe the smear away.

He chuckles and points at my car. "I'll follow you home."

"You don't have to do that." I take the keys out of my pocket and stuff the tissue away.

He just smiles at me again, the right edge of his nose wrinkling. "I'm going to do it whether you want me to or not. Sorry, but I need to make sure you get home safely. These spare tires aren't always that reliable."

"Oh." I glance at the car, then back at him. "But I don't want to be a pain."

He chuckles. "There's nothing painful about you, Bianca."

I like the way he says my name. People don't always pronounce it right, but the soft way he played with it just then was perfect.

My lips part as I watch him walk to his car, and then I realize that he's getting behind the wheel and will be waiting for me if I don't get a move on.

I kind of skip to my driver's door and jump in, checking the road before pulling out and having Cam follow right behind me.

It's kind of sweet that he's doing this. I'm sure the spare will be fine. The gesture only makes him more likable, though. It's the kind of thing Tane would do.

When I reach the driveway about fifteen minutes later, I honk my horn and wave goodbye out the window, but he doesn't keep going like I expect. Instead, he follows me down to the big white house.

What's he doing?

He's going to be late for work.

I park the car and jump out quickly so I don't delay him more than I need to.

"It worked." I smile and walk around the car to make sure the spare tire is still sound.

"Yeah." He lightly kicks it. "It held, but make sure you

mention it to Beck as soon as. Morley's does tires. If he comes down tomorrow, I'll try and get him a discount."

"Okay. I will." I nod and wonder why he's still standing there looking at me.

I glance at his car and then back up to him. He's watching me, like he's expecting me to say something else. But what?

I start playing with the ends of my hair, combing my fingers through it and giving him an edgy smile.

Do I say thanks again?

Why is he looking at me like this?

"Hey, um." He scuffs the dirt between us, shoving his hands into his pockets and looking at the ground. "Have you seen the trailer for that new movie, *The King's Man*?"

"Oh yeah. That looks really good. The other *Kingsmen* movies were great. I expect it'll be a fun ride."

"Yeah. Yeah, definitely." Cam glances up with a breathy laugh. "Um, so, maybe… Would you… Do you want to go see it with me?"

I can't help a confused frown and don't know what to say. I'm waiting for the *your sister can come too, if she wants* line, but he doesn't say it. He just stands there with this hopeful smile on his face.

What is going on right now?

"Hey, Cam! What are you doing here?" Tane appears around the side of the house, and as he lopes over to the car, I use it as the perfect excuse to get out of answering Cam's weird question.

I mean, maybe he's just being nice because he knows I love movies, but it almost sounded like he was asking me out on a date, which can't be right.

"Thanks for your help," I murmur before darting away. I kind of feel bad for not giving him an answer, but that feeling is being countered by this heat inside my chest. It's not a painful heat, more like a tingling warmth— that giddy feeling you get when you start to crush on someone. Kind of like how I felt when Riku was being all nice to me.

I can't go there.

Not again.

But as I reach the stairs, I head up to my room with a little bounce in my step, and when I dump my bag on the floor and spin to catch a glimpse of my dirty face in the mirror, I'm smiling.

20

TANE

Cam's glaring at me, and I'm not sure why. Shading my eyes from the late afternoon sun, I can't help admiring the rich golden light as it bathes the side of the garage. I love that color so much, and with the new coat of paint on the structure, it practically glows.

Beck doesn't need me for milking, so I'm about to go check on the horses. It's a nice surprise to clomp around the house in my gumboots and spot my best mate. I know he's got work today, so why's he here?

Planting my feet in front of Cam, I look up at him and cross my arms.

"Everything okay?"

With an irritated huff, Cam rakes a hand through his hair and, after a quick headshake, mutters, "Bianca got a flat tire. I helped her change it and followed her home to make sure she was okay."

"Nice." I grin, giving him a quick slap on the arm and wiggling my eyebrows. "I bet she appreciated that."

"Yeah." Cam's eyebrows dip, and I wonder yet again why he's glaring at me. What the hell did I do?

Or maybe he's annoyed that he's going to be late for work.

That's weird. He doesn't usually get pissed about that kind of thing. His boss is a sweet old grandpa. All Cam has to do is call him and explain. It won't be a big deal.

I'm about to reassure him of this when my words are cut off by the sight of a car taking the corner too fast and then tearing down our driveway like the driver thinks the accelerator is the brake or something.

Dust billows out behind the sedan, and tension spikes inside of me as it draws close to the house. Cam and I both turn and step forward, but the car doesn't seem to be slowing because the driver is too busy making out with the passenger.

Stacey?

"Oi!" I shout, raising my hands and trying to get his attention.

The car jerks to a stop and Stacey lurches forward in her seat, nearly whacking her head on the dashboard. Jonas grabs her shirt, pulling her back against him, and they fall against each other in fits of giggles.

"What the hell?" Cam mutters under his breath.

"Is she drunk?" I snap and send a sharp look up at my friend.

Cam winces, telling me my instincts are right. I work my jaw to the side and storm toward the car. "If he's drunk, I'm killing him."

I wrench open the passenger door and Stacey jumps, letting out a surprised scream before flopping onto Jonas's shoulder with another giggle.

"Get out of the car," I bark.

She scoffs and points at me like I'm crazy. Jonas laughs and riles me with a piss-poor imitation of my grumpy voice. "Get out of the car."

They burst into laughter again.

With a growl, I snatch Stacey's arm and haul her out of the vehicle.

"Hey, get your hands off me!" she shouts in my face.

I let her go immediately, thrown by the fact that I could be so rough. Images of my dad thrash my brain, sharp and painful. I'm not going to be that guy. I won't get rough when I'm pissed off. Clenching my fist, I swallow and turn my back on Stacey, instead directing my wrath at a guy who fully deserves it.

Leaning down into the car, I snatch Jonas's shirt collar and give him a little shake. "Are you drunk?"

"No!" Jonas frowns and looks at Stacey through the windscreen, but his eyes are kind of glassy.

"You lying shit!" I jerk him around to look at me, my voice rough with warning. "If you're driving her around when you're wasted, I'm going to pummel you into the ground."

Jonas's door flings open and Cam appears behind the idiot. "Let him go, mate. I've got this."

I reluctantly loosen my grip so Cam can pull Jonas out of the car. After getting over the shock of being manhandled, Jonas lets out a caustic laugh, looking right up at Cam and burping in his face.

This sends Stacey into another fit of giggles while Cam stares Jonas down with a glare that could melt titanium. "You have been drinking."

Jonas scoffs. "But I'm not drunk, so get your hands off me."

He tries to shove Cam away, but his spindly body does nothing to move Mount Cameron.

"I'm driving you home," he grits out, tugging Jonas toward his ute.

"Hey! Let me go! I'm not drunk!"

"You shouldn't even have passengers!" I walk around

the car, ranting at Jonas while he's dragged after Cam. "There's no way you're on your full license yet."

Jonas ignores me, instead trying to fight Cam's hold on him.

He doesn't have a chance. His arms are like toothpicks compared to Cam's tree branches.

"I've had like two drinks! I can drive myself home. Let me bloody go!"

"Not a chance," Cam mutters.

"I can't leave Mum's car here! My old man'll kill me!

"We don't give shit." I open the passenger door and help Cam haul Jonas's stupid ass into the ute. "You can come and pick it up tomorrow. When you're sober."

Jonas gives up the fight and flops into the seat, cursing under his breath and glaring at me before busting into a snicker. I turn to see what he's laughing at.

Stacey's pulling a face behind my back.

I shoot her an incredulous scowl, but she just grins at me and flips me off.

This cracks Jonas up, and he throws her a kiss goodbye. "See you tomorrow, baby! I'll come back and rescue you from these assholes!"

She laughs as Cam slams the door in Jonas's face. My

best mate bulges his eyes at me, and I suddenly feel like we're both way older than seventeen.

"Do you know where he lives?"

"Same street as Eddie." Cam walks around to his door. "I know his house."

"Okay. Thanks for your help. Hope you're not too late for work."

Cam glances up at the house with a slightly disappointed frown before shaking his head and muttering, "Don't worry about it."

I watch him do a three-point turn, then raise my hand in farewell before spinning on Stacey to let her have it.

But she beats me to it, slapping my arm and spitting, "Don't you ever humiliate me like that again!"

"He was driving you around drunk! That's not okay, Stace! You shouldn't be dating that asshole."

"He wasn't drunk, he's not an asshole, and you're not my father." She goes to hit me again, but I block her sloppy punch and shunt her shoulder.

She stumbles back with a gasp, but then her face morphs into this lioness ready to pounce. I prepare myself for her to scream or growl and then lunge at me with her claws out, but she's stopped by a loud shout.

"What the hell is going on?" Beck appears around the corner of the house, barking at us.

Stacey pings tight and bulges her eyes at me. "You tell him, I'll never speak to you again."

I give her a withering look, but know I have to keep her on side. I'm so tempted to tell Beck, but if I do that, I'll have zero sway with Stacey, and she strikes me as the kind of girl you don't want to make enemies with.

So, against every instinct in my gut, I point my thumb at her and fudge the truth. "Just a little disagreement."

Stacey spins and no doubt flashes a dazzling, plastic smile at Beck while pointing over her shoulder. "He's an idiot."

Beck gives her a dry glare. "So are you with that look on your face." His forehead wrinkles. "Have you been drinking?"

"No!" she snaps and storms into the house before he can ask her any more questions.

Beck gives me a quizzical frown, but all I can do is shrug.

"Whose car is that?" He points past me.

"Oh, uh..." I spin to look at it, then walk over to retrieve Stacey's bag. I check for bottles in the back while I'm doing it but can't see any evidence of alcohol, just idiotic behavior from two morons. "Stacey's borrowing it off one of her friends from school. I don't know all the details, but they'll collect it, or I'll help her return it, tomorrow."

"Weird," Beck mutters as I hand him Stacey's bag. He takes it, still shaking his head like it's all a big mystery. "I don't know why Richie wanted daughters."

I give him a tight smile and start walking for the barn. "I'm checking on the horses."

"Yeah, all right. I'll radio you when dinner's ready."

I wave my hand in thanks but don't say anything. Guilt is clogging up my throat. I don't usually lie to Beck. Sure, he can be scary and gruff, but it's all an act. He's actually got a heart of putty, and if you tell him the truth, he's not going to get pissed.

But I can't tell him the truth this time, because I can't break Stacey's trust.

Yes, she's in the wrong, but I helped her out today, which means she'll probably let me keep an eye on her at school. If I don't keep her on side, she'll pull even further away, and then no one in the family will be able to protect her.

21

HARPER

Crossing my arms, I head through the darkness, my pulse racing as I make my way toward the blasting music in the garage. The stars are out in all their glory, and I stop for just a second to admire them. You don't get stars like this in the city. They twinkle so much brighter out here, the sky an endless pool of diamonds.

A cool night breeze brushes my skin, and a few stray locks of hair tickle my neck. I gather them up and drape them over my shoulder, forcing my eyes back to the garage and my mission.

I've been putting this off all evening.

Dinner was awkward.

Stacey didn't feel like eating and went to bed early, Bianca was away with the fairies, Willow wouldn't even look at me, and Tane was avoiding my gaze as well. It made mealtime conversation nothing but hard work, and although I can't fix it all right now, I can work on one of those things.

Tane acting all quiet and morose was the worst of the lot, so I'm starting with him.

Oscar told me, just ten minutes ago when I was saying good night to him, that he spied Tane and Stacey arguing this afternoon.

I grilled him for every detail I could, and even though he couldn't hear all of their disagreement, I think I've managed to piece it together. The blonde guy with scarecrow hair must be Jonas, and the fact that Cam drove him home is a sure sign that he was either driving illegally, or he was drunk.

I'm guessing the latter because of the way Oscar said, "They were acting like idiots. It was weird. Cam and Tane looked super pissed."

I checked in with Bianca on my way out of the house. "Was Stacey drinking this afternoon?" The way her cheeks flared red and she looked down at her curling toes told me everything I needed to know.

No wonder Tane was so sullen at dinner.

And I probably didn't help the situation either. I hurt his feelings this afternoon, even though I didn't really say anything wrong.

I don't need him.

At least I don't think I do.

I don't want to, anyway.

I want to do this on my own.

But I also don't want to live in a house where people can't talk to each other, so I'm going to make it right.

Pausing by the narrow side door, I gaze at the brass ball handle, the round bulb now dented after years of use. It's a little rattly and loose when I turn it, and I have to use my shoulder to shunt open the door and my butt to close it again.

Rock music is blaring from the old stereo on the shelf, a heavy, throbbing beat that gives away Tane's mood. The treadmill whirs beneath him as he runs, his arms and legs working in a smooth rhythm that's actually pretty fast.

Man, he's gorgeous.

I stop and let myself stare at him for just a minute.

A fine sheen of sweat makes his skin glisten, and the loose singlet he's wearing has a few damp patches under the arms and spotting his stomach. He must have been running for a while.

Creeping forward, I rest my hip against the pool table, transfixed by his power, the shape of his muscles and the sexy manliness that oozes out of him. He doesn't even have to try. It's like he was born to be great.

Desire stirs strong and fast inside of me and I swallow, unnerved by just how much I want him.

You're not here for that.

Dipping my head, I tuck a lock of hair behind my ear and am about to wave for his attention, but he spots me first.

Slapping the Stop button, he slows to a jog, then a walk before jumping off the treadmill and grabbing the hand towel off the floor.

"Hey," he puffs, wiping his face down as he heads for the mini fridge. Grabbing a bottle of water, he chugs it down.

I watch his throat work, can't take my eyes off the dribbles of water slipping down his chin, beading on his evening stubble.

He swipes the back of his hand over his mouth and screws the lid back on. "What are you doing here?"

"Sorry to interrupt your workout."

"No problem." He turns down the music, then whips off his shirt, throwing it by the door before wiping down his chest with his towel.

Suddenly I can't remember why I came in here. Suddenly it's hard to inhale a full breath. My lips part without my say-so, and I just stare at him until his head pops up and he catches me ogling.

I flush and turn away, gripping the edge of the pool table and trying to say something even vaguely coherent.

"I came in here to…um… to talk to you. About…"

Come on, brain!

"Stacey." I spin with relief, determined not to get thrown by his way-too-hot body again.

It's pretty hard, and I have to blink twice, then lick my lips in order to find my voice again. My insides are trembling, yearning, begging for another taste of him. Crossing my legs at the ankles, I lean back against the table and try for a casual stance.

"What about Stacey?" His forehead wrinkles, and I'm lost in the unrest of his eyes for a minute.

My heart curls with affection, and I give him a sympathetic smile. "Don't feel bad about her ranting. She's more hot air than anything."

"She was drunk." Tane slaps his towel onto the concrete floor and stalks toward me, resting his hands on the edge of the pool table, his stance tense and stormy.

"Yeah." I purse my lips. "I figured that part out. Not sure what to do about that one."

Tane scrapes a hand through his hair, then crosses his arms and leans his hip close to mine. "I should have told Beck."

"I understand why you didn't." I avert my gaze from his biceps; they look even bigger when he crosses his arms like that.

"Thanks," he murmurs. His smile tells me he appreciates the support.

Once again, affection blooms inside of me.

This is dangerous. I should get the hell out of here.

But I can't.

"Hey, um..." I cringe and start sketching invisible lines on the green felt surface. My index finger creates a circle and then a swirl as I try not to look at him. "I'm sorry about this afternoon. In the kitchen. I know you were just trying to be nice and help. I didn't mean to hurt your feelings or anything." He doesn't reply and I can't look at him, so I just keep talking, giving him a little peace offering. "Willow doesn't want to do ballet anymore. It threw me." I raise my hands in the air, surprised by how fast the statement can rile me all over again. "I just... it's her thing. It's her *passion,* and she doesn't want to do it. She won't even attend one class!"

I hold up my finger and look at Tane, my chest heaving and my hand starting to tremble. I quickly drop it, resting it on the soft green felt of the pool table.

He gives me a calm smile that takes the edge off my heat, until he asks, "Do you want me to try talking to her?"

"No," I practically snap.

Why does he think he can convince Willow when I can't?

I don't want to say that to him. He's only trying to help, to be kind. That's all he ever wants to do.

Which is why it's so impossible not to like him.

I should say good night and get going. I can feel myself weakening even as I stand here, but the idea of going back to the house is... well, it's not exactly appealing.

What am I going to do? Crawl into bed and try to read a book when my mind will be plagued with images of Tane, and my body will be sizzling as I picture him standing here shirtless?

But staying here isn't exactly safe for me either. He's standing there all gorgeous and sweet and—

Snatching a ball off the pool table, I grip it in my hand and blurt, "Feel like losing a game of pool to me?"

This could be the worst decision I've made all day, but when I catch the look of glee on his face, I don't care.

22

TANE

"I don't know if you want to take me on." I grin. "I'm pretty good."

"We'll see."

Her smirk is the sexiest thing I've ever seen—the way her eyebrow arches, that challenging sparkle in her eye. The dim garage lighting casts a cool glow over her, and I'm captured by her beauty once again. She has so many shades of prettiness, and I just caught another one tonight.

It's washing away the shit from my afternoon, and with a smile I grab a couple of cues and throw Harper the rack so she can get the balls ready. She sets it up, taking the time to make sure it's lined up exactly where it should be before removing the plastic triangle.

I rub chalk over the end of my cue, wondering how

many games she's played in her life. She seems pretty confident.

"Do you want to break?" I hand her the chalk.

"You go for it."

"No *ladies first* with you, huh?"

"I'll go first next round. In our family the rule was always winner gets to break for the next game."

I chuckle at her cockiness and bend down, lining up the white ball and doing a quick jab. The balls scatter, and I cringe at the striped yellow that ends up right next to the pocket.

"Thanks." She winks at me and sashays around the table to claim stripes, then goes on to take me down with easy precision. I manage to sink three balls before she completely cleans me out.

And so she breaks for the second game.

And the third.

Damn.

If I was playing Cam right now, my competitive side would be riled. But Harper Hughes playing pool is all kinds of luscious. Plus it's nice to see her relax. She has a great laugh. When she sets it free all loose and easy like that, it's music. Her hazel eyes are bright and playful, and if I wasn't crushing on her before, I am so gone now there will be absolutely no recovery.

I have to have this woman.

I have to win her heart if it's the last thing I ever do.

Putting the cues away, I can't help noticing the way Harper's jean shorts hug the curve of her butt as she leans over the table to grab the chalk square.

I walk across to her, drawn by a force I can't counter.

I need to touch her. Even just a brush down her back, a skim of my knuckle across her forearm. I'll take anything.

Standing tall, she throws the chalk cube at me and sticks her tongue out the side of her mouth. "Maybe we can place a little bet next time." She winks, and I can no longer control myself.

Throwing the chalk over my shoulder, I close the gap in two easy strides and place my mouth on hers, winding my arm around her waist and clutching her against me.

She stiffens in surprise, then quickly melts into the kiss, her hand gliding up my bare back. It's all the permission I need. Swiping my tongue across her bottom lip, I claim her mouth the way I've been wanting to since that day she kissed me in the barn.

Heat sears every part of me, traveling through my body at light speed. Curling my fingers into her hair, I rest my thumb behind her ear, cupping the back of her head and deepening the kiss even more.

Her fingers dig into my skin as she matches me beat for beat, our mouths working in perfect unison as our tongues dance and my heart burns brighter than it ever has before.

Stepping toward the table, I take her with me, hefting her up with one arm so her legs can wrap around me. And they do. It's the best feeling in the whole freaking world.

Her knee curves over my hip as she lets out a soft sigh, her fingers skimming my bare shoulder and up my neck as I trail kisses from her mouth to her chin before my greedy tongue wants another taste of her.

She tips her head, owning me with her scent, her taste, her touch. The pads of her fingers are only a light caress, yet they wake every nerve in my body until I'm vibrating with need, want, desire.

It's a powerful, heady effect. I get lost in it, so lost that I don't notice her stiffen. I don't become aware of her retreat until she's pushing on my shoulders and murmuring, "No. No. I can't do this."

I jerk back like she's slapped me, my pulse beating so loud in my chest that it's hard to think straight.

"Please." She pushes me back and jumps down from the table. "We can't. I can't kiss you. I…"

"Why not?" I whisper. "You want to."

She averts her gaze, swallowing and turning her back to

me. Her arms cross, the shield put into place as she locks me out again.

It kills me. I've been thrown out of the oven and straight into the freezer. It's weird how ice can hurt more than fire. It's a different kind of burn.

Gripping the edge of the table, I bite my lips together and try to think of the right thing to say. I could royally screw this up if I don't pick my words carefully.

I want to grab her against me and tell her she's full of shit. That we *can* kiss. That we *should*.

I know she wants me. It's obvious in the way she reacted just then.

But something's holding her back.

Her fingers skim up her arm and she grips her shoulder. I wish she'd turn around and look at me, but I don't think she wants me touching her right now.

So I talk to her back, willing my voice to come out smooth and gentle. "I really like you, City. So much I almost don't know what to do."

She spins, her expression folding for just a second before she sniffs and squeezes her biceps. "I know. I know you do. And I'm sorry I can't offer you anything right now."

Her words are fists to the gut, but I try not to let it show. "Will I ever get a chance?"

"I don't know," she whispers, looking pained as she rubs her forehead with shaking fingers. "I don't know anything at the moment except that I'm here for Willow and Oscar."

"Us making out or being together isn't going to change that."

"You make me—" She shakes her head and looks at the wall. "You don't understand."

I would if she'd let me, but I can sense she's not going to do that.

"You want me, City. You're fighting it right now, and it'd be a whole lot easier if you just let go. Let me in."

Her chin bunches, but her headshake is firm. "I can't."

With a thick swallow, I quietly relent, nodding a couple of times before giving her space to leave.

When she reaches the door, I call out on impulse, "We're good for each other. I know you don't want to see that right now, but it's true. So I'm not going to stop trying."

I hold my breath while I wait for her response.

I expect the door to rattle and hit the wall as she flings it open to escape me.

Instead I hear a very soft "Okay."

And it gives me hope.

23

HARPER

The house is quiet except for Mr. Grandpa Clock, my constant companion during the school days. He ticks away, keeping me on track. And although it used to irritate me, it's becoming a comfort. The silence can be almost daunting when I first get home from dropping Oscar at school. After the chaos of the morning, it's a striking contrast.

Sometimes I fill it with music, but not this morning. I don't know why.

Putting the final pot away, I dry my hands on the tea towel, then use it to wipe down the bench and sink until the surface is sparkling. I then head to the laundry to pull the load of towels into the basket.

It's a nice enough day—a little cloud cover, with patches of sun and a decent breeze—so I'll hang them on the line and then get the second load in. Trying to keep on top of washing for seven people is full-on. I don't know how Mum did it for a household of five.

Dumping the wet towels into the basket, I try to dodge thoughts of Tane. He's been plaguing my dreams since our Friday night pool game. It's now Tuesday, and it hasn't lessened one little bit. Every time I see him, my body crackles with yearning, but I can't give in right now.

Tane will be a distraction I can't afford. I'll end up ignoring my siblings because all I'll want to do is make out with him. I remember what it was like when Dylan and I first got together. We were always trying to steal kisses and be together. It'd be even worse with Tane. My attraction for him is stronger than anything I've ever experienced.

But it's more than that. It's not just the physical desire, it's the fact that he's so damn kind and nice and sweet. Everything about him draws me in, and for some reason, that makes me feel weak and fluffy. And if I'm weak and fluffy, I might just fall apart. I need to be steel right now. I need to hold myself together in order to run this home and do the best job I can for my parents.

That's what they'd want from me, and I won't let them down.

A gentle wind catches my hair as I step out the door. The sun is a warm kiss on my face, and I can't help a satisfied little sigh as I walk to the clothesline.

A satisfied sigh?

What is wrong with me?

I frown, wondering if I'm starting to enjoy this country life, the song of the chirping birds and the squawk of the chickens.

"No, that can't be right." I shake my head.

I'm a city girl. I miss the city. I know that because I spoke to Zoey and Alaina this weekend. They'd been out shopping and then to the movies while I was helping out around the farm and then shoveling horse crap in the stables. It wasn't fun, although the horse ride in the afternoon was. I actually got Jax up to a short canter, which was thrilling.

"But not as thrilling as a new pair of heels." I flick out the towel and try to conjure up some of that envy I felt when Zoey was showing off her silver stilettos to me, but my brain keeps getting interrupted by Tane and the grin on his face when I pulled Jax to a stop beside him.

"Good job, City. Abby would be proud." He winked and my heart melted in my chest.

He always knows the right thing to say to me.

Maybe I shouldn't have said "okay" when he told me he wasn't going to stop trying to win me over. Maybe then he'd stop being so nice and I could focus on my job here—my mission to do what's right for Ozzy and Will.

Snatching out another towel, I flick it so hard it makes a sharp snapping sound and then hang it on the line. I end up scowling as I hang the rest of the laundry, trying to ignore the mix of emotions raging inside of me. Guilt for stringing Tane along wrestles with an overwhelming desire to swoon at his sweet words and melt against him.

"You can't melt!" I growl. "Harper, there will be no melting!"

Plucking the basket off the ground, I rest it against my hip and head for the back steps. But then I notice a roaming chicken.

"What are you doing?" I chase after it, but she just picks up her pace and scuttles away from me, flapping her wings and freaking me out when I get too close.

There's no way I'm picking that thing up, but what's it doing out of its penned-in yard?

I wander back to the chicken coop and see the problem immediately. Some of the wiring that forms a side of the fence has broken loose of the post, and it's a big enough gap for a brave chicken to fit through.

I shoot a scowl over my shoulder. "Dammit, why'd you have to be brave?"

The chicken ignores me, strutting around under the clothesline and making me worry that it'll take off and we'll never see her again.

The breadth of my chicken knowledge is pretty much confined to what to feed them and then anything I gleaned from the movie *Chicken Run,* which is hardly much to go on.

Dropping the laundry basket, I take a closer look at the fence and figure I better do something to fix it before more chickens escape.

I have no idea where Beck is on the farm right now, but surely I can mend this. Even if it's just a temporary job.

The idea of doing something non-house related is actually kind of fun, so I head to the tool shed and clumsily gather together the materials I think I might need. Hopefully Beck won't mind me taking the initiative. Dad always loved it when I did, so I'm going to go with that.

Laying the equipment down next to the fence, I study the problem and try to come up with a solution that will at least last until Beck can come check on it.

I glance at my watch. I have to go and get Ozzy from school in about forty minutes, and Beck usually heads up to the house before milking, so I'll figure out something that can hold for an hour or so.

"Right." I crouch down and get to work, pulling at the broken wiring and trying to be careful with the razor-sharp edges.

I should probably have some work gloves on, but I

couldn't immediately see them in the shed, and I want to get this done. Wrapping my hands carefully around the wire, I give it a tug and it slowly starts to loosen. I figure if I pull the whole thing free, I'll have a better chance of lining it up and securing it to the post. Although, the post is looking kind of old and rotten, with rusty nails sticking out of it. Replacing it can be a job for the weekend.

The weekend. It's my birthday on Monday. I don't want to think about the fact that it'll be my first one without Mum and Dad around. I wonder if I should head into Hamilton on Sunday and treat myself to a little birthday gift. Or a whole lot of them. It might make me feel better to go on a shopping spree. Maybe it'll take the edge off the pain. I bet The Base shopping mall has something good. Although Willow and Oscar might be secretly planning a surprise, and I don't want to spoil anything for them.

I get caught up thinking about what I want and don't notice the brown, speckled chicken until it's trotting toward me.

"Don't even think about it," I mutter. "I'm not letting you escape too."

Suddenly it rushes at me, flapping its wings like it wants a challenge and bawking loudly.

I scream and jump away but lose my footing and end

up lurching forward, scraping my arm down the post as I try to catch myself and not get cut by the wiring.

"OW!" I shout, landing sideways on the fencing and quickly snatching my arm against my chest. I don't know what I've done, but it bloody hurts.

Wrestling into a sitting position, I ignore the ache of landing on the fence wire and inspect my outer forearm. Blood is oozing from beneath my fingers, and I'm almost afraid to look. Pain pulses from my elbow to my wrist as I carefully lift my hand and spot the ragged gash tearing down my arm. The fine hairs are matted and coated with sticky red liquid.

"How the hell...?" My voice trails off when I spot the thick rusty nail sticking out of the fence post. A droplet of my blood is about to drip off the end of its point.

Oh. That's how.

"Right." My teeth start to chatter as I force my body up and slap a hand back over my oozing wound.

Stumbling up the back steps, I wrestle with the door handle, smearing blood all over it and feeling slightly light-headed as I fall against the laundry tub.

It freaking hurts, but I rinse the wound under cold water and snatch out a clean rag from the cupboard. Clamping it over the wound, it soon starts turning red and I cringe, lifting the rag to inspect the gash again.

I doubt Band-Aids are going to be enough.

This thing needs stitches.

Dammit.

Closing my eyes, I pull in a breath, trying not to let the pain get the better of me.

"Just stay calm," I grit out, shuffling through the laundry and grabbing the radio off the dining room table. "Hey, Beck, you there?"

"Yeah, what's up?" He sounds harried and stressed.

"Are you okay?"

"Just dealing with a cow in a ditch. Little bugger rolled in and I've just found her. Need to get her out as quick as I can." He huffs before tersely asking, "You right? You need something?"

I shake my head, not wanting to burden him with a little cut. He's got enough on his plate right now. "It's nothing. Don't worry about it. I just have to...pop out for a little while."

"Okay. See ya later."

"B-bye." I set the radio back down and check the wound again. The rag I'm using to stem the blood is going to need replacing already.

"Crap." I head back to the laundry and dump the rag in the sink before collecting a clean one, then grabbing the car keys out of the bowl. I manage to smear blood on the keychain and my phone when I snatch it off the bench, but I can't care about that right now.

Stumbling out the front door, I ask Siri to find me the closest Accident and Emergency center and just hope it won't hurt too much to drive there.

24

TANE

I don't have any responsibilities after school on Tuesdays this term. Preseason rugby training doesn't start for a few more weeks yet, so I take advantage and head out to the car as fast as I can. Hopefully the girls won't keep me waiting too long.

I'm keen to get home. The teachers are already piling on the pressure, and as much as I want to ignore school-work and just play rugby and work the farm, I can't do it. Beck made me promise that I'd get good grades so I had options after school. I'm pretty sure he's going to convince me to only work the farm part-time next year so I can still fit in some university study. I hate the idea, but he's probably right. Having a degree or diploma in something isn't a bad idea.

It's the homework that puts me off more than anything, but maybe if I'm studying something about farming, which I'm interested in, it won't be so painful.

"Homework," I mutter, feeling the weight of the books in my bag and wondering how fast I can get through it. I want to get it done so I can hang out with Harper after dinner. Maybe I can convince her to play another game of pool.

She probably won't want to, but it's worth a shot.

I grin. I know I need to take it slow. She's obviously not ready, but she wants me. She said *okay,* and that feels so freaking good.

"See ya, Tane!"

I glance up and wave goodbye to Manu, Tameka and Logan, then spot Stacey walking out beside Willow. Stacey's chirping away while Willow bobs her head, obviously not that interested but too polite to really let on.

Harper's like that too. Politeness must have been a big deal in their house growing up. It's not a bad thing, but I can't help wondering if they sometimes use it as a shield. Smile, talk nice, and that way people won't see what's really going on beneath the surface.

I'd love to get beneath Harper's surface.

I'm not thinking about the physical one, although I'm sure that would be lush, but the emotional one. She's got things locked up pretty tight, and I know she'd feel better if she'd just talk about it. Her independent stubborn streak is going to be her undoing. I can't let it go that far. I just need to patiently keep working on her until she can see that letting me in is going to make her life better. I'm there to help her. I want to be the guy she calls when she needs something.

The girls reach the car and jump in, Willow taking the front seat and rolling her eyes at me while Stacey finishes her story about the evils of statistics and how horrible Mr. Cho is.

He's not that bad. I had him in Year 11 and yeah, he's boring as, but that doesn't make him mean.

"Where is Bianca?" Stacey tips her head back as if we've been waiting a lifetime when she only hopped in the car thirty seconds ago.

"There she is." I point out my window as Bianca shuffles out of school by herself. Her red hair is falling loose from its braid, and a few tendrils dance around her face as the wind has a play.

She tucks her long fringe back and gives the person walking past her a kind smile.

I see what Cam's saying about her aura. She does kind of ooze this sweet goodness.

Willow's phone dings in her hand. I glance at her, about to hassle her for not being able to last a minute past the bell before pulling out her device.

But she's got this confused frown on her face, so instead I say, "What's up?"

"We have to go and get Oscar from school."

"Why?" I start the engine as Bianca slips into the car.

I wonder why Harper can't do it today. I hope everything's okay.

"Does the text say anything else?" I ask when Willow gives me no more than a shrug to my first question.

"Hang on."

Her thumbs fly over the screen while Bianca quietly asks, "What's happening?"

"We have to pick up Oz from his school on the way home."

"Oh, okay. But he gets out earlier than us, right? So he's just sitting there waiting?"

"Yeah," I mutter, pulling out of my parking space and gunning it to the exit.

Something's really off. Oscar's only fifteen minutes away, but if he's already been waiting twenty, it'll feel like a freaking lifetime before we arrive.

Willow's phone starts to ring as I pull onto North Ridge Road. She looks loath to answer it, and I nearly snap, "*Just give it to me*," because I know it'll be Harper with an explanation.

After a little sigh, Willow slides her thumb across the

screen. "Hey, Harp. I got your message, we'll go get Ozzy now. Why can't you do it?"

I wish I could hear the conversation, but all I can do is drive and hope she'll tell me when she's done. I keep glancing at her, then nearly lose all concentration when her eyes bulge and she gasps, "Are you okay?"

"What happened?" I snap, my stomach knotting.

Willow raises her hand to shut me up. "Do you want us to come?" Willow nods. "It's okay. We'll get Ozzy. Don't worry about it. You just look after you... Okay. No, he'll understand."

I don't think I've ever heard Willow talk this much. It's freaking me out. As soon as she hangs up, I ask again, "What happened?"

"Harper cut her arm, and she's at Tui Medical waiting to get stitches."

I nearly slam on the brakes and do a U-turn, wanting to get to her as fast as I can, but dammit, Oscar is waiting for us.

Gripping the wheel, I clench my jaw and try to calmly ask, "Is Beck with her?"

"I don't think so."

"She went on her own?" I'm stating the obvious right now, but I don't give a shit.

Harper needs stitches, which means she's obviously in

pain, and she's currently sitting in some medical waiting room all by herself.

I'm not okay with that.

With a low growl, I press the accelerator and break the speed limit to get to Oscar. Harper had been nice enough to get a message to his teacher, so he's not too stressed waiting for us. We find him sitting on a post by the front entrance, messing around on his phone.

"Why did Harper bail?" He throws his bag into the back, accidentally clipping Stacey on the head.

"Hey!" She rubs the spot and scowls at him.

He snickers, then mumbles an apology before she can deck him one, but it still doesn't stop a bickering match from starting.

I want to bark at them to shut up and sit still. I don't know why I'm suddenly so grumpy. It's probably this worry eating at my guts.

Tearing down our driveway, I'm about to order everyone out of the car so I can take off for the medical center, but then the thought hits me that if she drove herself there, she'll have the car, and there's no way I'm letting her drive home by herself.

Running into the house, I dump my bag by the stairs and then go to snatch the radio off the kitchen table. That's when I spot the blood. It's smeared on the black plastic, and it makes my heart jump right into my throat.

I'm about to press the button and go apeshit on Beck for not taking Harper to Accident and Emergency when the phone in my bag starts ringing.

"Cam. Where are you, mate?"

"I'm heading to your place. I forgot to—"

"Excellent. I need a ride. I'll meet you at the end of the driveway."

I hang up before he can ask why and race out the front door.

25

HARPER

I've been waiting for what feels like forever.

When I first arrived, I walked up to the counter, scanning the crowded waiting room and knowing the inevitable before I even asked.

"Will the wait be long?"

"It's about ninety minutes to two hours at the moment." The receptionist smiled at me. "Is this accident or medical?"

"Accident," I murmured.

"Have you ever been to Tui Medical before?"

"No, I'm new to the area."

"Okay." Her fingers tapped on her keyboard while she softly asked for my details. And then she gave me two forms to fill out. Trying to write with my aching arm was draining, and by the time I shuffled back to the counter with my paperwork, I felt like keeling over.

My head is still spinning a little. I rest my cheek against my hand, feeling weak and useless. The fluorescent lights are merciless as they highlight people's tired, sick expressions. Some people murmur quietly to each other, and another guy is awkwardly stretched out in his chair, one leg sticking out far enough to trip people, but he's too wiped out to care. Two little girls play with half-dressed Barbie dolls in the children's area, wiping snot from under their noses and coughing all over the toys, which are probably hand-me-downs from some staff member's family supply. One of the dolls is missing a limb while the other has had a gnarly haircut.

A little boy sniffles beside me. I glance at him, and he blinks his big glassy eyes before turning his face into his mother's chest. She brushes the blond tendrils off his forehead and kisses him.

I miss Mum.

She was always the one to deal with us when we were sick. I miss the feel of her hand brushing the hair off my face. When I was sick, she'd take the day off work so we could watch movies together. She'd make me toast and bring me lemon and honey tea to soothe my throat. Then she'd sit on the couch with me, and I'd rest my head on her knee. And she'd stroke my hair.

The ache in my chest blooms as my breaths start to quicken.

Tears scorch my insides when my chest constricts. Flashes of light and pain blur my vision.

Hating that sizzling panic that seems to build inside me without warning, I do my best to counter it by squeezing my wounded arm.

It works. Sort of. Pain stabs me, harsh enough to make me squirm in my seat. But it's working. I'm breathing again, and I've got something else to focus on.

With a soft hiss, I let go of my arm, wondering if the medication the nurse gave me has had any affect at all. She called me through about fifteen minutes after I arrived to check the wound and grab some more details, like my height, weight and medical history. She took my blood pressure and told me it was a little on the low side.

"I've always been like that," I murmured, and she noted it down.

Her gloved hands gently poked at the gash on my arm. "Hmm. Yes, that'll need stitching. And because of the rusty nail, you'll probably need a tetanus shot as well. How's the pain?"

"It's pretty sore."

"Okay. I'll give you some paracetamol to take the edge

off. The bleeding is under control, so I'll just wrap a temporary bandage over it while you're waiting."

And wait I have.

I check my watch, relieved that Willow got my message. I should probably text again to check in, but I'm too exhausted to even pull the phone out of my pocket.

"Harper," an older woman with a black-and-gray stubby ponytail and pale brown skin calls into the waiting room, checking her clipboard again before saying my name for a second time.

"Here." I raise my hand and shoot out of my chair. It's obvious she's harried, and I don't want to keep her waiting.

As soon as I'm on my feet, I start to sway, the world spinning in a blur as black splotches dance in front of me.

Oh crap, I'm going to keel over right on the waiting room floor.

I hold out my hands to steady myself and stagger right, only to be caught around the waist by a steady hand.

"I'm here," a voice murmurs, pulling me against him.

Relief floods me, the dots dissipating as I look over at Tane's worried face.

His expression is kind of endearing, like he's ready to

swoop me into his arms and carry me to an examination room.

In front of all these people? That would be so humiliating.

So I force a smile and point toward the doctor. "I just stood up too fast."

"Hmm," he grunts and holds me against his side while we shuffle after the doctor.

She leads us into Room 2 and I take a seat on the chair beside the doctor's desk. Tane plunks down in the chair adjacent to me and I glance at him, wondering why he's here.

I mean, I know *why* he's here. I just wonder why he felt he needed to be.

"Sorry for the wait today. We had a doctor call in sick, and the other one had to leave early for a family emergency, so it's just me."

She gives me a polite smile and I try to return it, although my lips only twitch at the corners.

"So, you have a gash on your arm?" The doctor checks her clipboard. She has a mild Indian accent, but she's obviously been living in New Zealand long enough to pick up a few kiwi nuances as well. "How'd this happen?"

"Uh, I was trying to fix a fence."

Tane shuffles in his seat beside me, his eyes darting from me to the doctor and back again.

"For chickens," I clarify for his sake, but it doesn't ease the expression on his face. I can't tell if he's still worried or just plain angry now. Why is he frowning like that?

"And you cut yourself on what?"

"Oh, um, one of the chickens gave me a fright, and I lost my balance and fell. Then I noticed my arm was bleeding, and there was blood on one of the nails sticking out of the post. It's a pretty old fence. The nail was rusty."

"Right." The doctor nods and types on her computer before she pulls on some gloves and gently lifts the bandage.

Her face remains bland and unreadable while she inspects the wound, ignoring my hisses and clenched fist.

"Okay, I'll go and get a suture kit. You might be more comfortable on the bed." She points and leaves the room.

"I'll help you." Tane jumps up and treats me like an old woman, gently helping me out of the chair and guiding me over to the bed.

He doesn't have to, but he picks me up anyway and sets me on the bed like I'm a child. I should be annoyed by it, but my legs start to swing back and forth in spite of myself.

He crosses his arms and leans against the thin, plastic-covered mattress.

He's still in his school uniform. I've only just noticed. He must have dumped everyone home, then rushed straight out the door again.

That's kind of sweet, although a little unnecessary. It's only stitches.

"Was Ozzy okay when you picked him up?"

"Yeah. He was fine. Wanted to know why you weren't there, but then he ended up accidentally whacking Stacey in the head with his school bag. Her indignation was enough to distract him."

My lips twitch as I picture the bickering match that no doubt filled the drive home.

"And Willow?"

"Yeah, she was fine. Worried about you, of course, but she'll look after Oz."

"I hope they're okay. I feel bad that I'm not there to make them afternoon tea. I just rushed out of the house, and there's probably blood in the laundry and aw, crap." I squeeze my eyes shut and hope like hell they both just went up to their rooms. It'd be so disconcerting to walk into what no doubt looks like a crime scene. "I left the house in such a mess."

Tane scoffs. "No one expects you to tidy up after your-self when you're bleeding and in pain."

"I just don't want to freak anybody out."

Tane's eyebrows dip with annoyance again and he's about to say something when the door pops back open.

"Okay." The doctor wheels in a trolley loaded with wrapped and sterilized weapons.

Tools.

Things that are going to both hurt and heal me.

I avert my gaze from the two syringes resting beside the wrapped needle that's curved—a lethal hook.

With a thick swallow, I glance at Tane. His anger, or whatever that was, has slipped behind a tender smile, and I'm suddenly grateful that he's here.

When he reaches out his hand, I take it without think-ing. His big thumb rubs gentle circles over my knuckles as the doctor gets to work.

It's impossible not to whimper just a little when she injects the area around the wound.

"This will numb the area," the doctor tells me while preparing the other syringe. "And this is the tetanus shot to make sure you don't get any infections."

Lifting my shirtsleeve, she wipes my upper arm with an alcohol swab, then injects me. It freaking hurts as she gently pushes the liquid medicine into my bloodstream. I feel kind of ridiculous wincing this way, but bloody hell!

She pulls the needle out and pops a little white bandage over the spot before turning her attention back to my wound.

"Can you feel that?" She presses around the gash.

"Barely. Just a little pressure."

"Okay. Good." She smiles at me, then rests my arm on a sterilized pad before unwrapping the needle and thread.

Closing my eyes, I turn my head away, swallowing convulsively.

"Look at me," Tane whispers, and I open my eyes, gazing straight into a set of brown orbs that welcome me home.

He smiles without moving his mouth, then softly tells me a little about his day. I can't help a grin at the way he describes Manu's antics at lunchtime.

"The guy can't cartwheel to save his life, but he was determined to be better than Kim. We were all in hysterics watching him. He's such a clown. I'm surprised he didn't break his arm."

It's sweet that he's trying to distract me, but his story only makes me miss school. I've spent the last two weeks at home alone, cleaning and acting like a domestic goddess while he's been hanging out with his mates.

I get to have lunch with Beck—sometimes—and then he'll take an hour off to read a book or do admin work at his computer before disappearing onto the farm again.

"Thanks for lunch, Harper."

"That's okay."

That was pretty much our entire conversation today.

Self-pity scrapes through me, a longing for my friends, my old life.

Stupid bloody farm with its fresh air and crazy chickens. I don't care that their eggs are awesome. I shouldn't be here. I should be shopping with my besties in Wellington!

Tane's fingers give me a little squeeze and I'm brought back to him, to the feel of my hand wrapped inside of his. I gaze down at our connection, my insides softening as tears start to bubble up my throat. How good would it feel to fist his shirt and pull him close so I could rest my head against his chest and just cry? Cry until there was nothing left of me.

You can't do that! my brain snaps at me, a sharp, cold slap against my senses.

I don't have the luxury of tears or falling apart. I have to get home and put on a bright smile for my siblings, downplay this whole thing so they won't worry.

"All right, you're done." The doctor secures a bandage over my wound. "You need to keep this dry for a few days." Removing her gloves, she washes her hands, then gives me a piece of paper. "Here are all the home care instructions, and you'll need to come back in ten days to get the stitches removed."

"O-okay." I nod as Tane takes the paper.

"I've also given you a prescription for paracetamol and Nurofen. You can alternate them every four hours to manage the pain, and try to go easy on that arm for a few days. You don't want to pull any of the stitches."

I bob my head, hating the idea of having to take it easy, but it's not like I can stand there disagreeing with the doctor. The way I'm feeling right now, doing nothing is kind of appealing. I'm no doubt as pasty and pale on the outside as I feel on the inside.

"Thank you." Tane smiles at the doctor while helping me off the bed.

The doctor opens the door for us. "You take care."

I let Tane help me out of the medical center after we collect my prescription from the pharmacy. We stop just outside the sliding doors.

"Where'd you park?" He holds out his hand for the keys.

"Um…" I blink and try to remember, then point in the direction of the pub. "Over there."

"Let's go. I'll drive you home."

"What about the other car? How'd you get here?"

"I got Cam to drop me off."

"You didn't need to do that." I check the road for traffic before crossing toward the pub. "I'll be fine."

"You're not fine!" Tane suddenly explodes.

I whip my head to look at him, surprise making my eyes bulge.

The anger on his face is back, and I'm struggling to understand it. What the hell did I do wrong?

He huffs and stops by the car. "You have stitches in your arm. Why were you even trying to fix that fence?"

"Because the chickens were getting out."

"I could have done that for you when I got home. Or you could have called Beck."

"Beck was dealing with a cow."

"You should have called him when you hurt yourself."

"I did! And he was dealing with a cow in a ditch or something. He said he had to work fast!" I yell loud enough for the people passing us to stop and give me a curious look.

With a sigh, I cradle my aching arm against my stomach.

"Did you tell him you'd hurt yourself?" Tane's voice softens, but his gaze doesn't let up and I'm forced to look to the ground, answering him with nothing more than a thick swallow.

He tuts and holds out his hand for the keys. "You should have called *me*."

"You were at school."

"Which I would have left in a heartbeat if it meant helping you."

I don't know how to respond to that. To that pained look on his face right now.

Digging into my pocket, I pull out my keys and slap them into his hand.

I don't want this feeling inside of me. I don't even know what it is. Guilt? Yearning?

Just stick with anger. It's easier.

So I do.

"You're not ditching school to fix a fence," I grumble, shoving past him to get to the passenger door.

"I'm not talking about the fence anymore and you

know it." He follows me, catching the door when I swing it open and bending down to talk to me. "It's not a bad thing to ask for help. It's not a sign of weakness to need someone!"

He shuts my door and stalks around the car, getting into the driver's seat and adjusting it to accommodate his longer legs and arms. He goes to grab the wheel and jerks to a stop when he notices my dried bloody fingerprints all over it.

With a heated stare that says everything it needs to, he gives me a pointed look and starts the engine, grabbing a couple of tissues to try wiping away the worst of the blood.

Irritated, I turn to look out the window and bite my lips together.

I wish I was driving myself home. I wish I could tell him to piss off, but the truth is, I'm relieved he's sitting behind the wheel. The twenty-five-minute drive to get here was so freaking painful, and I doubt I have the energy to safely make it home.

Dammit!

I don't want to need him.

I just want Mum! Or Dad! Or Wellington… or anything that will take away this hollow, raw feeling in my chest.

Leaning my head back against the seat, I close my burning eyes and try to ward off another round of those quick breaths. I hate the way they punch out of me and make my heart race.

I just want calm.

I want peace.

I want oblivion.

26

TANE

It's nearly dark, but I keep working anyway. I'm determined to get this bloody fence fixed before the morning. The light from the kitchen and laundry are casting enough of a glow that I can keep going until the sun really is a memory.

The heat from the day has basically disappeared, and I can sense a dampness starting to brew. Rain could be coming. It's not a bad thing. The tanks need a top-up.

I wipe the back of my hand over my forehead and adjust the backward cap that's soaking up the sweat from my hair.

By the time we got home, it was dinnertime and everyone was starving, but Harper was white as a ghost. I refused to let her do anything, and Beck backed me up until she was propped on the couch with her arm on a pillow, watching (or not watching) TV. Willow sat with her, not saying anything—of course—but holding her sister's hand, so at least that was something.

Beck did a fish and chips run and we ate straight off the paper, crowding around the table and getting our fingers greasy with oil and tomato sauce.

Harper nibbled at her food and eventually caved to pressure halfway through her piece of fish.

"Just go to bed, Harp. Sleep it off. You'll feel better in the morning." Beck sent her upstairs.

She shuffled away from the table, and I swear she would have keeled over if the wall hadn't been there to catch her. It took everything in me not to bolt from my chair and help her up to her room, but she'd already barked at me once when I'd tried to help her out of the car. She didn't say a word to me on the drive home. It was the longest frickin' twenty-five minutes of my life.

She was pissed that I told her off.

But she needed to hear it!

I hate the idea of her driving all the way into Rototuna with blood running down her arm. It must have hurt like hell. And the idea of her in pain kills me a little bit. I would have been there for her in a shot. If only she'd let me.

With a grunt, I start hammering in the new pins. I replaced the post. Thankfully, Beck had some precut ones already stored away, so I nicked one of those and got to work. It's been good to burn off some steam, and by the time Beck saunters out to check on me, I'm actually feeling better, although my simmering anger isn't far from the surface.

I can feel my stomach knotting as he plants his feet near mine.

"You right, mate? You seem kind of edgy."

I give him a sideways glance before wiping the sweat from under my nose and picking up another pin.

"She shouldn't have been fixing this on her own."

"Yeah. Don't think she really knew what she was doing." Beck grinned. "Scared by a chicken. It's a little funny."

"It's not funny," I snap. "She really hurt herself!"

"Yeah, I know." His eyebrows pucker as he tries to read me.

I turn away before he sees something I don't want him to.

"We can finish this up in the morning, mate. The chooks are all tucked in for the night."

"I want to get it done," I bark.

Beck crosses his arms and gives me one of his long

assessing looks that makes me feel like he's stripping off my skin.

"What?"

"Why so grumpy?"

"Because she shouldn't have had to deal with this on her own." The truth spurts out of me, and I check myself to make sure I don't say anything that will give me away.

I don't want Beck reading into it. He'll probably jump to all the right conclusions, and it's just awkward. I want to be with Harper, there's no denying that. But it's not like I want Beck to know about it. He thinks of me as a son, and even though she's not his niece, she kind of is, which means I'm essentially falling for my cousin. It's weird.

"Look, mate, I would have been there if she'd told me. She's way more important than a cow. I could have left Linc to deal with that. When I got home and saw all the blood in the laundry, I didn't know what the hell had been going on. I called her straight away, and she gave me a quick rundown. She seemed okay."

"She nearly keeled over on the emergency room floor." I scowl at him. "She was *not* okay."

"Yeah, all right, all right." Beck holds up his hands, his eyes narrowing at the corners.

I turn my back to him and hammer in another pin.

"She's just so freaking stubborn," I mutter. "She doesn't think she needs anybody."

I pound in another two pins, wondering why my heart seems so sold on this girl when she drives me crazy. It'd be so much easier to pine for one of the sweet girls at school who'd give me no trouble.

And no challenge.

And no excitement.

Beck clears his throat, crouching down to check out my work.

"It's looking good." He points at it.

I grunt in thanks and pull across the last of the wire fencing so it sits tight against the pole. Beck holds it in place for me.

"You know her dad was just the same."

"Huh?"

"Harper's dad. He was annoyingly independent." Beck starts to chuckle. "I remember this one game. It was club rugby, so we must have only been about ten or eleven. Lance hit the ground pretty hard. It was a brutal tackle, and I thought he'd be off for sure, but he staggered back to his feet and assured everyone he was fine. He played the rest of the game, and no one even knew he had a broken arm until he walked off the field and fainted, right there at his mum's feet." Beck's chuckle turns into a laugh, and I can't help a short, sharp snicker.

"His mum gave him an earful for that one. Poor kid. Never could ask for help. Wanted to be in charge or do it on his own. I mean, he was always nice about it. Sometimes bossy, I guess. But mostly, he was just... independent."

"Bloody Hughes trait, I guess."

"Too right." Beck steps back after I've hammered in the last pin and checks how secure it is. "You've done a good job, mate."

Is it weird that no matter how many times I hear those words, they always make me feel good?

Even tonight, when my insides are storming, my lips still curl up at the corners.

Slapping his hand over my shoulder, he gives it a little squeeze. "You know, one of your best—and maybe most painful—traits is that you care too much. You want to be there to fix it all for everybody, and some-times you just can't. Today, you arrived for the after-math, and I get it... you'd rather save the day than clean up the mess. But she's going to be okay, mate. It's just a few stitches. They'll heal up quick."

"If she takes it easy," I grumble.

Beck snickers and shakes his head. "We'll have to make

her. Between the two of us, we should be able to get her bum on that couch more than she wants it to be."

I grin at him, already anticipating Harper's fight against it. She's going to make it hard on me, but I'm strong enough to deal with her stubborn streak. I just wish I didn't have to.

"Hey." Beck points at me, his expression flashing with pain before landing on a sad smile. "It's been less than two months since the funerals. We're doing okay."

I don't say anything as he walks back into the house. The blood's been cleaned off the back door handle, but I still notice spots of it on the ground around the coop.

I scuff my gumboot over the dirt, trying to clean it up and wondering if Beck's actually right.

Are we doing okay?

Between Harper's bullheadedness and Stacey's recklessness, I'm not sure we are.

27

BIANCA

I stand by the kitchen window and listen to Tane and Beck. I'm holding a hot chocolate from the machine Harper brought up from Wellington. She loves that thing. It makes a perfect latte (according to her) and for me, it makes the perfect hot chocolate with the frothy milk and everything. I wrap my fingers around the mug and listen to Beck's footsteps in the laundry.

I should probably head upstairs before he sees me. I don't really want him knowing that I was eavesdropping on their conversation. Creeping across the wooden floors, I make my way upstairs, listening for noises in the house. I kind of love the old creak and murmur of this place, and I definitely love the sounds of nature as opposed to traffic.

Apartment living in a city is so far removed from this.

The hum of traffic, the whiff of smog in the air, the

constant bustle of people. Everything was so closed in and claustrophobic.

Out here the noises are wide and far apart. Everything's so vast and open. I could stretch my arms wide and spin a dozen circles without hitting anything.

I understand why Dad loved it so much. It would have been a great place to grow up. Hearing Beck talk about that rugby game where Lance broke his arm conjured up pictures in my mind. They're probably a blend of my imagination and the photos Dad showed me of him as a kid—that shock of red hair, the cheesy smile, the dirt on his shirt.

I can remember one really clearly with the three of them standing in a row after a muddy rugby game. They were brown from head to toe, their arms around each other's shoulders and these stunning white smiles that seemed to glow that much brighter because of the mud.

Walking into my room with a grin, I set my hot chocolate down.

"What are you smiling about?" Stacey glances up from her phone.

"Oh, I was just..." I plunk onto my bed and glance at her. "I was thinking about Dad."

"Oh." She stiffens and looks back down at her phone. "Hey, do you know Jonas is over at Leon's and they're doing a *Matrix* marathon? He keeps texting me with updates."

I watch my sister, disappointment curling inside of me.

I don't want to talk about Jonas. I want to talk about Dad!

"It's hard being here and not imagining Dad around the place. I can see him as a little kid, darting into the kitchen and stealing a cookie from the tin. You know what I mean? I don't know if Beck's mum had a cookie tin or not, but I can imagine it."

"They've just started the second movie. I think he's staying the night at Leon's. You know, to get away from his psycho dad. He was so pissed over Jonas leaving his mum's car here. Apparently, he tried to ground him for a week, but it's all BS. There's no way Jonas is going to hang out at home this week. His dad is such a loser."

My eyebrows dip into a sharp frown and I cross my arms, irritation blooming inside of me. I don't want to fight with my sister, but I hate it when she does this. She's not ignoring me, per se. I know she can hear every word out of my mouth. She just does that thing where she refuses to respond to it. She'll go all freaking night until I'm driven to the point of complete insanity.

"So, do you know what I heard today?" Her blue eyes sparkle as she glances across the room at me.

I want to tell her that I don't give a shit, but she starts talking before I can even open my mouth.

"Apparently Luka used to hang out with Kim and Tameka and those netball girls. They were really tight, but then she started falling for Leon and they completely shut her out."

"Really?" I hate that I'm even responding to this, but that doesn't feel right to me. I watch Tameka and Kim and Melina. They seem like really kind, friendly people. "I can't imagine them doing that. They seem nice."

"They're not. They're total bitches. Luka was completely shunned when she started dating Leon. They're narrow-minded and clique-y. That's what Jonas and Dee told me."

I want to roll my eyes and tell her that's hardly solid proof, but she'll just get pissy with me. Still, I'm not sure I believe it. Cam and Tane's group don't strike me as the clique-y kind. Cam was nice to me my first day, and he always smiles at me when we pass each other at school. Melina asked me to join them for lunch the other day. I chickened out and said I was busy, which in retrospect, I wish I hadn't, because I spent lunch with Stacey's friends instead and that was so much worse.

The thing I don't get is that Melina and those girls are exactly the kind Stacey *used* to hang out with—sporty, fun, charismatic. But now she's spending her time with a bunch of deadbeats. I bet Luka wasn't shunned at all.

I bet she turned her back on all the good people in her life just to please Leon.

"I don't like Leon," I murmur.

"Yeah, he can be a dick, but he's Jonas's best friend, so…" Stacey shrugs. "I put up with him."

Stacey grins at her phone, then holds it out in front of her, blowing a kiss at the camera and snapping a few pics—the last one is of her winking with an open mouth and the tip of her tongue touching her top lip. It's all sexy sweet, and it makes my upper like curl.

She fires them off to Jonas with a little giggle, and I shake my head.

"Why do you like him so much?"

"He's a good kisser."

"Come on." I spin on the bed so I can face her properly. "That can't be the only reason you like someone."

"Okay, fine. He makes me laugh."

"Really?"

"Yes." Stacey gives me an emphatic look, her blonde curls tumbling off her shoulder as she tips her head. "He makes me feel happy."

"As happy as you did when you played sport and didn't drink after school?"

Her blue glare makes me swallow and scratch the side

of my nose. I don't want to piss her off, but she can't deny the fact that she's changed since hooking up with Jonas. I wonder if they're having sex like Leon and Luka are.

I cringe but manage to stop myself from asking. I don't think I want to know.

"Okay, fine." Stacey drops her phone on her duvet cover. "You want the truth? He makes me forget. He's the perfect distraction. When I'm with him, I'm not remembering everything we've lost." Her voice wobbles, her blue eyes turning vibrant as they glass over.

"But I don't want to forget," I whisper. "Forgetting doesn't change what happened. I want to be able to talk about it. About *them*. It keeps them alive."

"But they're not alive! They're not here!" Stacey slams her fist into the mattress. "I *can't* talk about them. I won't do it, so stop trying to make me!"

I gaze at her, sorrow filling my heart until it's over-flowing with aching pain.

I miss them.

I miss them so much.

If they were here, Stacey probably wouldn't even be dating Jonas. She'd be playing touch and begging Dad to come down and watch after school. Mum would come too, and we'd stand on the sidelines cheering and making up chants until all three of us were the loudest supporters there.

They brought out the happy in me. The loud. The silly.

But that's all gone now.

Curling my fist against my chest, I fold in on myself, shuffling down the bed until I'm a tight ball on the mattress.

Stacey sniffs and snatches her phone. "I'm going downstairs."

She thumps out the door and that country quiet covers me again. A morepork hoots outside the window and I close my eyes, focusing on the soft, soothing sound and letting thoughts of my parents float and swirl through my brain until I'm drifting on a cloud of memories that both comfort and destroy me.

28

HARPER

I'm going out of my mind!

It's been a full day and one morning since the accident, and my arm still hurts. I thought it'd be better by now, but every time I try to get some work done, it starts to ache and throb again.

Beck's told me not to lift a finger around here, but the place will fall into complete filth if I don't keep pottering. He swung by the house after milking and caught me doing the dishes.

"Oi. What are you doing?"

"The dishes have to get done. There's only one decent fry pan in this house."

"Sit down." He ordered me into the lounge, and I had to sit there listening to him clunk around in the kitchen. He then came through and propped my arm on a pillow, handed me the TV remote and two magazines, and then ordered me to stay put.

I waited twenty minutes after he left before getting up and going to check the laundry baskets in the bathroom and wiping down wet surfaces.

There's a load of clothes in the washing machine that will need hanging out soon. I wonder if it'll hurt to lift and peg.

A smattering of rain hits the window, and I jump up with a frown. "What?"

Pulling the net curtain aside, I watch the rain increase and start hitting the ground with gusto, pelting into the dirt and stealing any chance of hanging out the washing.

I guess I'll have to use the dryer, although it's so old and clunky it takes freaking hours to get anything dry. I should have brought our dryer up from Wellington, but I decided to rent out the house with whiteware included.

At least that's sorted now. A family of four is living there. It kind of kills me to think about them making my home theirs. I should be happy for them, but all I can think about is how wrong and unjust it all is.

That should be my family in there. *My* parents using the en suite, *my* clothes in the fully functioning dryer.

Sagging against the wall with a sigh, I stare at the grandfather clock.

"I wish you'd just shut up," I mumble, shuffling back to my spot on the couch and flopping down too hard.

Pain shoots up my arm and I wince. I cradle it gently back onto the pillow, hating that I'm in this situation.

I had to thank Tane for showing up at A&E for me. That was a hard pill to swallow, but the right thing to do. I think he appreciated it, but things are still awkward between us. He wants to treat me like a piece of cracked porcelain. I'm sure if he had his way, I'd be wrapped in cotton wool and carried everywhere for the next week.

As much as I'd love the feel of being in his arms, I can't allow that to happen. For one, I'm not some weak woman who needs pampering, and two, even just one look from him can turn my insides to mush. If I let him look after me the way he wants to, I'll fall so hard and far I'll never be able to get up again.

I need to keep my distance.

Rubbing my forehead, I pick up my phone and text Zoey and Alaina. I need the distraction right now.

Me: Going insane! Tell me what you're doing.

Zoey: Orientation starts next week, so I'm making the most of my final days of freedom.

She sends me a photo of her at the beach. The sky is a

crisp blue behind her, the waves gently rolling in and the white sand looking warm and inviting. Her turquoise bikini looks stunning.

Me: New bikini? It's gorgeous. And I love the shades too.

Zoey: Last week's shopping spree in effect. What are you doing with your wounded self?

Me: Sitting around, bored out of my brain, and going insane! I miss you guys.

Alaina: Hey, chicken hater. How's it?

I grin as Alaina's message buzzes over top of Zoey's.

Me: I'm sitting here feeling sorry for myself. What are you doing?

Alaina: Gettin' me nails done. Want to look all pretty for the first day.

My insides clench. She's talking about orientation too. I should be happy for them. This jealousy ripping through me is unhealthy, but it's hard not to feel it when come Monday, they'll be at Victoria University, checking out the buildings and buying new textbooks while I'll be folding washing, dusting or cleaning a bathroom.

I should be there with them.

I should—

The landline phone rings, and I throw the cushion aside

and rush over to it before it goes to answer phone. I usually wouldn't care, but today I'm desperate for any kind of interaction.

I don't recognize the number flashing up on the screen, so I have my polite voice on when I press OK. "The Connell farm, Harper speaking."

"Miss Hughes?"

I hate it when people call me that. It's so formal and, in my experience, usually followed by bad news.

"Yes," I rasp, my fingers clutching the phone a little harder.

"It's Helen, from Norton Primary School."

My heart rate spikes, the room spinning for just a second. "Is Oscar okay?"

"Uh, well, yes. He's… we need you to come down to the school."

"Is he hurt?"

"He's fine, Miss Hughes, but he is in a bit of trouble, and the principal needs to talk to you. Are you available to come down now?"

"Um…uh, yes. Yes, of course. I'll be there shortly."

I hang up, my mind racing as I try to figure out what *a bit of trouble* means.

My phone buzzes with a text, but I ignore it, figuring

I've got bigger things to worry about than turquoise bikinis and painted nails.

Snatching my wallet, I grab the keys and head for the car, wondering what the hell awaits me at Oscar's primary school.

"Bit of trouble," I mutter, starting up the car and ignoring the pain slicing up my arm as I grip the wheel and reverse into a three-point turn.

The drive to the school is quicker than usual because I speed without meaning to. I park haphazardly in the drop-off zone, figuring it's okay because school doesn't get out for another couple of hours. I rush through the rain to the entrance, hissing at the strain on my arm when I pull back the door. Flexing out my fingers, I lay them on the reception counter and try for a demure smile while swiping the drops of rain off my forehead and nose.

"I'm Harper Hughes. You called me a little while ago about my brother, Oscar."

"Yes." The receptionist smiles and stands. "If you could just sign in as a visitor, and I'll let Mrs. Gillies know that you're here."

I follow the instructions on the iPad until a sticker shoots out from the mini printer. I stick it onto my shirt before smoothing down my clothing and trying to look a little more presentable and mature than I actually feel.

"Miss Hughes." A lady with short blonde hair and a kind smile appears in the waiting area and extends her hand to me. "It's nice to see you again."

"Hello, Mrs. Gillies. I'm sorry about whatever trouble Oscar might have caused."

Her expression turns serious as she indicates for me to follow her into her office.

As I walk through the door, I spot my brother slumped down in a chair by the window. His expression is thunderous, his angry gaze warning me not to sit too close.

"Hey." I take the seat beside him anyway and reach out my hand, but he snatches his away, tucking it under his armpit before I can touch him.

"Unfortunately, Oscar has been having a pretty bad day." Mrs. Gillies gives him a sad, pointed look before turning back to me. "He's been struggling to settle in at school here. His teacher, Ms. Andrews, is having a hard time getting him to complete tasks in class and to even be involved with discussions."

"Why has no one contacted me about this?"

"She was planning on emailing you this afternoon and setting up a parent meeting. We wanted to give him a couple of weeks to settle in, but it's apparent that Oscar is not very keen on doing that." She shuffles some papers on her desk and murmurs, "His actions today have made that abundantly clear."

I whip a sharp look at my brother before turning back to the principal.

"What did he do?"

She looks to my brother and points at me. "Would you like to tell her?"

Oscar shakes his head and slumps even farther down in his seat. His butt's going to be on the floor in a minute.

I shuffle in the chair and try to come across as composed and unruffled, but my insides are going nuts.

Mum and Dad would be so disappointed.

Oscar usually loves school. He's always been a go-getter on the field and in the classroom. Teachers usually think Oscar is awesome, their only complaint being that he talks a little too much in class, but that's it.

"It appears that Oscar has deliberately destroyed another student's belongings. Using a pair of scissors, he has cut this student's school bag to shreds, dumped his homework in the sink and deflated his soccer ball, which he brought from home to share with his friends during lunchtime play."

"What?" I shoot Oscar an incredulous look.

"That's not the worst of it, I'm afraid. When this student tried to challenge Oscar on his behavior, Oscar became very agitated and ended up attacking him with fists and scissors."

I gasp and cover my mouth with my hand.

"The student has left for the day."

"Is he okay?"

"His injuries are not serious; however, Oscar's actions very much are." Her eyes tinge with sadness as she threads her fingers together and rests them on the desk. "We don't tolerate violence at this school. My primary concern is the safety and well-being of my students."

"Of course." I nod, trying to figure out what the pained look on her face might be leading to.

"So, it's my decision to stand Oscar down for two full days."

"Stand him down? What does that mean?"

"He'll be suspended from school until Tuesday, February twenty-fifth, at which time he is welcome to return to us, and we will do our best to avoid any of this kind of behavior again."

"Suspended?"

"A stand down is a milder form of suspension, Miss Hughes." Her eyes dart between us. "I hope you understand that it pains me to make this decision. I know your family has been through some terrible heartache recently, and we want to help."

I don't know how to respond to that. My mind is still thrumming with the whole stand down thing.

Dad would be mortified. His precious boy, stood down for acting like an asshole.

The principal picks up a letter and hands it to me. "Here is a formal letter outlining my decision, and I'd also like to give you this card."

I take it numbly, struggling to read the words.

"Keryn has been counseling children for years now. She's one of the best in the area. Can I suggest calling her might be a good way to go? After a tragedy like you've faced, it would be good for Oscar to have someone to talk to."

I nod, still not managing words as I blink and stare at the card.

Counseling.

I hadn't really thought about that.

Folding the letter in half, I figure I'll read it later. All that's left to do now is get my destructive brother back to the farm.

"I'll take Oscar with me now."

"That's probably for the best." The principal stands up with a genial smile, smoothing down her jacket and making me feel like a frumpy housemaid beside her.

"Uh… thank you."

I think that's what I'm supposed to say.

Clicking my fingers, I order Oscar up and out with a little flick of my head. That's what Mum used to do, and he gives me a baleful glare before shuffling through the doorway.

Why's he looking at me like that?

I'm not the one who attacked another kid!

We don't say anything as we storm out to the car. The rain has stopped, but gray clouds hover over us. We're both pissed, although I feel like I'm the only one with a right to be.

I want to slam the car door and start ranting at him, but I don't even know what the hell I'm supposed to say.

This isn't my job!

Mum and Dad should be the ones down here. They would have sat in that office and known exactly what to say. They wouldn't be sitting in the car, gripping the wheel and fighting a racing heart and the inability to breathe right.

Gripping my mouth, I hold myself together while shakes course through my body.

"Just drive," Oscar whines. "I want to get out of here."

It takes everything in me to start the car and not scream in his face for acting the way he did. I need to stay calm. I need to hear his side, figure this out.

By the time we've pulled away from the school, my

breathing is starting to regulate and I'm able to ask in a voice that I think is extremely calm. "So, what happened?"

"I don't want to talk about it."

"I don't care if you don't want to talk about it. I deserve an explanation! Who cuts up a kid's school bag?"

Oscar snorts like a bull ready to charge.

"Ozzy, come on. What's going on?"

I brake at the intersection and take a minute to look at him before pulling out.

All he gives me is a stony glare before crossing his arms and staring out the window.

Surly little butthead.

Dad would so not let him get away with that.

And I'm not Dad.

But Dad's not here, so I have to deal with this shit!

Panic sizzles through me again, and I ward it off with a few calming breaths. We make it home in one piece, and as soon as I pull up to the house, Oscar slams out of the car and heads inside.

"What's going on?" Beck appears around the side of the house. "Where'd you go? I tried to call, but you didn't take your phone with you."

"Sorry." I rub my forehead, leaning against the open car door for support. "I had to go and collect Ozzy from school."

"Is he all right?"

"He's in trouble." I cringe. "Damaged some kid's personal property and then attacked him."

"Attacked him?"

I shrug. "That's what the principal said. Oscar won't talk to me about it."

"You should have radioed me. I would have come to the school with you."

I give him another lame shrug, not sure what else to do. It didn't even occur to me to radio Beck. Oscar's my responsibility.

"So, how long is he home for, then?"

"He's been stood down for two full days." I reach into the car and pull out the letter, passing it over with the card.

Beck stands there reading it, his forehead wrinkling and his thick eyebrows bunching together.

"Geez Louise. Scissors?"

"Yep."

"Okay." Beck lets out a heavy sigh and nods. "Let's just leave him to cool off for the afternoon, and I'll have a chat with him tonight." He glances at me. "*We* can chat with him."

"He doesn't want to talk to me." I slam the door shut and wince, catching my arm against my chest and holding my elbow.

"Yeah, well, he's just gunna have to get over that. There's no way a kid as good-hearted as Oscar behaves like this." He shakes the letter. "There's got to be a reason, and we're going to find out what it is."

I nod, appreciating his determination, needing it. Because, to be honest, right now... I just want to give up.

29

TANE

I'm late home because Cam needed a mate to have dinner with.

After dropping the girls off, I ignored the urge to go in and check on Harper, instead staying in the car and driving straight to Hamilton. Cam and I grabbed sushi, flavored water, and salt and vinegar chips from the supermarket, then headed to a park on the east side of the Waikato River. Although the sky was overcast and it'd been raining on and off all day, we risked eating at a picnic table. The air was cool with just a hint of dampness in it, and I breathed it in, hoping it could soothe whatever seemed to be raging inside of me.

The river flowed past, the leaves above our heads rustled in the breeze, and birds chirped their conversations, bobbing near our feet and looking for crumbs.

The way nature was so unaffected by my inner turmoil calmed me a little, and I was able to relax. We didn't talk about Cam's dad or Harper or any of the shit we're both dealing with. Instead, we spent the whole time bouncing from rugby to the movies and music, then over to school… and for that couple of hours, it was like we were two teenagers with happy homes and normal lives.

At least I'm lucky enough to have the happy home thing.

I get out of the wagon, checking the house for lights and movement, trying to figure out where everyone is.

A murmured conversation is coming from around the side of the house. I approach quietly and peek my head around the corner. Beck and Oscar are leaning against the fence, facing out toward the milking shed.

The conversation must be pretty serious. I can tell by the morose look on Oscar's face and the way Beck pats his shoulder. I know that pat; I've experienced that pat. It's the one where you're in trouble, and not just tantrum trouble but serious *crossed the line* trouble. Beck's trying to ease Oscar into the lecture. A consequence is just around the corner, but Beck has this way of laying it out nice and mild so it takes the sting out of it.

Sort of.

I wonder what Oscar did that was so bad.

Curious, I head inside to get the goss and find Harper in the kitchen, unloading the dishwasher.

"Should you be doing that?" I place my bag at the bottom of the stairs and rush over to help her.

"Shut up." She gives me a pleading look that gives away just how rough her day was.

I take the stack of plates out of her hands and slide them into the cupboard.

She uses the tea towel to dry off the tops of the glasses and we silently unstack them together, her passing me the cups and me reaching up to put them away. She'll never admit it, but I think she's relieved I came along to help.

"So, what's up with Oz?"

Harper tuts and hands me two mugs, shaking her head.

"That bad, huh?"

"I had to go and pick him up from school today. He's been stood down for... being a little shit."

I wince and hiss in a breath. "What'd he do?"

"Destroyed this kid's stuff, then attacked him with a pair of scissors?"

"Are you serious?" I can't help a surprised laugh.

A pair of scissors?

What the hell?

"Don't," she pleads again. "It's not funny."

"No. You're right. It's just… insane?"

She snorts and lets out a hard laugh. "Yep." Her laughter soon becomes a desperate kind of sigh, and I can't help myself.

Walking around the open dishwasher, I gently glide my hand across her shoulders and kiss her forehead.

She lets me do it but doesn't sink into me like she's done before, so I pull back and try to smile down at her.

Her eyes are dark with warning. "If you tell me it's going to be okay, I may have to punch you in the gut."

I bite my lips together, swallowing down my words and backing away from her.

Her lips twitch with what could be the beginnings of a grin, and I really want to turn that thing into a proper smile.

"Well…" I pick up the last glass and slide it into the cupboard while Harper closes the dishwasher. "I guess you're just gunna have to put him to work, then." She glances up and I wink at her. "Want me to help you write a list?"

And there it is.

That smile I was hoping for.

It pulls her mouth wide, showing off her straight teeth and making me feel like I've just won the Rugby World Cup final.

30

HARPER

I wake up before the alarm, which isn't unusual.

The thing that's weird is that my mum isn't walking through the bedroom door singing "Happy Birthday" to me. It was one of her many birthday traditions, and I miss it with an ache so strong my stomach hurts.

Every year on our birthdays, Mum made sure we felt like the most important person in the world. She was the queen of birthdays, and this year...she's not here.

I gaze up at the white ceiling, lightly running my fingers through my hair and thinking about the fact that I am now nineteen years old. It's tempting to think about all the things I *should* be doing, like attending day one of orientation at Victoria University with Zoey and Alaina.

But my alarm starts buzzing, and there's seriously no time to lament or dream about anything. I have lunches to prepare and people to organize so no one will be late for school.

It's Oscar's last day of stand down. He was a total shit on Friday. I tried being nice and seeing if I could cajole a little truth out of him—any kind of reason as to why he acted like a complete psycho—but he kept shutting me down. He wouldn't budge with Beck either, even after their lengthy chat, so there was nothing left to do but take Tane's advice and put him to work, making him do all the chores I found too painful with my stitched-up arm. He complained and whined the entire time, arguing with me over every single task. It did my head in.

Thankfully Beck's bark brought him into line, but as soon as the big guy walked away, the bitching kicked in again.

Hopefully today, being my birthday and all, he'll show a little mercy. Maybe that can be his gift to me: chores without complaint. I'll take it!

Willow moans in the bed beside me.

"Morning," I softly greet her.

She rolls over and looks at me, her eyes smiling for just a moment. I pause, waiting for her to acknowledge my special day, but she doesn't say anything. She's obviously got something else planned for me, so I get up with a smile and head to the bathroom.

The rest of the morning runs like every other morning since school began. I rush around the kitchen, getting everyone organized while trying not to bump my arm or spill anything. Bianca, inevitably, knocks into someone, but she's pretty awesome at cleaning up her own mess, so I jump around her and set out filled lunchboxes on the end of the dining table.

Everyone sits around eating, sipping coffee and talking about the day ahead.

What everyone doesn't do is mention my birthday.

Not one single person says anything.

Maybe they're planning some mondo surprise I'm unaware of.

Or, more likely, my first birthday without Mum and Dad around has been forgotten.

I don't want it to hurt as much as it does, so I square my shoulders, clench my jaw and just get on with the day.

Once everyone but Oscar has left for school, Zoey and Alaina call and I chat with them briefly while my brother takes forever in the toilet. All I know is that he can clean up whatever stink he's leaving behind.

"So, happy birthday again." Zoey blows a kiss at her camera phone.

"Thanks." I wave goodbye, knowing they're about to head out to uni.

Lucky little tarts.

"Wait, wait, before we go, what are you doing to celebrate tonight?"

"Oh, um…" I lick my lips and suddenly can't tell them.

For some reason, everyone forgetting my special day makes me feel like a total loser, and I just can't admit it to my best friends. Not when they're about to walk out the door and start the life I'm supposed to be living with them.

"I think we're celebrating this weekend." I shrug. "It's just easier. School days are so busy."

"Makes sense." Alaina nods. "But make sure you still treat yourself today. You deserve it, babe."

"Thanks. Love you guys."

"We love you!"

"Have an amazing day."

They both grin at me and blow more kisses. I hang up and drop the phone on the kitchen counter, gazing out the window at the chicken coop. They're all securely back in their yard, strutting around, and all I can think is they need feeding. And these kitchen windows need a good clean.

With a resigned sigh, I head out back and shove my gumboots on. Looks like today is going to be a day like any other.

But it's not.

Not really.

Because Oscar's home, and now that the weekend is over, he's back to being a turd again. Making him clean the bathroom is a battle royal. It takes me an hour of arguing before it's finished to a standard that is only barely reasonable. I seriously thought he was going to maim me when I made him redo the toilet.

I lost him after that.

He was pissed, and I was going to pay the price.

By lunchtime we were both edgy and foul, and when he refused to empty the dishwasher while I prepared the food, I lost it.

"What is your problem? Why are you being like this?"

"Because you're treating me like a damn slave!"

"I have to do all this stuff while you're normally at school, so what the hell does that make me?"

"It's your job! I shouldn't be doing this stuff."

"My job? You sexist little shithead!" I jab my finger at him. "You were the one that screwed up, okay? *You're* in the wrong, yet somehow I'm feeling completely punished. I didn't cut up someone's school bag and attack them with a pair of scissors!"

His face bunches. A hurricane is brewing, and I don't have it in me to try and stop it.

But then Oscar's eyes glass with sudden tears, his anger ducking behind a cloud of misery. I was preparing myself for vile words and insults. There's a perfectly good bowl of fruit on the counter that I thought might end up on the floor, but instead he bunches his fist and practically wails, "You don't know! You weren't there. You didn't hear all the stuff he kept saying to me!"

His words shock my anger away, and I stare at my distraught brother, my voice dropping with concern. "What who was saying to you?"

He sucks in a ragged breath, this weird moan coming out of him.

"The kid from school? The one you attacked?"

Tears spill free as Oscar bobs his head.

"What was he saying?"

"From day one he tortured me, followed me around the school calling me a fat loser. He stole my lunch, and he wouldn't let any of the guys in Year 8 include me in any games at lunchtime." The tears dribble down his red cheeks, but he doesn't bother swiping them away. "The day I got stood down, that morning, when I arrived at school, when I walked into class, he like pointed at me and just got to work, you know? It was brutal! But the thing that made me want to kill him was when he said

Mum and Dad probably died on purpose so they didn't have to look at my ugly face every morning." Oscar's voice is overrun with tears, blurring his words together, but I get the gist.

The cruelty of those taunts spears me right through the heart, unearthing a torrent of tears that I am struggling to blink back. My nose tingles, my throat aches, but Oscar's crying enough for the both of us. My body is practically shaking as I try to muster the strength to be what he needs.

Moving around the dishwasher, I cautiously wrap my arms around him. He may not want a hug. He hasn't let me hug him in days, but as soon as I'm close enough, he wraps his arms around my waist and sobs into my shirt. His tears instantly create a wet patch just beneath my collarbone. I rest my cheek on the top of his head and stroke his back the way Mum would.

Beck appears in the laundry room door, obviously having heard it all. His face is a mix of rage and heartache. I know exactly how he feels.

I wish Oscar had told us this earlier. All that gentle persuasion and he gave us nothing. Who knew he'd respond so well to a little explosive yelling?

Weirdo.

Poor kid.

No wonder he's hating school so much. I want to kick

that kid's ass for being so horrible to my brother. I'm not exactly sure how I'm supposed to handle this, and worry stirs in my belly, knotting it until I'm struggling to breathe again.

"Hey." Beck steps into the kitchen, concern wrinkling his brow.

I force a smile, not wanting to worry him. Oscar's our primary concern right now.

As soon as he hears Beck approaching, he whips out of my arms and starts slashing the tears off his face. Beck rests a hand on his shoulder and gives it a little squeeze.

"You're all right, mate." His voice has a little tremble in it. "A story like that deserves a few tears. And that little bastard deserves a thrashing."

My heart is aching for Oscar and the torment he's faced... all on his own, because he wouldn't tell us. It kills me. I should have probed him more, made him talk. Instead I let him stew until he exploded.

Running a hand down my face, I squeeze my mouth and try to figure out what our next step will be.

"I'm taking him for the day." Beck tips his head toward the stairwell. "Go get your shoes, mate. It's just you and me this afternoon."

"Where are we going?" Oscar blinks, still trying to get control of his tears.

Beck gives him a little wink. "Figure you're due a man's lunch at the pub, and then I've got something else I think you're old enough for as well. Trust me?"

Oscar's lips rise into a small grin as he bobs his head.

"Go get your shoes on, then."

I rest my hand on the counter as Oscar darts upstairs. "Thanks, Beck."

"Poor kid." His expression crumples.

"What are we going to do?"

"We're going to be having words with the school, that's what."

"Do I have to call them? I mean, what do I say?"

"I'm not making you do it on your own." He lightly pinches my chin. "Why don't you call and say we want to meet with the principal first thing tomorrow morning. I'm not sending Oscar back into his class without this resolved. We'll both take him to school, and if they can't sort it out, he'll just come back home with us. We'll look for a new school for him if we have to, but I'm hoping the principal will take this seriously."

Relief washes through me. "Okay."

"Right, then." He runs a hand over his beard. "I'll just go change my shirt." He walks off before I can ask him what he's doing with Oscar this afternoon.

They drive off about ten minutes later, and I'm left with nothing but the tick of the grandfather clock and dishwasher to unload. I glare at the clock and then sigh, my shoulders deflating as I feel the weight of everything bearing down on me.

Plunking into a dining room chair, I draw invisible circles on the wooden table and think about my parents. They'd be grateful for Beck right now. Grateful that he's taking Oscar under his wing.

I am.

Thank God for Beck.

Although it's hard not to lament that if my parents were still around, Oscar wouldn't even be in this situation. He'd be at his school in Wellington, surrounded by his friends.

But he didn't want that without Mum and Dad, and I get it.

Everything is different without them.

I draw a heart with my finger and softly sing, "Happy birthday to me. Happy—" The words get clogged in my throat and I lean forward, resting my forehead on my good arm and closing my eyes.

I used to love my birthday, but this year, I just want it to be over.

Oscar and Beck arrive back thirty minutes before milking.

And they have a little something extra with them.

Well, kind of little.

My mouth drops open as Oscar rushes into the house with a huge smile on his face and a wriggling black-and-white puppy in his arms.

"Wow." It's all I can manage.

"I know! It's a Labrador/Heading cross. And it just turned nine weeks old today!" Oscar grins, dropping to his knees and placing the dog down. It lets out this high-pitched puppy bark, then starts sniffing any and everything. "I always wanted a dog. Beck took me out to this farm in Te Awamutu and said I could pick whichever one I wanted."

"Is... is it like a farm dog or...?" I shuffle back a little when the puppy prances over to me, its tail going nuts as it sniffs around my feet.

"It's mine. I'm allowed to have it in the house and everything."

"He'll be all right around the farm." Beck walks into the house. "Once he's trained, I might use him a little, but we've been coping fine without one, so I mainly want him for Ozzy."

Beck's smile is all proud, like he's done so well with Oscar today.

I mean, maybe he has. My brother hasn't smiled this big since…

Swallowing back the thought, I crouch down and greet the puppy.

"Hey."

"It's a boy, and I've named him Rocket."

"Rocket." I nod, forcing a smile while I try not to think about the idea of having to cope with a puppy in the house. It's easy for them to all stand around beaming, but they're not the ones who'll have to deal with it day to day. I've never trained a puppy before; I don't know what the hell I'm doing! All I do know is that it'll chew stuff and pee everywhere, and he'll no doubt leave black bits of fur on every surface of this house.

It's going to be impossible to keep it clean!

I press my hand into my stomach, forcing a smile at Beck and Oscar before excusing myself to the bathroom. As soon as the door clicks shut behind me, I hold my hand against my forehead and just let the panic take me.

I managed to stave it off this morning, but I can't do it right now.

There's no fight left in me.

A puppy.

Now I have to cope with a puppy.

How something so cute and adorable can send me off the deep end like this, I'm not sure.

Plunking onto the toilet seat, I rest my elbows on my knees and cradle my head. My breath picks up until I'm gasping for air and shudders are rippling through my body, one after the other.

31

BIANCA

Something's off at the breakfast table this morning. I spoon the cereal into my mouth and dart a glance at Stacey. She's watching Tane, who keeps gazing into the kitchen with a worried frown on his face.

The puppy scampers around under the table, his tail hitting everything he walks past and his claws clicking on the wooden floor. Oscar is completely distracted and trying to feed him morsels of Weet-Bix while Harper bangs around in the kitchen like she's preparing for war.

Slapping my lunchbox onto the counter, I wince and berate myself for the fact that I keep forgetting to make my own. Harper's so quick and efficient in the mornings and she's already working on it by the time I get downstairs. I need to offer my help the night before, but I just keep forgetting.

"Thank you," I call out to her.

She doesn't respond and something plops into the sink, followed by a clatter of cutlery that's being shoved into the dishwasher with venom.

Harper was kind of quiet and sullen last night. After she cooked dinner and we sat down, she just picked at her food, barely involving herself in the mealtime conversation. She's probably worried about this meeting with the principal at Oscar's school. I'd be dreading it.

Poor Oscar. We're all pissed off on his behalf. I can't believe someone would treat him that way. Stacey was furious too. She listed a bunch of ways to torture the kid, but Beck shut her up and said we were going to deal with this the right way.

"What's the point of retaliation like that? Oscar will only get in trouble again."

She hitched her shoulder and muttered, "It'd just be fun to see that little dickhead squirm."

Oscar laughed at that, and it lightened the mood around the table. But not for Harper. She obviously took her mood to bed with her, and a night's sleep has done nothing to alleviate it.

Maybe she didn't sleep well.

Maybe her arm hurts.

Tane tips his chair back and stares in the kitchen, trying to catch her eye, but she's refusing to look out at the table.

"Coffee's great this morning." Tane lifts his mug. "Think you've won me over."

She throws a twitchy, half-hearted smile over her shoulder.

"Come have breakfast with us."

"I will in a minute. I just need to—" She jerks to a stop as the puppy trots into the kitchen, lifts his leg and promptly pees on her.

"Are you f—argh!" she screams.

The puppy yelps and scampers away.

Stacey slaps her hand over her mouth to stop the laughter coming out. I kick her under the table, warning her to shut up. I doubt Harper's in the mood to see the funny side of this. Stacey dips her head, but her shoulders are still shaking.

Oscar quickly grabs the pup, cradling him against his chest. "He doesn't know any better. It takes time to train him."

"I know that," Harper grits out, shaking pee off her foot.

"Oscar, you better clean that up." Tane stands from the table. "And put the pup outside."

"I don't want him running off!" Oscar argues. "Beck's building me an outdoor area today."

"He'll be late for school." Harper shakes her head.

"So let him be." Tane crosses his arms. "You shouldn't have to do everything, Harper."

"We can't be late today. We have a meeting!" she snaps. "And who the hell is going to do this stuff if I don't?"

"Well, maybe it doesn't need doing for a day."

"You want me to leave pee on the floor? That's disgusting!"

"I'm not talking about the pee, I'm talking about all the other stuff you're constantly doing around here. This place doesn't need to be so spotless all the time. We're not the Ritz."

Harper's eyes flash, her expression morphing to… well, kind of scary actually.

"I'll clean it! I'll clean it!" Oscar shoves between them, snatching up the paper towel roll and pulling it too hard so about twenty squares fly out and puddle onto the floor.

Harper growls in her throat and storms past Tane. "Fine! You clean up the mess, then. I'm having a shower. A long one!"

Her feet thump on the floor as she disappears, and

we're all left staring after her, no doubt wondering where Harper the elegant and serene has disappeared to.

32

TANE

"**H**oly crap," I mutter under my breath, scraping a hand through my hair before crouching down to help Oscar. He seems flustered by his sister's outburst. I get it. Harper's the master of keeping her emotions in check. If anything, she doesn't let them out enough, but this morning she sure as shit showed us how she was feeling.

I wonder what's got her so riled up.

I guess it's kind of good that she let off a little steam this morning, but there's something that doesn't sit pretty in my guts. Her angst has a dark, brooding edge to it, and I'm worried what it might turn into if we don't figure out what's wrong.

"Here." I pass Oscar a clump of sodden, yellow-stained paper towels. He pulls a face, and I give him an impatient frown.

He takes it with a sigh, throwing it out and then promptly washing his hands.

"You'll need to mop too." I point at the floor. "You can use the bucket in the laundry tub. I think there's some floor cleaner in the cupboard above it. Just squirt a little into the hot water."

I wander back to the table to finish off my breakfast, although my appetite has basically disappeared. The puppy dances around my feet, nearly tripping me up. I snicker and reach down, scooping him up and tapping the end of his nose.

"No peeing in the house, you little creep."

He barks and tries to nibble my finger, so I plop him on his feet and sit back down at the table.

"What is up with her today?" Stacey asks the question we're all thinking.

I scratch the back of my head, wishing I knew. Harper could be worried about this meeting with Principal Gillies this morning, but Beck will be there with her. He should have been there when she first picked Oscar up, but of course she didn't bother telling him.

I shake my head, irritated yet again by her stubborn independence. She's so quietly strong, which I actually really love, but the flip side is she ends up pushing everyone away in the process. That's the part that kills me.

No one can respond to Stacey's question. I glance at Willow, but she's got her earbuds in and is focusing on her toast like it will somehow transport her to another dimension. So helpful.

I stare at her until I know she can feel it. She refuses to look at me the whole time and eventually jumps up from the table, clearing her plate and wandering around Oscar when he carries a bucket of steaming water in from the laundry.

"Mop's against the wall by the dryer," I murmur.

He runs back to get it, then starts mopping the floor. Someone's phone dings on the kitchen counter and Willow glances down at it, her eyes suddenly bulging and the plate rattling as she dumps it onto the counter.

"What's wrong?" I ask, giving up on my breakfast and standing up.

"Oh crap," she hisses.

"What!" Stacey throws her hands up. "What other drama are we about to face this morning?"

Willow pulls the buds from her ears. "I think I know why Harper's pissed." She looks sick as she rushes past Oscar with the phone in her hand.

I meet her halfway, reading over her shoulder and frowning at the name in the text box.

"Who's Dylan?"

"Her boyfriend," Oscar mutters.

I whip around to face him. "Her what?"

"Her *ex*-boyfriend," Willow clarifies, settling my nerves, but not by much.

"Why is he texting her?"

"Read it." Willow unlocks the phone and hands it to me.

I try to ignore the name at the top of the box and focus instead on the smaller white words.

Happy birthday! Sorry it's a day late. I got the time zone wrong on this one. Hope you had an awesome day anyway xx

"We forgot her birthday," I croak, closing my eyes and feeling like crap.

"What?" Oscar stops mopping and then gasps. "Oh shit! When was it?"

"Yesterday." Willow's face crumples like she's on the verge of tears. "I can't believe we forgot. Mum always made everything so special. She was the birthday queen."

And now she's not here.

Harper will be feeling it like a knife blade through the chest.

We forgot. I mean, I didn't know, but still. I should have found out.

Shit, I feel rotten. I can't believe we all walked around her yesterday, completely ignoring the fact that she just turned nineteen.

"We have to make it up to her." I dump the phone face-down on the counter, trying to ignore the jealousy ripping through me after spotting the Valentine's Day text as well.

Freaking Dylan.

I don't even know the guy and I already dislike him.

I hate that he's remembering stuff I should be!

Valentine's Day. A chance to show a little romance and I didn't do a damn thing.

And now her birthday, which is so much worse.

"We could throw her a party," Stacey suggests. "Is she into that kind of thing?"

"Mum always insisted on parties or at least a dinner." Willow tucks a lock of long brown hair behind her ears, looking more animated than I've ever seen her. Guilt must be driving the words out of her mouth.

"Do you remember Dad's karaoke party last year?" Oscar grins, but his expression quickly turns sad.

"Karaoke, yes!" Stacey claps her hands together. "I love it!"

"We could deck out the barn." Bianca starts to smile. "It'd be fun to do like a cowboy theme or something."

"Harp loves country music." Willow cringes while I just let the smile spread across my face.

"I used to want to be a cowgirl."

That's what she told me. Well, we're gunna make that wish come true.

"Really? Country music?" Stacey's surprised laughter makes everyone grin.

"We have to do this." Bianca claps her hands together. "Let's make it a surprise. We could invite everyone over this Saturday."

"I love it." I snap my fingers and point at her. "Who are we going to invite?"

Willow bounces up on her tiptoes. "I'll call Alaina and Zoey today. As long as they're here, Harper won't mind about anyone else."

"What about Dylan?" My voice is stiff and edgy, making it hard to hide how dark I feel over the guy.

"He's in Europe." Oscar washes his hands. "That's why

they broke up. He left on his big OE, and Harper didn't want to go with him. She had other plans."

Oscar's smile fades again, like he's just realizing how much Harper's plans have changed in the last two months.

Drying his hands off, he then finishes them on his uniform shorts while Stacey feeds the puppy her toast crusts.

"Okay." I nod. "So we're going secret squirrel on this one, right?"

"Are we allowed to let her know that we forgot her birthday?" Willow looks worried. "I don't think we should wait until the weekend for that."

"No, let's do a nice dinner tonight or something, but we'll keep the party a surprise."

"And her friends coming up. She'll love that." Willow grins.

"So, we're agreed?" I grip the back of the chair and glance around the table. Everyone nods.

"I'll let Beck know. He's going to feel so bad about this, so I won't tell him until after school." I point at Oz. "Mouth shut, all right, mate? You have to get through this meeting first."

Oscar nods, collecting up the puppy and cuddling him like he needs the support.

I give him a kind smile. "It's going to be okay. You've got Big Beck and your sister right there fighting for you."

"Yeah." He starts to smile, and I wink at him, dashing up the stairs to finish getting ready for school. I grab my wallet and check how much money I've got. Should be enough to duck out at lunchtime and snatch Harper a little gift.

There's no way Dylan's going to outclass me with a simple text.

I'm making it up to Harper big-time.

33

HARPER

I walk out to the barn with a frown. Tane's text is a mystery that I really don't feel like solving this afternoon.

It's been a tough day. The meeting with the principal took ages. She seemed to believe Oscar's story but still wanted a full rundown. She wrote detail after detail until he was fully spent from crying.

After that, she suggested he spend one more day at home, which he happily agreed to since he knew Rocket would be here waiting for him.

She promised she would start an investigation into the bullying and there would be a follow-up. Oscar is welcome back to school whenever he feels ready, which Beck is insisting be tomorrow.

"You can't just run and hide from your problems, mate. That doesn't make them go away. Now, you enjoy today, but tomorrow, you're gunna walk into that school with your head held high."

I don't know what this follow-up is going to look like, but it better be something decent, and Beck told the principal straight. She agreed with him. Hopefully it wasn't just politeness on her part. She asked again about the counseling sessions for Oscar, saying that it's probably even more important now that he's a victim of bullying as well.

I promised her I'd call. And I have. Oscar has an appointment lined up for next week. He seems vaguely open to going, so that's a relief. Hopefully I won't have to muscle him through the door.

With a sniff, I slide my phone into my back pocket and clomp down to the barn in my gumboots. The sky is clear and sunny, dust kicking up around my feet as I fidget with the edge of my bandage that's curling up at the corner. It's really tempting to peel it off, but I have to keep it covered for a few more days yet. It's starting to get itchy, which is a good sign apparently. It means it's healing.

I give it a light scratch with my short nails and wonder why Tane wants to see me all the way over in the barn. Probably so we can have a little privacy. The thought of what we could do in private makes my muscles vibrate. A little hot kissing in the hay. The horses wouldn't care, and they'd definitely keep it a secret.

A vivid image of bodies pressed into the hay, warm tongues, wandering hands, makes my pulse spike.

Stupid desire. Maybe I shouldn't be doing this.

But when I peek my head through the barn door and see him standing there chatting to his beautiful horse in a stream of golden sunlight, I can't help myself. I walk toward him as if my legs are being pulled of their own accord.

He turns and spots me coming, his eyes lighting with a smile that seems reserved for me. It makes my heart trill in ways I don't want it to, so I look down and shove my hand in my back pocket, then feel awkward and take it out again, fluffing up the back of my hair.

"So, um… you wanted to see me?"

Ugh, I sound so formal.

Clearing my throat, I scuff my boot through the hay and figure it's best if I just don't say anything.

Tane runs his hand down Copper's nose, his face crumpling with obvious remorse. "I'm sorry. I'm *so* sorry. "

His sincere tone makes me tip my head with a confused frown. "What are you talking about?"

"We forgot your birthday."

His school shoes scuff through the hay, and I watch them coming. His feet are so big and broad compared to mine. His long legs obliterate the space between us, and he's soon standing right in front of me.

And then he pulls out a small paper bag from behind his back.

It's a Paper Plus one. Someone's been shopping at a bookstore.

I don't reach for it immediately, instead letting out a little sigh. "How'd you find out?"

"Willow read your text from Dylan this morning. She's waiting inside to give you a *huge* apology hug. But I just wanted to give you a little something first." His voice has a nervous tremble to it, so I take the gift to help him out.

It's not wrapped or anything, just the store bag. The receipt flies out as I pull the book free and brush my thumb over the cover.

"How to Find Joy in the Little Things," I murmur and then thumb through the pages.

"It's a book of quotes. Positive messages, that kind of thing."

I nod and force a smile.

What is he trying to say? That I'm a grumpy bitch who needs a little help?

Do I not have enough on my plate? Now I need to act happy as well?

"Thank you," I murmur.

"I just thought it might be encouraging." He brushes his fingers down my cheek, and I force another smile.

"It's great. It was nice of you to think of me."

He lets his hand drop away, looking slightly gutted by my serious lack of enthusiasm.

Crap, what am I supposed to do?

I'm trying to be polite. And I don't want to be ungrateful, but this crappy, unwrapped book is nothing compared to what my mum would have pulled off. She always made everything so special. Treasure hunts to find our gifts, a chocolate cupcake with a single red candle, a special lunch if it was a school day, a massive party if it wasn't. She pulled out all the stops.

And I miss her so much.

It's killing me, but I don't know how to say that without crying.

And I can't cry.

If I start, I'm scared I won't stop. I'm scared that all the cracks inside of me will break for good and I'll be nothing but a shattered mess.

Tane's smile is sad and disappointed. "You probably wanted something else. I was kind of on the clock. I just wanted to show you that I care."

"I appreciate it."

And I do. The gesture's sweet. I think I'm just in a bad headspace or something. Mum used to talk about headspace when she was out of sorts.

That's what I am.

Out of sorts.

Lost.

Broken.

How do you accept a gift about enjoying the little things when every little thing feels like a boulder that's going to crush you?

Tane tuts and looks away from me. "It's probably not as cool as what Dylan would have gotten you."

My heartbeat goes dull, my stomach sinking as another *little* thing is slapped in my face. "What?"

"Your boyfriend. Your *ex*-boyfriend. I'm sure he bought you great gifts."

A wave of jealousy courses over his face. He's not quick enough to hide it.

Don't do this to me, Tane. Please! Don't be that type of guy.

His eyes meet mine for a brief moment before darting to Copper's stall.

The tense set of his jaw, the downturn of his lips... it pisses me off.

Why is he making this about him?

Isn't it *my* birthday? Isn't he trying to make *me* feel better?

Tucking the book under my arm, I snip, "We were never together for my birthday, so I wouldn't know. I've never had a boyfriend on my birthday, and I still don't." My last four words come out low and hard, but he's not put off by them. Instead he turns and looks directly at me, his expression a mix of pain and confusion.

"Only because you're too stubborn to admit your feelings. You could have a boyfriend right now." He jabs his finger into his chest. "A guy who would do anything for you, who just wants to help you, but you won't let him! And I have no idea why!" He throws his arms wide and paces away from me before spinning back to keep ranting. "Sometimes the way you look at me makes me think you're into me. The way you kiss me definitely gives it away, but each time I try to get close, to be what you need, you *always* pull away." He lets out a ragged breath. "What do I have to do to win you over?"

"I don't know, okay? Maybe I don't want to be won over right now." My voice starts to crack and shake. "Maybe you can't help me or fix this or make it better! Because being with you won't change the fact that my parents are gone! This birthday is not the same without them. No birthday *ever* will be! So maybe you should just stop trying to be what I need and leave me alone!" My eyes glass with tears, and I swear if I don't get out of here in a second, I'll break all the way in half.

I turn away from Tane's wounded expression, and my heart cracks a little further when he softly murmurs, "I thought you didn't want me to give up."

I close my eyes, guilt and regret coursing through me. I feel sick. My head is pounding, and I want to cry. I want to cry so frickin' badly.

And even worse, I want to turn into his arms and have him hold me so I can sob against his chest—big, ugly, wet sobs that will only humiliate me.

Trying to clench my trembling jaw is impossible. My teeth are chattering now, making it hard to do anything but stand there and hug this stupid little book.

"Your family's waiting for you." Tane's defeated voice breaks the silence between us. "You better go."

With a sniff, I quickly swallow back the tears, tighten up the dam and robotically walk for the house. I need to have a bright smile in place by the time I reach the front door. I practice it while walking, my stiff lips brittle and dry.

By the time I finally walk into the dining room and find my two siblings standing next to the table, I'm exhausted. But a chocolate cupcake with a single red candle sits between them.

I gaze at it, love for my mother overwhelming me as tears start to build on my lashes.

"No, please don't cry." Willow holds up her hands, shaking them in the air. "We're sorry we forgot."

"We can make it up to you." Oscar bobs his head, his eyes big and hopeful. "You don't have to cook dinner tonight and we…" He trails off, hesitating and glancing at Willow.

She just shakes her head, looking all awkward.

They didn't get me a gift, of course. I'm sure Willow feels bad about that.

Dropping the book on the couch, I catch her eye and smile. "Don't worry." I open my arms as wide as they'll go. "Just a monster hug is all I need."

They both grin, rushing away from the table and barreling into me. We create a tight circle, clinging to each other, and I tell myself that this is totally enough.

This is why I'm here, right?

So it's enough.

It has to be.

34

BIANCA

I roll over in bed, staring into the darkness and listening to the even rhythm of Stacey's breathing. Thankfully neither of us snores, so sharing a room with her isn't all bad. It's just the mess that drives me bonkers.

She's been putting in a big effort with the invisible line, though. I have to appreciate that about her. She is trying. I just wish she understood me better sometimes. I wish she'd let me talk about Mum and Dad. I wish I didn't have to be pulled into *her* world.

But I don't have another world, so…

With a sigh, I throw the sheets back and creep out of the room. I don't flush the toilet after using it, instead closing the lid and heading downstairs for a glass of water.

I don't know what it is about tonight, but the air feels

musty and thick. It could be the lingering tension from dinner. It wasn't a shouting tension, more like a quiet, unbearable one. We were all trying so hard to make up for the fact that we forgot Harper's birthday. We got her favorite takeaways—Indian—but not even a little curry could turn her smile from fake to genuine. Her lips curled upward when we sang her "Happy Birthday," and she blew out the little red candle, but once that flame had been extinguished, her smile fled with it and there was no bringing it back.

We all apologized so many times, in so many different ways. She forgave us, but it didn't take the edge off her sadness. Instead the emotion wafted in the air like a blinding fog. Saturday night will be better. I have to make sure it is.

My mind has been whirring with ideas. Maybe that's why I can't sleep.

I was hoping Stacey would get into it, but as soon as she found out Jonas couldn't make it, she lost all her enthusiasm and now I'm party planning on my own. At least it avoids Stacey dominating every decision—that part's nice—but I'm kind of overwhelmed with everything I need to organize in the next few days. Harper deserves a great party. I really want to give her one.

As I pop off the bottom step, a flickering light in the lounge catches my attention. Tane's sitting in the armchair, slowly blinking at the TV screen.

It's like two o'clock in the morning. What's he still doing up?

I pad across to him and notice he's in boxer shorts and a T-shirt. He probably went to bed but wasn't able to sleep, or he woke up and tossed and turned like me.

He hasn't seen me yet, which I find weird. Maybe he *has* seen me but just doesn't want to say. He looks kind of sad. Should I leave him to wallow alone?

"What are you watching?" The question slips out of my mouth, almost surprising me.

I obviously don't want him wallowing alone.

Tane glances up, lets out a resigned sigh and points at the TV. *"World's Fittest Human.* Just a doco on... CrossFit."

"My mum always loved those." I walk around the couch and plunk down on the adjacent couch.

Tane gives me a weak smile and I cross my arms, studying him. "Are you okay? You seem kind of down."

He lets out an awkward laugh and shuffles in his seat, keeping his eyes locked on the screen.

I should just walk away and head back upstairs, but for some reason, I don't want to drop this. Tane is not a down-in-the-dumps kind of guy. He's easygoing, warm... like a lazy Sunday afternoon. You want to hang out with him because it makes you feel better, more relaxed.

The guy I'm sitting with tonight is troubled, and if I can't sleep because of party planning, there's no way I'll be able to sleep if I can't help Tane even just a little.

"Can I watch with you for a bit?" I shuffle on the couch, turning to face the screen.

"Sure." He swings his leg over the arm of the chair, angling his body toward me—a silent invitation to join in.

I tuck my feet under my butt and try to focus on the super-strong, super-buff contestants, but my eyes keep darting to Tane. He's staring at the screen, but zero emotion is flickering on his face. It's like he's watching but not absorbing anything.

It's probably not my business, so I force my gaze to the screen and try to focus on the next event. It's like a gazillion pull-ups followed by these squat things where you lift a million kg before running through some other obstacle and then sprinting back to start all over again.

It's insane. These people are bone and muscle. Not an ounce of fat on them.

I shuffle around and curl my knees to my chest, trying to hide the pudge of my stomach. Resting my head against the back of the couch, I blink as a yawn stretches my mouth wide.

"You should head to bed. School tomorrow," Tane murmurs.

"You too."

He shrugs. "Can't sleep."

"Me neither. My head's been whirring with party details. I know exactly how I want it all to look, and I thought Stacey was going to help me, but she's..." I shake my head.

Tane rolls his eyes, knowing exactly what I'm not saying.

Glancing at me, he lightly taps my foot with his toe. "Well, what do you need?"

"Um..." I brush a hand through my hair. "Sound equipment set up in the barn, fairy lights, chairs, tables, food. I've made a list in my head."

"Cam and my mates will pitch in with that stuff. You just have to ask them."

My stomach clenches and I nearly squeak, "Can you ask them for me?" But I know that will be completely lame. He'll think I'm pathetic, and he seems to have enough on his plate right now.

"One of Cam's neighbors is in a band. They might let you borrow some sound equipment. You should talk to him about it." Tane's lips twitch as he raises his eyebrows at me.

"Um." I lick my lips and try to nod. "O-okay."

I've kind of been keeping Cam at a distance. I smile when he smiles at me, and I say hi if we get close enough to pass, but if I see him coming, I tend to dart the opposite direction. I know he's probably after Stacey, and I'm scared of doing that thing where I end up falling for him by mistake when he doesn't even want me in the first place. I just have this feeling like if I get to know him, it won't be hard to stumble right onto the love train without meaning to. He gets more handsome every time I see him, and I really wish he wouldn't. I just love that smile of his. It's so warm and sweet.

Whoever he ends up with is going to be one lucky girl.

But maybe I can ask him about Harper's party. I can be cool and professional about it all. It's just one little conversation, right?

"He won't mind." Tane winks, and I see a flash of his relaxed self come through, but it quickly dies away.

"What's bugging you?" I whisper. "I know I shouldn't pry, but I'm just not used to seeing you…blue."

He gives me a sad smile and shakes his head. "Gave Harper a birthday present today. She didn't really like it. All I wanted to do was make her feel better, but it was a complete fail."

"What was it?"

"Just, uh… this book of quotes. I thought it was great. Lots of encouraging messages to try and make you feel better about life. I know she's going through a hard time. She gave up her dreams to stay here, and she's working her bum off to keep the house tidy and… I don't know…I thought I could cheer her up. But it didn't work."

"You really like her, don't you?"

A muscle in his jaw clenches, and he looks back at the TV. "Like I said, I just wanted to make up for the fact that we forgot her birthday, but I may as well have gifted her a pile of steaming cow shit."

I snicker but quickly cut off the sound, pity for him coursing through me. He looks gutted.

Biting the edge of my lip, I try to think of the best thing to say and end up murmuring, "She's obviously not a 'words of affirmation' person."

"What does that mean?"

"You know. The love languages. Some people respond to encouraging words. It pushes all the right buttons for them. Obviously not Harper's jam, though."

"What are you talking about?" He shifts in his seat, turning to face me fully. "What are love languages?"

His full attention throws me a little. He's got this intense stare going on, like he's desperate for whatever I'm about to say.

I tuck my fringe behind my ear and start playing with the ends of my hair. "Oh, well, it's just this theory that my parents were really into. They had this book by a guy called Gary Chapman. He's done all this research on how humans show and respond to different forms of love. So, like, I respond really well to quality time and gifts. If someone buys me a present, it means a lot to me and I treasure it. Other people, like my dad, he was a physical touch person, always giving us hugs and holding Mum's hand and snuggling with her on the couch. She wasn't like that, and she sometimes felt a little smothered." I grin, picturing my sweet mother as she subtly tried to get herself a little breathing room. Not always—she knew how Dad ticked—but when she was angry, hugging her was not the right move. It didn't calm her the way a cuddle would calm my dad.

"What was your mum's...love language?"

"Oh, she was quality time, like me. So when she and Dad went on a date and she had his full attention for like the whole time, she would come home so happy and energized. Her love tank was all filled up."

Tane looks thoughtful for a minute, then reaches for the remote and mutes the TV. "Okay, so how would I know what someone's love language is?"

"Um, well, why don't we figure out yours first? So, just think about times in your life when someone has made you feel really good. Like, what makes you feel all warm and fuzzy?"

Tane looks to the ceiling, the light from the TV casting an eerie glow across one side of his face. "I know." He finally looks back to me. "When Beck tells me I've done a good job. That feels real good." He taps a hand over his heart. "Gets me every time."

"Okay." I smile. "And if you want to show someone that you really care about them, what would you do?"

"Uh…" He works his jaw to the side, then shrugs. "Probably give them a hug or tell them something really uplifting, so they'll feel better about themselves."

"Right." I grin, knowing exactly the love languages he talks in. "So, that means you're a words of affirmation guy and maybe a physical touch person. There's a test you can do to find out more, but from what you've said, that's my guess."

"What are you again?"

"I'm gifts and quality time."

"What do you think Harper is?"

My eyes narrow as I point at him with a teasing smile. "I knew you liked her."

He winces and scrubs a hand down his face.

"Don't worry, I won't tell anyone."

Tipping his head back with a sigh, he looks at the ceiling again. "Don't worry about it. She wants me to leave her alone right now anyway."

"She said that?"

"Pretty much," he mumbles.

"I'm sorry. She probably didn't mean it."

"I don't know, she seemed pretty adamant." The way he snaps off the ends of his words gives away how raw his emotions are over the whole thing.

I so want to make him feel better.

Tane's such a great guy. Harper would be lucky to have him.

And he'd be lucky to have her too. When I think about how hard she works for this family, how much she gives out… she deserves to be happy.

I want them together. It's a good fit.

The cupid in my chest flutters its wings, excitement twirling through me at the idea of spreading a little joy.

Although, I probably shouldn't meddle. It's not really my place, but—

"I don't know what to do." Tane's sigh is heavy and sad. "Probably just stay out of her way like she wants me to."

"Well, I guess it gives you time to figure out what works for her. Why don't you watch her over the next few days with the idea of love languages in mind?"

"What are they again?"

"Words of affirmation, physical touch, gifts, quality time and acts of service." I lift a finger for each one and stare at my pinky for a second. "You know what, I think that might be hers. Think about all the stuff she is constantly doing for us and we never have to ask her, she just swoops in to help. I bet that's her way of showing love—doing stuff for people."

Tane's lips dip into a thoughtful pout. "So if I did something for her, something practical, without her asking me, that might make her feel better?"

"Maybe." I shrug, too scared to guarantee it. What if it doesn't work? What if she does all this stuff out of duty, not love?

Suddenly doubting myself, I press my lips together.

"Problem is, she won't *let* me do anything for her."

Poor guy. He's back to being all cut up again.

"People are complex," I whisper. It was a line my mum always used to say. "Especially hurting people, and she's… well, we're all kind of fragile at the moment."

Tears sting my eyes and I sniff, not really in the mood to cry. Bringing the big loss into the lounge at two o'clock in the morning is not the best idea.

"Yeah, I guess we are," Tane murmurs, staring at the silent TV.

A guy with ridiculous muscles is punching his arms in

the air, his smile triumphant as sweat drips down his face.

"Hey." I rest my hand lightly on his ankle. "I hope you manage to figure it out. I like the idea of you two together."

Tane scoffs, but his lips tip into a smile. "Not sure Beck would."

"Yeah, I guess it could be kind of awkward."

"It'd just be so much easier if I didn't like her."

"The heart knows what it wants, I guess."

"Yeah." Tane lets out a sad, frustrated snicker. "Got any good tips for telling it to shut up?"

I giggle softly. "If I find any, I'll let you know."

"Thanks, cuz." He gives my wrist a little squeeze, his eyes glimmering with a grateful smile. "Now go to bed. You've got some party planning to do tomorrow, and you're gunna need your energy."

I stand up with a smile and kiss the top of his head. "Sleep well when you get there."

He gives me a thumbs-up and I head for the stairs, turning one last time to look at my cuz. Man, I'm stoked he called me that. Makes me feel like part of a family. Mum, Dad, me, Stace—we've been a unit of four for so long, but now there's more. The hole they've left behind is being slowly filled with other people. Good people, like Tane and Beck and Harper. It's not just me and Stace. Not really.

I'm becoming part of a new family, and in spite of the fact that I still desperately want my parents back, it feels good not to be alone.

Maybe there is a place for me here.

Maybe I do fit.

Maybe.

35

HARPER

The kitchen is starting to gleam, the scent of window cleaner and Ajax spray mingling into a heady cocktail. I sniff and dash a hand under my nose before getting back to the windows. The rag squeaks on the glass, and I push a little harder to eliminate any streaks.

This cleanliness should be making me feel better, but even the smear-free surfaces are doing nothing to bolster my mood. My arm twinges as I put a little more elbow grease into finishing off the window.

I hiss and back off for a second, dumping the rag onto the bench and pacing to the fridge. Misery nips at me, frying my nerve endings and making me edgy.

Tane barely looked at me this morning. He barely said hello when he stepped into the kitchen earlier than usual and started preparing his own lunch. He then went a step further and prepared Willow's and Stacey's as well. He could see what I was doing and just joined in. I silently worked on Bianca's and Oscar's. We moved around each other in a mute dance and I couldn't stop looking at him, but he didn't budge once. He just worked. Helped.

And it was really sweet.

I wanted to thank him, but my throat was too clogged with emotions to talk.

He even made sure the puppy was outside in his new area before he left for school. I heard him telling Oscar that Rocket wasn't to be messing up the house when I was the only one there to monitor him. It wasn't fair to me.

I couldn't believe it.

Oscar even bobbed his head before crouching down to cuddle Rocket goodbye. He did make me promise on the way to school that I'd take his dog for a walk when I got home. Which I did. The puppy skipped happily along on the lead, jerking me left and right as it wanted to sniff literally everything. When we got close to the house, I let him off-lead and he didn't run away, obviously too exhausted from the walk to do anything other than curl up on his cushion and fall asleep in the sunshine.

Rocket is kind of cute, I guess. I can see everyone in the family falling for him. As long as he doesn't terrorize the house. Although he won't if he's kept outside most of the day. It was so nice of Tane to do that for me.

Crap, I was mean to him yesterday. He gave me a gift and I repaid him by yelling in his face. What a bitchy thing to do.

"Have a good day" was all I managed to call when he grabbed his bag and headed for the front door.

He stopped and gave me a closed-mouth smile before ducking outside.

I drove Oscar to school in a mildly confused haze. Hadn't I wanted Tane to leave me alone? That's what I'd shouted at him. In the barn. He was just doing what I freaking asked him to do!

But then he helped me make lunches this morning. He worked beside me, not getting in my way and being awesome. And then he asked Oscar to help me out too.

"Argh!" I cover my face with my hands.

I don't know what to do! I wish I didn't like him so much. I wish he wasn't so sweet. Why does my heart feel like catapulting out of my chest every time I see him? Why can't he be flawed? Just an asshole? It'd be so much easier than this constant wrestling match in my chest.

I want him.

I like him so much.

But I can't let myself have him.

Why?

"Because I…" With a sad shake of my head, I pick up my rag and shrug.

I don't know why. I don't know freaking anything anymore. I thought I had it sorted. I was so motivated and in control when I first got back from Wellington, but everything keeps turning to custard and I'm sinking. I'm failing.

And I'm not used to that feeling.

I despise it.

Tears start to burn, my eyes glassing over and my vision blurring, but then a car horn beeps in the driveway. Rocket starts yapping, and it's enough to pull me together.

It's good. I don't want to cry.

I press my knuckles into my eyes before any tears can fall and run a hand through my hair. Glancing down at my dirty T-shirt, I nearly dart upstairs to change it, but someone's knocking on the door—sharp, urgent raps that demand attention.

Lifting my chin, I try for just a smidge of dignity and paste on a polite smile as I swing the door open. My mouth quickly drops into a wide O, and then the screaming begins.

"What are you guys doing here?" I yell above Zoey and Alaina's excitement.

They crack up laughing and wrap me in a monstrous hug so we're squished into the doorway like sardines.

Somehow Zoey pushes us through the gap, and then we dance in this little BFF circle until my shock has worn off enough to pull back and gape at them again.

They're both gorgeous. Smiling at me with bright, fresh eyes. Zoey's put pink streaks in her hair. They look awesome. And Alaina's floral boho dress is so cute.

They're here!

I can't believe they're here!

"Aren't you supposed to be at orientation this week?"

"We skipped it!" Zoey's hands fly through the air. "As soon as Willow called us, we knew we had to ditch everything to come and hang with you!"

"Willow called you?"

"We left last night and got as far as Turangi." Alaina starts scanning the house, her nose wrinkling as she snickers and points to a pale porcelain statue that belongs in a retirement home.

"I know." I grin at her, then turn back to Zoey. "But what are you missing?"

"Nothing much. Classes don't start until Monday. We'll be back in time."

"I can't believe you guys are here." I pat my chest, emotions rising like a tidal wave. I don't know whether to laugh or cry.

My best friends are here!

"Of course we are! You're our bestie, and after those little toe rags forgot your birthday, we've got some making up to do!"

"Aw, I think they felt pretty bad." I wince.

"Willow cried on the phone when she called me." Zoey tips her head. "Poor little thing."

"She called? When?"

"Yesterday morning on her way to school."

"We're your birthday present." Alaina wraps her arm around my shoulders and kisses my cheek. "Why didn't you tell us they forgot?"

"I don't know." I shrug. "Too busy wallowing in self-pity?"

They both snicker at me and I smile, feeling like an idiot.

"Well, that BS can stop right now, because we are here and ready to show you a good time, little lady." Alaina kisses my cheek.

I squeeze my girls close against me and start to laugh. I'll take that over crying. I can't believe the mix of joy and relief bursting through me right now. It's weird how sometimes you don't realize how much you miss your friends until you actually see them in the flesh.

36

BIANCA

I conceal myself behind the massive navy beam that holds up C Block. Tane and his mates always have lunch in the quad area just in front of my hiding spot. I scan the wooden bench seats but can't see Cam. I promised myself I'd talk to him today. I need to get organized for this party on Saturday, and I'm running out of time.

Tension wraps my stomach into a tight knot. I'm kind of terrified right now. Walking up to the crowd while they all stop to look at me will be so humiliating, but I have to get Cam's attention somehow. Will they assume all these weird things if I ask to talk to him privately?

I can't even see him yet. Maybe he'll pop out of a door soon and I can quickly speak with him before he joins his friends.

Students breeze past me, a few giving me odd glances before finding a spot to eat their food.

I'm supposed to be meeting Stacey for lunch, but I figured I could talk to Cam first and then use my sister as an excuse to leave what will no doubt be an embarrassing conversation. If he asks to join me, I've already devised a couple of lines to throw him off, my first being: "We're eating with her boyfriend, Jonas. They're really into each other. Kind of have to do everything together, you know?"

Maybe if Cam knows that Jonas and Stacey are a solid item, he'll stop trying to use me to get close to her.

"Are you pretending to be a spy, or is there someone in particular you're looking for?" Cam's voice makes me jump, and I spin around with a gasp before my cheeks go hot and no doubt crimson red.

I tuck my fringe behind my ear and look to the ground while Cam chuckles. "Sorry. Didn't mean to scare you."

"Oh, no. That's okay." I brush my hand through the air and find the courage to glance up at him.

He's smiling at me, that beautiful smile where his eyes dance just a little. This warm, yummy feeling starts creeping through me.

I swallow and order my brain to be professional, the way I'd planned. Clearing my throat, I play with the edges of my skirt and say, "I'm looking for you, actually."

"Oh yeah?" His face lights up even more.

I'm confused by what looks to be genuine pleasure. Like he's totally stoked I'm wanting to talk to him.

"Yeah, um, we're planning a surprise party for Harper."

"Tane told me."

"It's kind of fallen to me to organize it, and I... well, I need a little help, and Tane said I could ask you."

"Of course, what do you need?" He slides his hands into his pockets, and I can't ignore the way his muscles move. He's so broad and imposing, yet his smile and friendly eyes invite you in. Such a stunning contrast.

"Um." I wrestle with the zipper of my skirt pocket and finally pull a rumpled scrap of paper out. It's trembling a little in my hands. I hope he doesn't notice. "Sound equipment, mainly. Speakers, a couple of microphones, and well, it'd be great to track down a karaoke machine or something. I mean, we could use a computer or Play Station maybe. I..." Scratching the side of my nose, I glance up at him, but the sweet smile on his face throws me, so I dart my gaze back to the safety of the paper. "And then it'd be great to get help setting up on Saturday. Beck's sourced some chairs and tables from the local rugby club, but I need someone to help me pick it all up and then set it up. I don't know how to drive a trailer, and Beck's ute is kind of big and scary, so…"

Cam chuckles. "Yeah, we can do that. I'll get Sione and Logan to help me."

"Okay." I give him a relieved smile. That was so much easier than I thought it'd be.

"And you said something about sound equipment?"

"Yep. Tane said you've got a neighbor? Who's in a band?"

Cam clicks his fingers and points at me. "Actually, I know someone who might be even better. You said karaoke, right?"

I nod, entranced by the happy grin on his face.

"Come with me." He flicks his finger and I follow him without thought. He's my Pied Piper and I'm helpless against his charm. It's the weirdest feeling. As I walk beside him, completely unaware of where he's leading me, I actually start to relax. He's chatting away about the English class he just had, drawing me into the conversation like it's the easiest thing in the world.

I hear myself laugh at something he said, and it catches me off guard. The happy sound bounces from one side of my brain to the other, and I blink in surprise.

"Here we go." He points down the corridor heading to

the music suites and I turn right with him, slowing when he comes to a stop outside Practice Studio 1.

Someone is singing behind the closed door. She has a beautiful voice. Strong and sure, with depth and huskiness to it. My heart thrills like it always does when music gets within earshot.

I can't help a stunned smile. "She sounds so beautiful."

"Oh yeah, she's got a good set of pipes all right." Cam knocks on the door and winks at me.

My heart thrills in a different kind of way, and I have to look to the floor so he doesn't see my fierce blush. I hate to think how red my cheeks are right now. I'm probably a tomato with carrot top hair.

Ugh. So embarrassing.

The singing cuts off and the door handle clunks before being pulled back to reveal a gorgeous girl with black Afro curls and a stunning, toothy smile.

"Hey, Miss." Cam greets her.

"Hello, Cameron." She crosses her arms, a teasing gleam in her dark brown eyes. "What can I do you for?"

She's American. I pick up on the accent immediately.

He snickers. "Got someone here who's looking to set up a karaoke party for her...cousin?" He looks to me and I nod, liking the sound of that, loving the grin on Cam's face.

"Yay! Karaoke!" The singer glances at me, her white smile so bright it's hard not to mirror it. "Hey!" She sticks out her hand. "I'm Missy."

"Bianca." I shake it, feeling the warmth from her fingers travel straight into my soul.

"You're in my music class, right?"

"Uh... maybe. Yes, I mean, I recognize you." I feel bad for not being more sure about it. I don't want to offend her; I've just been keeping my head down a lot these last few weeks. Just trying to survive school and find my learning groove.

"Do you sing?"

"A little."

"And you play the piano, right?"

I nod. "I got up to Grade 6. Still trying to decide if I want to take it further."

"Nice! And you totally should. If you get up to Grade 8, you can start teaching. I mean, if you wanted to. I don't know what your aspirations are or anything, but I always figure why not aim for the best and if you don't quite make it, then you're still doing awesome, you know?"

Cam laughs and I smile up at him before looking back to Missy, who my heart is quickly falling for. She just oozes this niceness that I want to fall straight into. She's so enthusiastic and happy.

"Anyway, maybe you can come in and help me with this song, and then I'll chat karaoke gear with you."

I glance up to Cam, who gives me an encouraging smile and another little wink.

It's cute, that wink of his.

"Have fun." He wiggles his eyebrows at me, and my heart pitches in my chest.

Thankfully Missy takes my hand and drags me into the studio before I can turn into a tomato again. "I would ask Cam to help, but he can't sing to save himself."

"I heard that!" he calls through the closing door.

"You're good for other stuff, man!" Missy yells back. "You leave the sounding beautiful to us girls."

"Whatever," he shouts back. "Take care of her for me."

"You know I will!" She grins at me while my heart goes crazy at Cam's sweet sentiment. He wants Missy to take care of me. He spoke like I was his.

I shouldn't love this feeling in my chest so much.

It's not realistic.

Cam isn't after a girl like me. It's too far-fetched to even entertain the idea. But if I'm not careful, it could turn into another case of Bianca crushing on someone she'll never have. I'd really love to avoid that if I can.

"So…" Missy claps her hands together and gives them a rub. "I just downloaded the music to 'Love Me Anyway' by P!nk, because I adore everything about her and this song's my jam right now. But I can't really play the piano that well, and it's frustrating the heck out of me. Can you sight-read?"

I grin, because I'm really good at sight-reading, but I don't want to be all proud and boastful about it, so I just say, "I can give it a go."

"Yay!" Missy claps her hands again.

I skim the music on the keyboard stand and place my fingers into the right position. Softly counting under my breath, I find the beat and start to play. Missy comes in right on time, and her stunning voice makes my skin ripple with goose bumps. When she gets to the second chorus, I can't help myself. I join in, throwing in a high harmony that makes Missy's eyes bulge with delight.

She keeps singing and smiling at me, and when the song ends, she lets out a whoop and wraps me in a tight hug.

"That sounded so amazing! We blend, girl! We are awesome!" She raises her hands in the air and does a snazzy little dance, her narrow hips wiggling.

I chuckle, her praise reminding me of Mum. She used to

love singing with me. Sweet memories flood my brain, and before I can stop myself, I tell Missy.

"My mum had a really good voice. We used to sing together all the time. I really miss it." Tears pop into my eyes so suddenly I gasp and let out an embarrassed little squeak. "Sorry."

"Never apologize for crying." Missy pulls a tissue from her pocket and gives me a stunning smile. "It cleanses the soul. If you don't get that water out of there, all those hurts on the inside grow moldy and are so much harder to clean out later."

I wrinkle my brow, having never heard that imagery before. I kind of like it.

Missy shrugs. "That's just what I believe. And I'm really sorry your parents aren't here anymore. Losing them like that must have sucked." I don't know how she knows, but I can't be annoyed about it, because her expression is so filled with compassion that more tears spill out before I can stop them.

She gives my shoulder a squeeze. "Singing with your mum must have been so special. And I'd miss it too." She pulls in a breath, then lets out a sigh that turns into a smile. "You know my mom always says that when a door slams shut, God opens a window. Meaning He never lets us go without the things we really need."

My forehead wrinkles.

"What I'm trying to say is that your mum might not be here anymore, but now you've met me, and I will sing with you anytime you want. I'm like your window, so you don't have to live without that joy."

Swallowing becomes hard work as my throat swells and more tears spill over. They course down my cheeks, running to the edge of my mouth. I lick the salty taste away and sniff.

Missy looks worried for a second. "I'm sorry. I know that living without her must be awful on so many levels, not just the singing thing. And maybe I'm not your window. I feel like I just totally said the wrong thing when all I wanted to do was make you feel better."

Bunching the tissue into my eyes, I can't help a breathy laugh.

"What you said was great." I sniff and try to pull myself together. "I'm so glad I met you today, and I'd love to sing with you again."

More tears tumble free, but I brush those ones away, feeling the lightest I have in a long time.

Missy grins, her own eyes shimmering as she leans forward and kisses my cheek. "Right, we better talk party business or we'll be two blubbering messes by the time the bell rings. Can't have that." She sniffs and dashes a finger under her eye. "Now, you said a karaoke party, right?"

"Yep." I bob my head, and wipe away the tears with my sodden tissue. "Would you like to come?"

"Ah, yes please!" She opens her mouth and then giggles. "That'd be so cool, and I can come early and help you set everything up. You can borrow any sound equipment from my church. As long as it's back on Sunday morning by like eight, all will be well."

"Your pastor person won't mind?"

"It's my dad." She laughs. "He won't mind. There's no social events at the church this weekend, and you can borrow my karaoke machine from home. That thing is loaded up with so many songs you'll be singing until Christmas."

I laugh and have to fight the urge to hug this person. This girl who already feels like a best friend, even though I met her less than half an hour ago.

She nods and it's like she can read my mind. Wrapping her arms around my neck, she gives me a squeeze. "We're going to be really good friends. I can tell."

I pull out of the hug with a happy grin and am about to give her my contact details when the door bursts open and I spin to find an irate Stacey.

Her blonde curls are a wild mane, her eyes sparking with irritation.

"What are you doing in here?" she snaps and looks at Missy.

Missy glances between us. "Hi, I'm Missy."

"Stacey." She crosses her arms. "I'm Bianca's twin."

"You guys are twins?" Missy's mouth opens into a big smile. "Wow. That's cool."

"Yeah, it's supposed to be awesome… when your twin shows up." Stacey's voice is sharp and caustic. Her glare could melt the freckles off my face.

I glance at my watch and wince. "I forgot. I'm sorry."

"I waited basically half of lunchtime, and then I had to waste the rest of it looking for you!"

"Well, you didn't have to look for—"

"We agreed to meet up today!"

"I know, I just got distracted organizing the party. Missy's going to loan us all the sound gear and her karaoke machine."

"Great," Stacey clips.

My shoulders droop, and I know the only way to settle this is to leave with my sister. Hopefully I can calm her down before the bell rings. Hitching my bag onto my shoulder, I give Missy a sad smile. "I'll see you in music."

"You bet." Missy's voice is still bright and perky despite the storm cloud Stacey just threw over us. "I can grab your number then, and we can arrange this weekend."

"Thanks." I give her a grateful smile, which grows when Missy mouths, "Sisters!" and pulls a face. "I have three!"

I stifle a giggle as I walk out the door, but it quickly evaporates when it slams shut behind me and I'm left to face Queen Pissed Off on my own.

"I can't believe you ditched me like that. You *promised* you'd show up today." Stacey storms down the hallway, and I trot after her.

"I know. I just got…distracted."

She jerks to a stop and spins to face me, her ponytail dramatically arcing through the air before settling on her shoulder. "Do you have any idea how hard I am trying to make this work? To make you fit!"

My eyebrows pucker. "I don't need you to make me fit, Stace."

"My sister is not spending her lunchtimes hiding in secret alcoves throughout the school! You need to get a life!"

"I wasn't hiding just then." I point my thumb over my shoulder.

"Maybe not, but you have got to admit that you are acing Loner 101 right now."

I look to the ground, scrambling for a witty comeback. But I've got nothing.

"I'm trying to help you. I'm trying to give you friends, but you're just not making any effort."

Anger simmers in my stomach, my lips forming a hard line as I glare at my sister and go for a little honestly. "I don't fit with your friends. You can try all you like, but it won't change the fact that I don't belong with your group. Why do you keep pushing this so hard? Why can't I just go and hide? What's the big deal?"

"Because I need to make this work!"

"Why? We've never had the same friends before."

"We've never just been the two of us before!" Stacey shouts, her words echoing down the empty corridor, her expression a mask of pain and desperation.

The chilling silence that follows her outburst makes me shiver, and I'm actually grateful when the bell lets out a loud shrill ring. We both jump and gasp in unison, but then Stacey pulls herself together with a sniff.

She's always been so good at that. She can switch it on and off like a tap.

If only it were that easy for me.

My insides are going berserk and I cross my arms, smooshing them into my stomach to try and control the buzzing in my guts.

"We better get to class." Stacey sighs, her blue eyes

wounding me with their sadness. "I'll see you after school."

I watch her walk away, not sure how to feel.

Part of me is annoyed that she's forcing me into this place I don't belong, but another part feels really guilty. She's so obviously hurting, struggling with this whole mess, and I want to help her. I just wish that didn't mean hanging out with Jonas and Leon. I wish helping her meant spending my lunchtimes singing with Missy.

37

TANE

The car is stuffy and quiet. The window's down, but it's like the earth has gone stagnant and the air can't rush through the open space fast enough. I tap my index finger on the wheel and peek into the back. Yep. Something definitely went down between Stacey and Bianca today.

They have their backs to each other, both looking out their own windows while an icy chill vibrates between them.

The silence is painful. I mean, music is playing, but it's being drowned out by the ice storm in the back seat. I'm used to Stacey rabbiting on. Shit, I'll even put up with listening about Jonas for a couple of minutes if it'll break the tension. Thank God I have touch rugby this afternoon. I'm in desperate need of a good run around. I'm going to play hard today. I need to get away from all these brooding chicks and burn off some steam.

Willow's in the front, her lips drawn into their usual disinterested pout. She doesn't seem unhappy, and before I can stop myself, I go ahead and start up a conversation.

"How was your day?"

She glances at me and nods, but when I roll my eyes, she gives me a break and says, "Good."

I look at her with a smile. "You talk to anybody today?"

"I'm talking to you, aren't I?"

"Come on. You know what I mean."

She gives me a long, dry look and I wink at her, which has the intended effect of making her smile.

It's just a flash, but I'll take it. "I had lunch with this girl, April. She's in my homeroom, and my English class. And my maths class."

"Cool." I nod, not knowing who she is and hoping Willow will volunteer some more, but I'm pretty sure I've gotten everything I can from her. I did just get a full sentence. I should probably be celebrating over that one.

I glance between her and the road a couple of times before giving up and figuring I'll tackle the back seat before we turn into our driveway. Harper doesn't need two ice queens stalking into the house. She's icy enough for everyone at the moment.

Although she did tell me to have a good day this morning. I couldn't respond with anything more than a smile. I'm still kind of cut up over what she said to me yesterday, but then of course I had to help her make lunches. I wanted to test out Bianca's love language theory.

But Harper didn't even say thanks, so I'm wondering if my cuz is full of bull or whether I need to give it another go. There's plenty of practical stuff I could be doing to help Harper out.

Why I want to try and soften her up, I don't know.

It'd be easier on both of us if I just left her alone like she wants me to.

But I can't.

I don't know how to stop liking her or wanting to help her. She's hurting, and I want to make it better. It's all I can think about sometimes.

And it drives me crazy.

With a sigh, I look into the back and figure Bianca's a safer bet than Stacey.

"Hey, Bee." I put on a bright voice as I call into the back. "Cam tells me you're sorted for karaoke gear."

He also had the biggest smile on his face for like all of lunchtime, but I'm not sure that's my place to say.

Bianca glances at me, then shoots a quick look at her sister. "Yeah, Missy's gunna lend it to us."

"She's awesome." I grin.

Bianca smiles but then checks on her sister again before speaking. "She's like a ball of happiness or something."

"Literally never stops smiling."

Bianca laughs.

"I'm glad you met her."

"Yeah, me too."

Stacey humphs and shuffles around to face the window even more directly. If she turns any farther away from her sister, she'll be facing the back of her seat.

Bianca looks to the sky and shakes her head.

I wonder what it's all about but don't really want to get involved. Maybe I should take Harper's advice and just leave everyone alone. My need to help and make everything better has only led to a yelling match with Stacey and then the girl I like more than anyone telling me to leave her alone.

At this rate, I'll have everyone in the house hating me by the Easter break, or maybe even Year 9 camp. That's only three weeks away. I wince, thinking about all the stuff Cam and I need to organize beforehand. We're going as student leaders and will have a big role to play throughout the camp. I want to do a really good job and not let the teachers down. Should be a fun gig. I loved going when I was in Year 9—a fresh-faced little thirteen-year-old forced to challenge myself by rock climbing, abseiling, caving and playing a bunch of team-building games. It's a good way to help the new students get settled in at high school. I'm stoked to be a part of it at the other end now.

The Year 13 camp isn't until the end of the year. It's like a big hurrah to say goodbye to all our mates. Should be a fun week away.

But that's not for ages. Right now, I have to focus on the things for *this* term, like athletics day and camp.

My mind starts ticking over with lists I need to write. I might see if Cam wants to hang out after rugby so we can start working on a few things for tomorrow's prefect meeting. It'd be good to walk in prepared. I think Mr. Kingston would be impressed. He's the deputy principal and in charge of us this year. He's as tough as boot leather but a really good guy under the surface. I think he'll be proud of us for showing some initiative.

I turn into our driveway and immediately notice a blue VW Golf parked by the house.

"Anyone know that car?"

The girls all move in unison to check it out, and a smile blooms on Willow's face. "I think that's Alaina's."

"Who?" I ask as she darts out the door and starts running for the house.

I share a perplexed look with Stacey before Bianca murmurs, "Isn't she Harper's friend from Wellington?"

"Oh yeah. Zoey and Alaina. I'm not used to hearing one name without the other."

Stacey sniggers and gets out of the car, slamming the door behind her.

"Everything okay with you guys?" I can't help asking. Bianca's face is all wrinkled, and she helped me out last night. I owe it to her to return the favor.

Bianca gives me a sad half-smile. "I was supposed to meet her at lunch today but got distracted with Missy. I don't know if it's jealousy or... what?" She shrugs. "I just thought I'd let her cool off for a while before trying to fix it. If I even have the energy to fix it." Her shoulders droop, and I wish I had something to say that would cheer her up.

But I'm blank.

I've never had sisters, and when the girls I usually hang with get scrappy with each other, I can just walk away. I don't have to live under the same roof as them.

"Don't worry about it, Tane." Bianca smiles. "She'll cool off and then we'll talk and all will be right with the world again." Her expression falters like she doesn't believe herself, but she gets out of the car before I can respond.

Grabbing my bag from the passenger footwell, I slip out the door and head toward the raucous laughter inside. I can hear little puppy barks as well, like Rocket wants in on the action too.

My eyebrows dip. Why is everyone so freaking happy?

And why can't I get the people in this house making those kinds of noises?

I stop in the doorway and watch as one of Harper's pretty friends plasters kisses all over Willow's face until she can barely breathe from giggling so hard. The other friend is tickling Willow's stomach, and it's obvious there's some major history going on here.

Harper is grinning, her arm slung around Oscar's shoulders as I get a snapshot of what life used to be like for these guys. Before they moved here and all became miserable.

They were miserable before they arrived, mate. Get the order straight.

I try to talk myself out of the black mood brewing in my chest, but it's hard to shake the idea that I've tried everything to make these people happy and all it takes is two squealing girls from down south.

I'm not enough.

It feels like I've lost, and I hate that.

"Oh, hey." Harper notices me and flashes me a brief smile before pointing at her friends. "Tane, this is Zoey and Alaina."

They stop torturing Willow long enough to grin up at me. Rocket barks and scampers over to sniff my feet. I pick him up and kiss the top of his head while he tries to nip my finger.

"Hi!" The pixie elf with pink hair gives me a once-over, her smile growing.

The other one purrs out her greeting. "Hello there."

"G'day." I smile at them, because I know that's the polite thing to do, but it's a half-ass effort. Placing Rocket back down, I pat his head for a second, still feeling their curious, hot gazes on me.

When I stand up, I half expect them to start whooping and throwing dollar bills at me. I don't usually mind girls checking me out— helps boost the old ego—but not today. Not when I'm feeling raw and itchy…inept.

Not when the only girl I want looking at me that way is staring at the carpet.

"Well, I'm gunna go get ready for rugby." I tip my head toward the stairs and shuffle off, but not before catching Harper's gaze. Her eyes find mine when I reach the base of the stairs. I pause and give her a gentle smile, then shake my head as soon as I'm out of sight. My freaking heart betrays me every time.

A crescendo of noise rises from the lounge. I can't hear what they're saying, but laughter quickly follows and it grates pretty bad. I flick my bedroom door shut and kick off my shoes, ripping off my uniform and scattering it around the floor as I get ready for rugby.

I'm leaving early. I don't care if I'm there way before anyone else. I'll just do laps of the field until my mates arrive. I need to get out of here and clear my head. There are too many girls in this house. Too many emotions. It's enough to do a guy's head in.

38

HARPER

It's Friday night and I'm at a bar for birthday drinks with Zoey and Alaina. It brings back memories of my eighteenth birthday when they took me out and I proudly bought drinks for our table. I was eighteen, old enough to purchase alcohol, and feeling like a freaking queen.

I've aged a decade since then.

Leaning against the small, round table, I tip back on my heels while Alaina waits her turn at the bar.

Music is thumping, the bass making my rib cage vibrate. It's a thick cloud of rhythm swirling around us and making Zoey's hips jiggle.

She raises her arms in the air, her whole body getting into it. She's ready to let loose tonight, and I think she's pretty determined to include me in this equation. I brush my fingers over the bandage on my arm, resisting the urge to pick at that curling corner. I can't wait to get the stupid stitches out on Monday. I was supposed to go today, but I wanted to hang out with my girlfriends while they're in town, so I postponed the appointment. A few extra days isn't going to kill me.

Although, now that I'm all dolled up in my heels and sexy red dress, I'm wishing I didn't have this stupid white bandage dominating my arm. I tried to cover it up with bracelets, but they kept falling down my arm and getting jammed. I quickly gave those up and went jewelry free on my wrists.

Smoothing a hand down my drop earrings, I grin at Zoey, who lets out a loud whoop when Alaina arrives at the table with three beer bottles.

"Cheers!" She hands them out and we clink them together before taking a deep gulp. The cold liquid soothes my throat and I start to relax.

This is fun.

I haven't done this in ages.

It's good for me to get out of the house and live it up a little.

Although I'm acting like a mother/housekeeper right now, I'm still just a nineteen-year-old girl who likes a night out. I haven't been myself in so long. This is good for me.

For some reason, I have to keep reminding myself of that.

Taking another slug from my bottle, I smile at my friends, so grateful they're here. The last two days have been a whirlwind. Thursday I gave them a tour of the farm, and they teased the crap out of me when I told them about ruining my white sneakers in cow poo. Then today I took them shopping. We went a little crazy, coming back with piles of bags. It was mostly for them, but I bought the pair of heels I'm wearing tonight and a couple of new T-shirts. It was hard not being practical and reaching for clothes I can run a house in, but I kept getting scoffed at and, in the end, settled on a few favorites that I know I'll love wearing.

"Who cares if you get cleaner on it. That's what a washing machine's for," Zoey told me. "I don't care if you're feeding chickens and scooping up horse poo, you can still feel pretty while you're doing it."

She had a good point, and I was glad she was there to boss me around.

I was pretty exhausted by the time I dropped them back to their motel so they could get ready for our big night out. I still had the bathroom to clean and a load of laundry to deal with before I could even think about a shower and makeup.

I was running way later than I meant to be, but Beck offered to pick up Oscar for me, and when I walked in the door and ran upstairs, Tane was coming out of the bathroom with a bucket in his hands.

"What are you doing? Is something broken in there?"

I glanced down at the bucket, and to my surprise it was filled with cleaning products and dirty rags.

"Figured it was one less thing for you to deal with while your friends are here."

I could have kissed him on the spot.

I nearly did. My fingers were that close to grabbing his shirt and yanking his mouth to mine, but then Willow breezed past us, needing to use the toilet. Tane walked to the stairs before I could catch him.

"Thank you," I managed to rasp, but I don't know if he heard me or not.

Sweet Tane.

I don't know what to do. Maybe I should just give in to all the urges pulsing through my body. Would it make life easier to be able to sneak hot kisses, feel his gaze on me and be able to return it? Or would everything in the house be awkward? What would Beck think? How would my siblings feel?

I close my eyes, hammered by the doubt and uncertainties.

"So, Harp..." Zoey lays her hand on my arm, her ringed fingers locking me to the table. "Tell me...how do you live under the same roof as that sexy-ass rugby player and not want to jump his bones every night?"

"Tell me about it!" Alaina's talking way too loudly already. She's only got half a beer in her. "He's like two doors away from you. I'd be sneaking in there for some nooky any chance I could get."

"You guys, stop it." I force out a laugh, sipping my beer and scrambling to change the subject.

I knew it would come up at some point. The way they checked him out on Wednesday afternoon was almost embarrassing. They were hungry lionesses, and I think he could feel it. No wonder he escaped to rugby so early.

They were more controlled for dinner on Thursday night, but he stuck with polite conversation and definitely wasn't his normal, relaxed self. He hasn't been his normal, relaxed self since our little chat in the barn.

The heavy rock I've been carrying around lodges a little further into my belly. I can't believe I actually told him to leave me alone.

It was such a bitchy thing to say, especially when I was holding the gift he'd just given me.

I close my eyes and groan.

"Come on." Zoey nudges me with a laugh. "Don't try and tell me you don't think he's gorgeous."

My eyes pop open and I nod. "He is."

I can't deny it.

"I can't believe you didn't tell us about him." Alaina gives me a pointed look, but then her eyes narrow— sharp and dangerous, like she's reading straight from my soul. "You like him!"

Zoey opens her mouth with an excited grin. "Have you kissed him yet?"

My expression must give me away, because before I can even say one word, they both squeal and start laughing.

"Oh, you have!"

"Epic."

"What was it like?"

Images of a wet embrace in the barn are knocked aside by a sizzling encounter on the pool table. My body stirs with heat just thinking about it, and all I can do is tip my head back and tell them the truth. "So hot. So incredibly amazing."

The girls start jumping up and down, making the table rock.

"So are you guys together?" Zoey asks.

"No," I whine and snatch my beer, glugging down a quarter of the bottle in one hit.

Alaina stops jumping, obviously perplexed. "Why not?"

"Because!" I smack the bottle down. "My parents just died! I have responsibilities! I can't get into a relationship right now."

"Babe, we're just trying to get you laid." Alaina giggles, but I can't even raise a smile.

I shake my head. "I don't need random sex."

"Sex with that guy would *not* be random." Zoey raises her eyebrows and clinks bottles with Alaina.

They both start laughing again, but I cut off the happy, crazy sound with a little truth that I didn't have any intention of saying. "He's not an easy lay, you guys. He's the one you fall in love with."

The words make us all freeze for a second, and then my heart starts hammering. Heat flushes through my entire body as I take in my friends' shocked expressions.

"You're in love with him?" Zoey squeaks.

"I—I..." I shake my head, determined not to be. Falling for Tane is crazy.

Inevitable, you mean. He cleaned the freaking bathroom for you!

I swallow and ignore my losing battle with the first idea that pops into my head. "Shots? You guys want shots? I'm buying."

Alaina whoops and punches her arms in the air while I head for the bar before Zoey can grill me with the questions no doubt exploding in her brain. She'll have a whole heap of advice too, and then Alaina will jump on the bandwagon and I'll get pummeled. The only solution is to get deliriously drunk. I've never been wasted before, just a little tipsy, but I'm more than happy to push myself right over the edge tonight.

I'm craving it.

I can feel these claws inside of me, scraping and begging for the liquor. Begging for the chance not to think or analyze. I just want reckless fun.

It takes the girls four shots to stop hassling me. I can't even remember how I countered them, but I batted off repeated questions and comments like:

Why won't you get with him?

Is it because of Dylan?

Tane is hot and you like him. Just go for it.

Living in the same house doesn't have to be weird.

He's obviously a nice guy. Just let yourself be happy.

You're allowed to be happy, Harper.

Stop holding back.

I take the last piece of advice, but I'm not thinking

about Tane when I down my fifth and sixth shots. I'm consumed with the idea of letting go, letting loose, drowning in a sea of no responsibility. An ocean of numb.

I deserve it, don't I?

I'm young. I'm with my best friends. I should be living it up and partying, not playing mother to a bunch of teenagers and running a home like it's something I've always aspired to. I don't want to organize anybody or make a damn school lunch. I'm sick of trying to make the house tidy for people who don't even give a rat's ass.

I down the last shot on the table, then wobble my way to the bar, slapping my credit card on the shiny surface. "Shree more," I slur, holding up my fingers.

I have no idea how many I'm holding up right now, but it's enough to make the bartender shake his head.

"I think you girls have had enough." His smile is kind, I think. It's hard to tell through the blurry haze. "Let me call you a taxi."

"We don't need a ride." Alaina bumps into me and giggles, threading her arm around my elbow. "Come on, Harp, you can share my bed."

She drags me out of the bar and we stumble onto Victoria Street, laughing and swaying against each other. Zoey is mumbling a song to herself, but I hear the tune and gasp, hollering the lyrics at the top of my lungs. It's a favorite of mine — "MGNO" by... by... some guy who sings good.

Alaina cackles in my ear and joins in, but she doesn't know the lyrics and ends up just shouting out sounds that are off-key and make me laugh so hard my stomach hurts.

"Whoa." My heels wobble as the world starts falling and I stagger forward, catching myself against a tree. "Where do you guys live again?"

"Duh." Zoey giggles. "In Wellington."

I snort and point at her. "You're silly. Where am I sleeping tonight?"

"In Tane's bed!" Alaina raises her hands, and we all crack up laughing.

I don't even know why I'm laughing anymore.

I feel light and untethered. That usually scares me, but tonight, I embrace it. I am free! Reckless!

I kind of actually... I swallow, my stomach roiling like I've been out at sea in a rocking boat for too long. Rubbing my hand over my dress, I groan and tip my head back.

"I want to lie down now."

"Come on." Alaina flicks her floppy wrist at me. "Motel's this way."

She teeters off through a quad. It's a big open space breaking up Victoria Street. Cafes and storefronts open onto it, and there are bench seats and a couple of sculptures to pretty it up. I follow after my friends, but the stilts I'm walking on are making it impossible to keep up.

"Wait, you guys!" I call, laughing at how childlike I sound.

They stop and turn to giggle at me while I try to balance and remove my sandals. I end up falling over and landing on my ass. Throwing my head back, I let out a hooting wail—it's a cross between a cry of pain and a howling laugh. Yanking off my heels, I throw them at my hyena friends.

They scream and duck out of the way, hysterical and crazy as they start running.

The shoes land on the concrete and dance a few three-sixties before finally stopping at the base of another tree. Slapping my hands on the rough concrete, I push myself up, my dress riding so high that I probably flash the world my underwear. I yank it back down with a yelp and start giggling until my stomach pitches again.

I swallow to keep the burning bile at bay. Zoey and Alaina are on the other side of the quad now. They're singing and swaying against each other—two drunk idiots.

I laugh and stumble-run to get to them but end up tripping over again. My laughter's gone quiet now. It's so strong and intense, I can't even make a sound. My body vibrates out of control, and I wonder how I'm supposed to breathe when the giggles have got me in their clutches.

"Come on, dopey," Zoey calls over her shoulder, just before disappearing around the corner with Alaina.

I suck in a breath and shout, "Wait."

"Come on!" they holler back. I can't see them anymore.

I get to my feet and weave in their direction, but I don't even reach the corner before a police car pulls to a stop on the curb and flashes its lights.

The blue and red are kind of pretty in the darkness. Like colorful fairy lights.

A police officer climbs out of the passenger side and slowly walks toward me.

"Miss? Are you okay?"

"I'm fine." I drag my hand through air that seems thicker than it did before.

I glance down at my sluggish limb with a frown.

"We had a call about a public disturbance. Are you out here alone?"

"No, I..." I point to the corner and wonder where my friends have gone.

Are they playing hide-and-seek?

Maybe that's a good idea, because I'm talking to the police right now, and I don't think being drunk in front of cops is the best idea.

"I don't know." I shake my floppy head, then hold it with a groan.

"It's not a good idea for you to be out on the street at this time of night when you're intoxicated. Especially if you're alone."

"Can we offer you a ride home?" another officer asks.

Where did he come from?

I stare between them, their blue uniforms and serious expressions penetrating the fog in my brain.

There's something so familiar about it all.

Something so harrowing.

"No," I whisper, stumbling back from them, fear clutching me.

They're going to tell me that Oscar and Willow are dead. That's why they're here. To destroy my world completely.

They're going to look all sad and then say, "We're sorry to inform you, miss, but—"

"Don't say it!" I point at them. "Don't you say it!"

"Miss." One of the officers raises his palms and walks toward me. "You need to calm down. You're going to hurt yourself if you're not careful. Now, please. Let us help you. We can take you home."

"Who's dead?" I suck in a gasp, and they look at each other before turning back to me.

"No one is dead. We just want to get you somewhere safe so you can sober up."

"No one's dead?"

"No, miss."

"No one's dead," I whisper, my body starting to shake uncontrollably as my knees buckle.

An officer lurches forward, snatching my arm before I hit the pavement again.

"Let's get her into the car."

They each take a side and gently walk me to their cruiser. One of them guides my head while I slip into the back and resist the urge to flop right down and close my eyes.

Instead, my head lolls against the headrest, the storm in my stomach starting to surge up my throat.

"If you could please give us your address, then we can take you home."

"I don't…" My head rolls back and forth. "I don't know where I live."

The officer crouches down by the open door. "You don't know where you live?"

"Wellington."

"You live in Wellington?"

"No," I whine.

He gives me a tight-lipped smile before asking slowly, "Do you live in Hamilton, or are you just visiting?"

"Just for a year." I hold up my finger.

"You're visiting for a year? Are you on a travel visa?"

I snort and tip my head back with a laugh. "I wish I was traveling; then I wouldn't have to deal with all this shit." My arms dance up in the air, then crash back down again.

"Okay." The officer glances up at his mate, bulging his eyes a little before standing tall.

"Do you have any ID on you, miss?"

"I…" Fumbling for my purse, I let out another groan and lurch sideways out of the car. The waves inside of me crash together and spew out of my mouth… and all over a pair of black shoes that don't belong to me.

I gaze down at my vomit, the edges of my brain clearing just enough for me to realize what I've done.

"Sorry," I manage to rasp before looking up at the officer and puking all over again.

39

TANE

"Yeah, see ya, mate!" I hold up my hand and wave goodbye to Cam.

He's dropping Manu home on his way, and I smile as I watch them drive off into the darkness. It was a good night. Just what I needed.

A little pool. A little music. And a whole lot of laughter.

It dulled the jagged edges of my week and helped me feel normal for a bit.

It's annoying that the second they're gone, I'm swamped again. Harper's not back from her girls' night out. She looked so freaking hot when she left the house that I nearly volunteered to be her bodyguard.

The tight red dress that hugged her butt but then fell all loose at the top was mouth-watering. Any guy with even a quarter of a brain would be an idiot not to hit on her.

I hope no one tried. I hope her friends are watching her back right now.

"It's not your problem," I mutter, raking a hand through my hair and hating that it's not.

I want Harper to be my problem.

I want to care about her, worry about her, be the guy she calls when she's in trouble.

But she doesn't want that.

Glancing up at the sky, I gaze at the moon for a beat. It's a curved thumbnail—the classic shape you see in a kid's drawing. The stars are glowing bright tonight. I'd love it if Harper drove up the driveway right now. I'd open her door for her, snag her around the waist and make her stare at the sky with me.

I wonder how many seconds I'd get before she pushed me off and retreated into the house. My chest caves with a heavy sigh as my shoulders droop and I shuffle for the front door.

My phone vibrates in my hand and I glance down at the screen, surprised to see Harper's name on display.

I hesitate for just a moment. Does she even want me to answer it? But then curiosity kicks my ass. She's probably just calling to say she'll be staying at the motel with her mates. Couldn't she call Beck to tell him that? Why involve me? Especially when she doesn't want me.

"Hey, Harp." My greeting comes out terse, but my irritation evaporates the second I hear her tiny, broken voice.

"I need you."

"What?" I pause outside the front door.

She sniffs. "I need you."

Her voice wobbles and breaks around the words, making them a little hard to hear.

Is she crying?

That can't be right.

She never cries—not that she doesn't need to—but...

She needs me?

Hope tries to soar through my chest, but it hits a solid wall of confusion as I step into the house and have to ask, "Are you... are you drunk right now?"

That's the only logical explanation I can think of.

Beck, who I didn't notice on the couch, jerks up straight. "Who are you talking to?"

"Yes," Harper whimpers. "I'm at the police station. I threw up on a police officer, and they want someone to come get me."

"You...what?" I blink slowly, shock overriding any decent chance at a coherent sentence. "The police... what?"

Beck flicks off the TV and stands tall, crossing his arms and giving me a concerned look. "Who are you talking to?"

I ignore him and focus back on Harper, begging my brain to switch into thinking mode. "Okay." I squeeze my eyes shut and try again. "Which police station are you at?"

"I don't know."

"Who's at a police station?" Beck walks around to stand beside me.

"Where were you when they picked you up?"

"I don't know. Um... the... there was concrete... and my shoes! Shit! My shoes." Harper kind of whines, and I'm thrown into another ball of confusion. "I couldn't walk and I left them and then they were gone around the corner and I didn't mean to... I just... they pulled up and then now I don't know where I live."

"Harp, you're not making any sense. Just take a breath and—"

There's a shuffling in my ear and then a calm, deep voice I don't recognize. "Who am I speaking with, please?"

"Uh, Tane Smith. Who's this?"

"This is Officer Apriana. Who are you in relation to Harper Hughes?"

"She…lives in our house."

"Are you the owner of the house?"

"No, uh…"

Beck, having lost all his patience, is now standing right in my face and flicking his hands. "Give me the phone. Now."

I hand it over with a tut, my insides reeling. Harper's drunk and at the police station. This is unreal.

"This is Beckett Connell. Who am I speaking with? … Right… Yes, I'm her guardian… She what?" Beck starts pacing, brushing his hand over the back of his head. I can almost see the hairs turning grey. I guess Stacey's not the only one giving him a run for his money. "Yeah… Yeah, nah, I understand. I'll come get her now… Yeah, thanks, mate."

Beck hangs up and shakes his head.

"Of all of them," he mutters, passing back my phone.

I grab the keys from the bowl and head for the door. "Is she okay?"

"I don't know what the hell she is." Beck shoves his shoes on and snaps his fingers before opening his hand.

"I'll go. Which station is she at?"

"No." Beck takes the keys from my hand. "I need you to stay."

"But—"

He's stormed out before I can argue, the door rattling shut behind him.

"Is everything okay?" Stacey calls from the top of the stairs.

I walk to the foot and talk up to her. "All good. Beck's just popped out to... pick something up."

Giving her the thumbs-up, I wait until she's turned back toward her room before lightly kicking the bottom step and stalking back into the lounge.

Harper called *me.*

She needs me. That's what she said.

That's what her drunk-self said.

I flop onto the couch with an agitated sigh, wishing like anything that I was the guy driving out to collect her now. I want to be the shoulder she finally cries on. I want to gather her drunk, whimpering body into my arms and hold her until she feels sane again.

40

HARPER

The taste in my mouth is rancid.

I don't know when I drank a vat of acid with a side of possum poo, but whatever substance has congealed in my throat, nose and on my tongue is enough to make me want to puke all over again.

I clutch the bucket in my lap and rest my head on the rim.

Zoey called me in a frantic panic just as I was arriving at the police station. I'd sobered up enough to insist she didn't come find me. I told her I was fine and had decided to head home. She bought it without any fuss, not even asking how I was getting home. She probably assumed an Uber, or was too drunk to assume anything. She'd never know that Uber wasn't even an option for me. There was only one option. One person who I wanted to call. So I did. As soon as I was guided to a chair and handed a bucket, I shakily pulled up Tane's number.

I can't really remember what I said to him now. The words just tumbled out in this jumbled mess until the officer took the phone from me and finished up the call.

He told me Beck's coming to collect me, and all I have to do is sit in this chair and try not to throw up on anything.

"You just hold that bucket tight, okay?"

"Yes," I rasped and tipped my head back to rest on the wall.

I've been checked on a couple of times, offered some water. I've sipped at it, but the storm in my stomach is still surging every now and again.

I've never been this drunk before.

I threw up on a police officer.

My humiliation is complete. The depth of my shame can't possibly be deeper.

They've actually been really nice to me, considering.

The puking has sobered the silly out of me and now a pounding headache is setting in, spreading like a virus throughout my body until every muscle aches.

I can barely follow a straight line of thought. I've been darting from chaotic laughter, to the feel of Tane's hands on my body, to the harrowing loss that floats inside of me like a big, black hole.

My parents.

My dad.

Oh, what would Dad say?

Tears blur my vision as the shame washes over me again. It's red and black and smothers me.

"I tried," I whimper, my teeth chattering as my eyes burn and my nose stings. "I can't do it. I can't do this without you."

My body starts to tremble and I dip my head into the bucket, wishing it was a vortex I could disappear inside of.

"Harper?" a woman softly says. "Beck's here to collect you."

My head shoots up, and I gape at her wide-eyed.

She gives me a motherly smile and takes the bucket from me. With her other hand, she helps me up, and I shuffle out to reception where Beck is talking to an officer.

He glances at me, his big bear eyebrows dipping into a growly frown before he turns back to the tall man in blue.

"She'll be right. Just needs to sleep it off."

"Yeah, yeah. I'll get her home safe." Beck shakes his hand. "Thanks so much for taking care of her."

"It's what we do."

He gives us both a smile before holding open the glass door. Beck grips my elbow, steadying me down the stairs.

My legs are cooked fettuccine, making it hard to walk straight, and in the end Beck wraps his arm around my waist and half carries me to the car.

"You still need a puke bucket?"

"I think I'm all out," I croak.

"Let's hope so. If your body tells you otherwise, let me know so I can pull over. You've already puked on enough stuff you shouldn't have tonight."

The force of his disappointment slams into me as I wrestle my seat belt on and gaze across the street at the big, ethereal mural of the woman's head.

She looks so serene, floating there amongst the stars.

I'd like to float in the stars right now, but I can't see that happening any time soon. As Beck pulls away from the curb, I can feel myself plummeting like an asteroid. I already know that the landing is not going to be pretty.

41

TANE

I pace until my legs ache, not giving up the fight until I see headlights in the driveway. Scrambling to the window, I pull the curtain aside and watch Beck help Harper out of the car.

The front porch light highlights her pale and forlorn face. She's a wreck.

I wonder if she wants me to see her this way.

Probably not.

As much as I *want* to see her, I can't be another burden. I've never seen her so vulnerable before. As much as I want to wrap her in a hug, clean her up, tuck her into bed, that's not my place right now.

Even though she called me, I have no idea how she'll react now that she's sobered up a little. I mean, I assume she's sobered up a little. Surely a stint in the police station will have had that effect. She's probably humiliated beyond belief. Will she want to see my mug staring at her when she walks in the door?

"Watch your step." I hear Beck's voice outside the door and bolt to the stairwell, ducking out of sight but not earshot.

No one but the grandfather clock says anything, and I listen to the shuffling between ticks. The click of the door shutting, the slightly unsteady padding of feet across the wooden floor.

"You better go get cleaned up, then into bed. You're gunna have one doozy of a hangover in the morning."

"Yeah." Harper's voice is small and shaky.

Her feet pad across the floor and I tense, ready to creep up the stairs, when she stops moving again.

Curious, I peek my head around the corner in time to see her turn to face Beck. "I'm sorry."

"You should be," Beck snaps, throwing his keys onto the coffee table. "Drunk off your face in a police station? I expect more from you. You're the sensible one. The one I don't have to worry about! I should be able to rely on you."

Harper looks down and I watch her profile bunch, her chin trembling.

I grip the wall and nearly step out, ready to defend her, to tell Beck to take is easy. She's obviously hurting.

"You're nineteen, for crying out loud! That doesn't give you the right to go and get plastered."

"Yeah, I'm nineteen!" Harper shoots back. "Nineteen years old, yet I'm living like a forty-five-year-old woman! Stuck in this house cleaning and cooking and looking after teenagers!"

Beck pauses for a second, frowning at her like this is all some out-of-the-blue revelation. His jaw works to the side and he takes in a breath before muttering, "No one said you had to stay. You wanted to. That was your choice."

"No! My choice? What choice? I had to do the right thing. And staying is right!"

Beck huffs, pinching his mouth before stroking a hand down his beard. "I know it's hard. I get that. I mean I *know*." He pounds his chest with his fist, then gives her a sad, disappointed frown. "But getting drunk isn't the answer. I mean, what the hell would your father say if he was here right now?"

The air in the room goes suddenly still, like the earth is holding its breath, waiting for an answer no one really wants to hear. Because it's a question that shouldn't have to be asked.

Lance Hughes should be alive. It's not right that he was

taken so suddenly. That any of them were. This pain Harper's fighting is so damn unfair.

She turns sideways, not noticing me as her chest starts to heave. "He's not," she sobs. "He's not here. And he never will be again." Her breath catches and skips erratically, her entire body starting to tremble. "And he should be! I miss him. I miss them both so much, and I can't do this anymore. I can't be what they need me to be. And it's not fair that they're gone! It's not fair!" She lets out this gut-wrenching cry, and then it happens. She crumples to the floor like a worn-out rag doll and she breaks apart.

I mean, she really sobs.

These ugly, soul-crushing sounds punch out of her mouth. They're so filled with agony that my own vision starts to blur, and I can't stand in the shadows anymore.

Slipping into view, I kneel down beside her and gently coax her against my chest.

She moves into me, fisting the side of my shirt and clinging like she'll drown if I let go.

I glance up at Beck. His face is ashen, his eyes glassy. With a sniff, he moves across the room and awkwardly drops onto his butt so we're sandwiching her.

Rubbing gentle circles over her shoulder, he pinches his nose and sniffs, then gives up the fight, letting the tears trickle into his beard.

Resting my cheek on top of Harper's head, I hold her against me and close my eyes.

For once I'm not trying to think of the perfect words to make her smile or trying to come up with some way to get rid of the sadness.

This is one of the moments where you just have to soak in the despair.

Where there are no words.

Just tears.

42

BIANCA

I couldn't see Harper, but I could hear her. I think everyone in the house could. When Stacey and I crept out of bed to check out the scene, she was cocooned between Beck and Tane. I didn't think it was right to disturb that moment, so we shuffled back upstairs and lay in our beds, awake half the night.

I was, at least.

At one point I thought I heard Stacey crying, but I didn't have the courage to ask her because I knew that would only set off my own tears.

Harper's agony was so real. I could feel it in my soul. The injustice of life, the immense, painful hole that just won't go away. I feel hollow so much of the time, and I know it's only been a couple of months since we lost them, but I can't imagine this hole ever going away. How do you fill such a massive void?

Sleep must have caught me eventually, because I wake up to a sunny morning. The birds outside are playfully chatting to each other. I roll onto my side and listen to them for a moment, charmed by it all until a thought suddenly strikes me.

Harper's party is today.

Better get your A into G!

I gasp and bolt upright.

"What's wrong?" Stacey moans.

"The party." I snatch my watch off the nightstand to check the time. "I've got so much to do."

"Isn't Missy coming to help you?" Stacey grumbles, rolling over so she's facing the wall.

I glare at her back and mutter, "Yes, but that still doesn't mean there isn't heaps to do, and it all needs to get done without Harper noticing."

"She'll be completely hammered after that cry-fest. She's not getting up anytime soon, I bet a bajillion bucks on it."

Throwing on some old work clothes, I hope Stacey's right as I creep out of the room and head downstairs.

The house is like a tomb this morning. Is everyone sleeping in?

No, Beck must be milking.

I nearly jump out of my skin when he suddenly appears in the kitchen.

"What are you doing here? Is everything okay with the cows?"

"Having a weekend off," he mumbles. "Linc and Tane are covering for me this morning."

"That's nice of them."

He scrubs a hand over his face. "Didn't sleep too well last night."

"I don't think anyone did." I set the kettle boiling. "Is Harper okay?"

He gives me a long, thoughtful look while I grab a mug out of the cupboard and reach for the instant coffee. I've watched Beck make it enough times to be able to get it right. He doesn't like the fancy-pants machine Harper uses. He's a simple 'one coffee, two sugars' kind of guy.

Leaning against the counter, he crosses his arms and looks wretched. "I don't think she'll mind me telling you this. No point in being all secretive and fudging the truth."

The water in the kettle starts going nuts as I wait for the switch to automatically click off.

"She got drunk last night. Ended up at a police station to sober up, and I had to go get her."

I gape at him, actually jolting when the kettle clicks off

with a little snap. Reaching for the jug, I struggle to pour water into Beck's coffee. Harper got drunk? No way. I can't even imagine someone so sensible taking things that far.

"I should be livid with her for being so reckless, and part of me is annoyed, but another part thinks it was just what she needed. She's been wound up so tight, trying to be the perfect person and look after everyone but herself. She needed to cry." I pour a little milk in his coffee and hand it to him. He gives me a grateful smile and thanks me with a wink. "I remember drinking myself stupid a couple of times after Abby and the boys…" He trails off and I get it. Saying the people you love most are dead, like actually saying it… it's basically impossible.

"I'm just glad nothing bad happened to her."

"She looked a little banged up. Must have fallen over a couple of times. She had a few grazes. She'll be feeling it today. A mondo hangover, plus a few bruises?" He hisses, then takes a sip of his coffee.

"Do you think she'll be okay for the party?" I cringe.

Beck grins at me. "She's got all day to sober up. I think the party will be just what she needs. Let's just keep her away from the beers, though, aye?"

I chuckle.

"Need any help with anything?"

I pull my phone out of my pocket and check my To Do list. "I think I'm sorted. Tane's friends are coming to help me later, but if I need anything, I'll let you know. Why don't you take the chance to put your feet up and relax for a change?"

Without a word, he steps into my space and wraps his big arm around my shoulders. Kissing the top of my head, his voice is thick when he murmurs, "You're a good kid. Real good."

I lean into his embrace and blink rapidly, managing to stave off any tears even after he walks away. It's funny how one little gesture can mean so much. Beck's a good guy. My confusion over why Mum and Dad made him our guardian clears up a little more every time I'm around him. He may come across as a gruff grizzly bear sometimes, but he's just a big marshmallow on the inside. I don't ever want to give him a reason to worry like he must have last night.

I stay in the kitchen, puttering around—emptying the dishwasher and putting out breakfast food—until everyone dribbles down to the dining room table.

By the time Tane gets in from milking, we're all munching on toast and cereal while Rocket scampers around the floor, his cute tail wagging as he takes turns begging for scraps from each of us.

"What happened last night?" Stacey asks Tane, since

Beck is who knows where. Hopefully he took my advice and is resting in the sunshine or something.

Tane grunts and glances over his shoulder while preparing the coffee machine.

"Come on," Stacey whines. "You can't keep us in the dark when we all had to listen to her wailing."

Willow looks kind of pale as she adds in, "She looked awful this morning. Dead to the world. White skin. Was she sick or something?"

"She threw up." Tane's shoulder hitches.

Stacey snickers and shakes her head. "But not because she was sick, right? She got tanked."

"What's tanked?" Oscar asks.

I give him a sideways glance and softly murmur, "Drunk."

Oscar's spoon rattles in his bowl. "She got drunk?"

"Shhh!" Tane spins around and points at us. "I don't want you hassling her about this, okay? That's the last thing she needs."

"We won't." Stacey raises her hand in surrender as Tane plunks down at the table with his frothy cup of coffee.

Scrubbing a hand down his face, he looks exhausted, and I wonder yet again if we should cancel the party. But too many things have been set in motion. I've arranged everything. In a few hours, all the stuff will be arriving, and—

"We just need to let her sleep and rest as much as possible today." Tane sips his coffee and that one act seems to make him feel a little better.

"How are we going to keep her away from the party prep?" I ask.

"I'll sort that." Tane stares into the lounge, like his mind is whirring with a plan he's not willing to share. I watch him drink his coffee on autopilot until he suddenly jolts up from the table, gulping down the last of his drink before grabbing the keys from the bowl.

Rocket barks and skips around his feet. Tane steps over the puppy and heads for the front door.

"Where are you going?" Oscar stands as if he wants to go with him.

"Out, and you can't come."

"But—"

Stopping at the door, he spins to face us and softens his expression. "I need you to help Bee with whatever she needs, okay? I have to go out for a bit. I'll be back soon."

He doesn't give us a chance to ask any more questions, bolting out the door before Oscar has plunked back into the chair.

Leaning over his cereal bowl, he mutters a few dark thoughts until the pup at his feet lets out a little bark. An immediate smile twitches his lips, and he bends down to pick him up.

I rise from the table, going for cheerful and breezy. "Maybe your job can be keeping Rocket out of our way this afternoon. Think you can handle that?"

Oscar laughs and rubs the puppy's floppy ears.

Willow smiles at him, then rises gracefully from the table and joins me in the kitchen to pack away the breakfast stuff.

"Thanks for your help." I smile at her.

She just grins and silently finishes up before floating back upstairs.

It's such a shame she doesn't want to take ballet. She moves like a dancer whether she wants to or not. Maybe she just needs time, the same way Stacey does on the whole sports thing. Although I can't help wondering if Jonas is partly to blame for that.

She's changed so much since dating him.

And I guess other stuff I don't want to think about has contributed to it, but still... the fact that she's not even interested in helping with party prep. That's so not Stacey. She's usually the one bossing everyone around, all excited about the event. Parties are her thing, but now that Jonas can't make it, she doesn't care anymore.

I hate that she's so bound to him. It feels kind of unhealthy, but I don't know what to say to make her see that.

It's—

My phone dings on the dining room table, and Stacey snatches it up to clear the message for me.

"Hey!" I frown at her, but the way her eyebrows wrinkle in sympathy makes me pause. "What?"

She winces. "Missy has to bail."

"What?" I dash out of the kitchen and snatch my phone.

Missy: I'm so sorry. I can't come today! I have a fever and Mom's making me stay home. I've called Cam already. He's picking up the gear for you. I'm so gutted. I wanted to help you set up, but I feel so disgusting and I don't want to spread my germs around. I'm so so sorry.

My stomach clenches with disappointment, but I force back a nice reply. It's not her fault.

Bianca: Oh no! You poor thing. I hope you feel better soon. Don't worry. We'll be okay. I'll miss you, though. You take care of yourself.

. . .

395

She sends me back a smiley face and love heart emoji while I slide the phone onto the table and lament the fact that my new friend isn't going to be there. I was kind of counting on her, not just for the setup but also for someone to hang out with at the party.

Even though Jonas can't make it, Luka is apparently going to show up, which means Stacey will be with her and I'll be left floating like a solitary buoy in a great big ocean.

"I'm just gunna…" I point to the front door and head down to the barn.

Stepping into the wide open space, I look around at everything that needs doing. I'm suddenly over-whelmed and wondering how the hell I'm going to pull it off. Missy was going to be here to kind of take charge, but now that's up to me. I'm used to quietly organizing behind the scenes while someone else takes the lead, bossing everyone around. Is that my place now?

Crap!

I can't do that.

Chewing on my lip, I shuffle over the packed dirt and up onto the mini staging area. It needs sweeping. Maybe I should start with that.

Finding the big broom, I get to work, my mind racing with a million different things until I'm actually sweating with stress.

"You okay, sis? You look like you're about to pass out." Stacey appears with a mug of coffee in her hand, scaring the crap out of me.

I jump a mile and have to pat my chest a few times.

"Sorry." She grins.

"I didn't hear you."

"Think your messy brain has something to do with that?" She tips her head at me.

"There's just so much to get through, and even though I have a list and everything, I almost don't know where to start." I chew my lip and probably look as worried as I feel. "I don't want to let Harper down."

Stacey purses her lips and wanders over to me in her red gumboots with yellow flowers. Harper bought them for her after she lost her last pair. They're so Stacey. So happy and bright and loud. Glancing down at my plain black pair, I'm struck again by our contrast.

"I can help." Stacey stops by the stage, tipping back on her heels.

It's impossible to hide my surprise. "You want to help?"

"Well, why wouldn't I?"

"I don't know. You just seemed...not interested, and then a little... pissed off with me."

Stacey wraps her fingers around the mug, kind of

curling in on herself. "Only because you've been shutting me out."

"Shutting you out?" I grip the broom handle. "What do you mean?"

"Not showing up at lunchtime, ditching me early whenever you can."

"I haven't meant to," I quickly explain, then grimace. "I just find your friends hard work. I—"

Stacey raises her hands to shut me up. "I get it. We don't socialize in the same circles. We never really have." She lets out a sad sigh and starts drawing circles in the hay with her boot. "I guess I'm just afraid that... if I don't keep you nearby you'll... you'll leave me again."

Her eyes start to water, and my heart stops beating for a second.

"I don't want to lose you again." Her voice wobbles out of control, followed by a few tears that start to leak from her eyes.

"You never will." I rest the broom against the wall and quickly jump down to stand beside her. "I love you, Stacey. You're my sister, and I promise I'm not taking off like that again. I was in a really bad place and I needed... I *thought* I needed to get away. But I was wrong. And then you came and got me, and..." I run my hands down her arms and smile at her. "I'm not running again, okay? You and me. We're family. We come before anything else."

Stacey gives me a watery smile. "Promise? We'll stick together no matter what?"

"No matter what," I whisper, pulling her into a hug.

She gets the coffee mug out of the way just in time, and I feel it pressing against my back when she squeezes me.

With a little laugh, she pulls back and wipes the tears off her face. "Come on, then. Let's get this party set up."

"Thank you." I give her a grateful smile and pull out my phone, ready to go through the list with her.

We manage to tick off a few more things and figure out a streamline food plan. Stacey gave me a couple of ideas I hadn't thought of, and we're just heading to the garage when Cam pulls up in his ute.

"Hey, Cam." Stacey gives him her stunning smile.

He grins at her, lifting his eyebrows before looking at me. "Where's the big setup happening?"

"The barn."

"Sweet, I'll give the others a call and tell them to drive the trailer down there." His warm gaze is so sweet and kind, it's hard not to smile at him.

Stacey clears her throat and walks up to his ute,

popping the back door open and jumping in. "We better work fast. Harper was supposed to be out shopping with her girls, but now she's upstairs sleeping."

"Really?" Cam looks intrigued as he hops behind the wheel.

I slip into the passenger seat, wondering why Stacey didn't take this spot. I would have sat in the back with her, but there's a speaker in the way, so I'm kind of forced into the front seat position.

Cam and Stacey start chatting as we drive down to the barn. She's so animated, and Cam responds. Two friendly people bouncing off each other, it'd make sense that their conversation is so bright and sparkling.

I stare down at my phone screen, focusing on the list and trying to tune them out.

This was bound to happen—Cam and Stacey making a connection.

It's not a bad thing. If it gets my sister away from Jonas, then I'm all for it.

But still, a little root of sadness is threading through my belly. I don't want it to grow and choke me like some toxic vine, so I pull in a breath and gaze out the window, thinking about the fact that I've met Missy—a new friend. And Stacey and I managed to clear the air this morning.

I don't need a boyfriend, or a crush, or anything like that.

I've got a home, people around me who are starting to feel like real family, and someone I can sing with.

That's enough.

That's all I need.

43

TANE

The motel is one road back from Victoria Street. I pull up outside reception, my anger starting to bubble over. I've had the entire forty-minute trip to really get the juices flowing, and now they're spurting inside of me, a mini volcano ready to throw some ash and lava all over Harper's "friends." I can't believe they just ditched her to deal with the cops on her own.

I don't know the full story, and I guess I should really get that before dishing out a little hell, but I'm not sure my temper will let me.

I can still feel Harper sobbing in my arms, her pain echoing in the back of my mind. Her tears soaked right through my shirt, and her clenched fists left permanent wrinkles where she held on and bled her soul all over me.

It was impossible not to cry as well. I let the tears silently slip out but made sure my eyes were good and dry by the time she was completely spent. I carried her up to bed, Beck following me to tuck her in and check on everyone. They were all asleep, or at least pretending to be.

I barely caught two winks last night. I knew I'd struggle to switch off, which is why I told Beck I'd deal with the milking so he could finally have a morning off. He agreed without too much of a fight. Just goes to show how exhausted he must be. Everything is catching up to us, and it feels like a freight train barreling right through the house.

"Yeah, hi." I smile at the receptionist who just greeted me. "I'm looking for Zoey and Alaina. They're staying here for one more night."

"Do you have a last name?" the receptionist asks.

"Uh-huh." I nod and hope I'm pronouncing it correctly. "Zoey Beynon."

"Beynon. Oh yes, I see." She picks up the phone and dials. "Good morning. I just wanted to let you know that there's a Mr…"

"Tane Smith." I force a calm smile.

"A Mr. Tane Smith here to see you… Yes… Of course… Thank you." She hangs up the phone and gives me a polite, professional smile. "They're in Room 8, second floor, first on your right."

"Thank you." I slip out the door and easily find the room, knocking once and sliding my hands into my pockets while I wait.

I guess I should be grateful they're willing to see me, but maybe they wouldn't have said yes if they knew what I want to say to them.

I snuck a look at Harper's phone while Willow was in the bathroom and Harper was still dead to the world. Zoey did try to contact her last night, but I'm still pissed that they didn't head down to the police station themselves. Where the hell were they when the cops pulled up and started talking to Harper? That's what I want to know.

A blurry-eyed Zoey opens the door, squinting against the sunlight behind me.

"Hey." She licks her lips, her face bunching like even talking hurts. "Is Harper okay?"

"She's sleeping it off." I give her a dry glare and peek into the room.

It's a shambles—clothes strewn everywhere, the duvet on one of the beds drooping onto the floor. The stench of liquor and perfume wafts lightly in the air while a lump in the other bed groans and starts to stir.

Zoey glances over her shoulder, then rests her head on the door. I wouldn't be surprised if she is literally using the door to stay upright. They must have been just as trashed as Harper last night.

My anger simmers again. Last night could have gone so much worse. Three scantily clad, intoxicated girls. I'm actually grateful the cops showed up. What if they'd come around the corner and bumped into some guys looking for a free thrill?

I shudder at the thought and cross my arms.

"Why are you looking so angry?" Alaina shuffles to the door. Black mascara streaks her cheeks, along with a smear of red lipstick. If hungover were a painting, she'd be it, with her mane of tangled, knotty hair and the pained expression on her face when she stops by the door and cradles her head.

"You idiots," I mutter. "I'm pissed off because you all got dangerously drunk and then left your best friend to deal with the cops on her own last night!"

Alaina groans, nursing her head again. "Can you like not yell? My head is literally cracking in half."

"I don't give a shit about your head! You abandoned her when she needed you most! And it's her birthday party tonight. Willow didn't invite you up here to ruin everything. You were supposed to be making Harper feel better!"

"Look, we thought she was behind us, okay?" Zoey licks her lips and winces. Her mouth is probably parched as, but I'm not letting up. She can get some water after I'm done.

"You should have stuck with her."

"We didn't notice until too late, and when we got back, she was gone." Alaina blinks slowly.

"Did you try to find her?"

"Of course we did! Zoey called her, all stressing, and Harper said she was fine."

I roll my eyes. Of course she did.

"Yeah, and…" Zoey goes still, her pixie face turning from white to gray as she holds up her index finger. "Wait a second, did you say cops?"

Took her long enough!

"Yeah. They picked her up in the quad, and she was taken to the police station. Beck had to go and collect her."

"Why didn't she tell me that?"

"Because she's allergic to asking for help!" I huff and pace away from the door, my mind starting to settle when a thought hits me. She told her friends she was fine, but she called me.

She called *me*.

Because she does need me.

"No wonder she got plastered last night." Zoey gives me a dopey smile when I turn back to face the door. "She likes you hard, Tane Smith. She's already falling."

I frown. Did they talk about me last night?

Alaina points a floppy finger at me. "You catch her and you don't let go until she admits that she's completely gone for you. She's a tough nut to crack. Always has been."

"She lets logic get in the way," Zoey explains. "Emotions scare her."

I let out a disbelieving laugh. "And how am I supposed to *logically* win her over?"

"Pfft." Zoey waves her hand like it's made of rubber. "She doesn't need *more* logic. She needs a man who's gunna sweep her off her feet. Give her all that loved-up stuff she doesn't think she needs."

That sounds pretty awesome to me, but... "She asked me to leave her alone."

"She was lying." Alaina shakes her head and then winces, lightly pressing her fingers against her forehead before croaking, "Don't let her get away with it. She wants you, and not just for an easy lay. She said that. She said 'he's not an easy lay, he's the guy you fall for.'"

My head jolts back in surprise while Alaina shuffles into the room and drops like a stone onto the mattress.

She follows it up with a quaking groan, and I can't help a snicker.

"Don't worry." Zoey looks at her, then gives me a sleepy smile. "She'll be right by the party."

I give her a skeptical frown and she just giggles, then presses her cheek against the door again.

"Harper needs you," she whispers. "The fact that you're standing at my door telling me off is proof that you're the right guy for her. She doesn't want to believe it, but don't you let her tell you otherwise. You're way more healthy than a bottle of liquor, and I've never heard her talk about a guy the way she talks about you."

I don't know what to say. I feel like I've just been handed gold, and I want to cradle it carefully so I don't lose one speck of it.

"See you tonight, farm boy." Zoey closes the door and I stay put for a minute, trying to absorb everything I've just heard.

I want so badly to believe them. To trust them.

But I don't really know these girls.

There's only one real way to find out how Harper truly feels. I know she wanted me to leave her alone, but I can't do that anymore.

44

HARPER

The birds outside the bedroom window are chirping. They sound like freaking chainsaws. Cracking my eyes open, I take in the glare that renders the pale curtains freaking useless. With a groan, I cover my head with my pillow, but I hate that suffocating feeling and am soon throwing the covers off.

The air has a warm stickiness to it, warning me that morning has come and probably well gone. Sitting up with a groan, I check my phone screen: 2:13 p.m.

I've never slept this late. Ever.

Shame washes through me again, my swollen, aching eyes beginning to shimmer.

"No," I mumble. "No more crying."

Gently patting my eyes, I force myself out of bed and head to the bathroom.

I have no idea where everyone is, but I'm sure they won't need me for a few more minutes. Flicking on the shower, I guzzle down a glass of water before stepping under the tepid spray. I can't handle heat right now, so I force my head into the coolish water and just stand there for who knows how long.

I'm sure I break the five-minute rule, but hopefully Beck's not around to know. Once I've dried myself off and am brushing out my shampooed hair, I'm starting to feel slightly better. Like on my way to being human again.

I throw on a white sleeveless top and my pair of jeans that are so worn the denim is actually soft. I'm seeking comfort over fashion today. I don't care what I look like. I'm not even going to bother with makeup.

Clomping downstairs, I get the coffee machine going and wonder again where everyone is. Checking my phone for messages, I find only one.

Zoey: Sorry about last night. We were terrible friends. Take care of you today. Be kind to yourself and let your heart do the thinking for you.

I don't know what that means, but I can't be bothered texting back to find out. I'll catch them tonight and ask then. My brain should be working a little better by that stage. A sadness creeps through me when I think about them driving home tomorrow. They need to be back in time for classes on Monday.

Wrenching the cupboard open, I seek out the Panadol and also grab the loaf of bread. I don't even bother buttering a slice and just start shoving hunks into my mouth. After one piece, I'm starting to feel kind of green again, so I down the medication and shuffle my coffee to the dining room table.

Where is everyone?

I should go looking, but I don't really have the energy to think where they might be, let alone actually go and find them.

The grandfather clock keeps me company as I quietly sip my coffee and patch together memories from last night. Some things are fuzzy—like my conversation with the police. I remember red and blue lights, but I don't remember what I said to them. I remember puking in a bucket. That part's crystal clear, as is Beck's dismay and my paralyzing tears.

Tane was there. He appeared out of nowhere and knelt beside me, and I lost the fight. I surrendered right there on the floor, ugly crying against him like I promised myself I wouldn't. I knew once the dam opened I wouldn't be able to stop.

My eyes still hurt. My limbs are weak and exhausted, yet the rock in my belly seems to have gone. Rubbing my stomach, I try to figure out where it went or how I could possibly feel lighter on the inside.

I failed.

I let everybody down.

I hit the bottom of the ocean.

Rock bottom.

Tipping my head to the side, I think about that expression and how people say you can only go up from there.

Is that right?

I don't deserve to go up after the way I behaved, yet Beck and Tane were right there beside me. They let me sob and wail. They carried me to bed and one of them kissed my forehead, tucking me in like I didn't have to worry about a thing.

They let me sleep this morning.

Tane cleaned the bathroom.

I smile, wondering how long I'm going to be thrilled by that. It was just so sweet.

He's so sweet.

The usual fight that rears its head when I start thinking about him has lost some of its bluster, so I let my mind waltz with thoughts of Tane—his strength, his smile, the tender look he gets in his eyes sometimes.

I like him so much.

The front door clicks open and I jump, scrambling to hide what was no doubt a stupid grin.

Tane walks into the house and my breath catches. He spots me and his face lights with a kind smile that thrills me from my eyes to my toes.

He's so freaking beautiful, I can feel my heart straining toward him. It nearly lifts me from my seat.

"How you feelin'?" He ambles past the TV.

I hitch my shoulder and make this weird groaning-grunting type nose.

He snickers. "Dumb question, I know."

"Do you?" I wince. "Have you ever been plastered before?"

Spinning one of the dining room chairs around, he straddles it and rests his arms along the top. "Once. When I was fourteen. I was on a scouts-type camping trip, and our leader was only eighteen. He thought it'd be fun to bring along a bottle of rum and a bottle of Coke." He sniffs. "As I'm sure you can imagine, the Coke got used up pretty quick, and then we were just downing straight rum."

I grimace and he starts to laugh. "I know! Apparently I spent the night passed out in the grass, woke up covered in mozzie bites, freezing cold and lying in my own puke."

I can't help a soft snort. He tells a good story.

"Needless to say, I didn't touch alcohol for a long time after that, and even now, it's like one or two beers and I'm good."

"You're a smart man." I point at him.

His expression turns serious. "I'm just glad nothing worse happened to you last night."

I swallow and start spinning my empty coffee mug on the table. "Should have asked you to come and be my bodyguard or something."

"I would have." He grins. "But… you know… maybe you just needed to get smashed. Something had to tip you over that edge. You needed to cry."

My vision starts to blur as tears quickly build on my lashes. I want to thank him for being there, for holding me in spite of the wails and the snot.

"Come on." He stands up, holding out his hand to me.

I gaze at it for a moment.

"Trust me." His smile pulls me from my chair and I take his hand, loving the way his fingers curl around mine, the warm comfort of such a simple thing.

"Where are we going?"

"Thought you could use a ride and some fresh air."

I pull out of his grasp. "My head hurts too much to ride."

He grabs a bottle of water from the fridge and takes my hand again. "We'll just take one horse, then."

Pulling me out the back door, he walks us outside where Copper is saddled up and waiting.

I narrow my eyes at him.

"What?" He winks and holds out a cowboy hat.

I've always wanted one of those. It looks like it's been salvaged from an old Western movie. I carefully take the worn hat off him and admire the stitching, tracing my fingers over the shape of it.

"Used to be Abby's. Beck said it was okay."

My eyes glisten as I reverently place it on my head.

"Looks good on you." Tane gently leads me off the last step and mounts the horse before reaching down to help me. I put my foot in the stirrup, and he pulls me up like I'm a featherweight. I nestle behind him, nearly moving to wrap my arms around his waist.

I catch myself just in time, but then he grabs my hands and guides my arms around him.

"That's better." He pats my wrist.

I smile against his shoulder while he clicks to get the

horse moving and we amble away from the house. We're heading in a direction I've never been before. There aren't any paddocks past the chicken coop, just a crop of trees. We wind down the narrow path in silence, my sore eyes slowly adjusting to the sunlight and starting to feel better when we enter the woods.

A stream bubbles somewhere to our right. I love the soothing sound of the water and let myself relax a little more, resting my cheek against Tane's shoulder. He's a solid rock I can lean on, holding me up when I feel weak and useless.

Tears line my lashes and I close my eyes, letting them slip down my cheeks unchecked. They don't hurt the way they did last night. These tears are soft, more like a cleanse than an outright scouring.

I still feel kind of brutalized by last night.

All that pain inside of me just bubbled out. Some of it left me, but there's still this hollow ache inside. It's not as raw around the edges as it has been before. I don't understand why. Maybe it's because of Tane.

Maybe my fight to do it all alone has been a waste of energy.

I was alone last night. All alone in that police car and sitting at the station.

It made me realize that there's nothing glamorous about

trying to do everything in my own strength. All it's brought me is more heartache.

As much as I hate relying on other people, when I called last night, in my darkest hour, Tane was there to answer me. Beck arrived to collect me, and rather than being shunned for my idiocy, I was comforted. When I broke down completely, I was held together.

I sniffle and wipe my face against Tane's shirt. He's not saying anything, and I'm so relieved. I don't think I could voice what I'm thinking right now. I just want to hold him and weep.

He lets me, not stopping our slow stroll through the woods until we reach a patch of sunlight. The small creek runs through the trees, making this glade idyllic. The only noises out here belong to nature—birds calling to each other, the rush of wings as they explode off the branches and into the air. I watch a little fantail flutter around like it's playing and then listen to the rush of the wood pigeon's wings.

"It's so peaceful here," I whisper, slipping off my hat so the light breeze can play with my hair.

"Yeah. It's one of my favorite spots."

Copper walks forward and dips her head to drink from the stream.

"Want to get down for a minute?"

"Okay." I sniff and brush my damp cheeks before reaching down to let him help me off.

I must look like such a mess, but he still smiles at me, making me feel pretty.

I swallow, dropping the hat in the lush grass and moving away from him, needing to compose myself.

"You don't have to wipe those tears away for me."

I spin and can't help a bashful grin. "I've never liked crying."

"I don't think anyone actually enjoys it." He chuckles. "But sometimes you gotta let it out, and I think you feel better afterward."

"Not physically." I shake my head, then wince and glance up at his face, having to concede. "Maybe on an emotional level."

He walks toward me and I take a few steps back until I hit a tree and have nowhere else to go.

He stops walking. "I'm not going to touch you if you don't want me to."

I'm surprised by how disappointing that is.

Lightly rubbing my forehead, I force my eyes up to his and for once don't bother hiding any of it. I want him. My body wants him. My heart wants him. Unchecked, I can't even imagine how eager my face must look right now.

Tane's lips lift at the corners as he slowly closes the gap between us.

He's still too far away to kiss, but he's close enough to reach out and lightly run his fingers down my cheek. "You don't have to be anything but you around me. I know you're tough, but you don't always have to be. Sometimes others can do the fighting for you."

I swallow my heart back into my chest.

"I'd fight for you. I'd… do anything for you." He rests his hand on the side of my neck, his thumb lightly brushing along my jawline.

"I know," I whisper. "I guess I do need you."

"I want you to need me. Everybody needs someone. More than just one, usually. That's what families are for." He dips his head, pursing his lips before smiling at me. "Although… I wouldn't mind being the person you call first. The one you go to when you want to feel better. Your…your special someone."

Leaning forward, he presses his lips to my forehead. I rest my hand against his chest, enjoying the feel of him this close. I've never felt so protected and secure. Not even with Dad. This thing with Tane is a new level for me.

And I'm scared.

But I don't want fear to stop me anymore. I want my

head to just shut the hell up for once so my heart can do the thinking.

"I could be good for you," Tane whispers against my skin. "I could be so good."

"I know," I breathe.

Tane pulls back and looks down at me, his eyes so full of hope.

"I know." I say it again, louder this time, more sure of myself. "I know." Taking his face in my hands, I beam him a smile that hides nothing and rise to my tiptoes, planting my lips against his.

He captures my hips, holding them lightly as I slowly explore the wonder of his mouth. There's no urgency or desperation in this kiss. It's long and languid, an unhurried saunter into new territory.

When his arms wind around me and fuse us together, I smile against his mouth and whisper one more time, "I know."

He chuckles and captures my tongue with his, gently lifting me off my feet. His strength envelops me, smoothing the edges of the cavity just a little more. It surprises me. I thought giving in to Tane would weaken me somehow, yet I feel stronger in his arms, like maybe I can take on this year and not be an epic fail.

Who knew surrender could be so empowering?

45

BIANCA

Organized chaos reigns in the barn as people buzz around like worker ants, moving furniture and setting up decorations. Cam's friends are freaking amazing, doing anything I ask of them. It's like they've been drilled to obey me or something, and they keep coming up to ask what's next as soon as one job is finished.

Tane moved the horses out of the barn an hour ago and said he'd keep Harper out of the way for us so we didn't have to sneak around.

I sent Kim and Tameka up to check on the house a few minutes ago, and they came rushing back to let me know it's all clear.

"Great. Okay, well, can you go and start organizing the food? It's all stored in the garage; you just have to get it out and cut up a few things, then plate the food. Beck said all the platters and serving dishes are scattered throughout the kitchen and in the cabinets in the lounge and dining room."

"Sweet as." Kim gives me a thumbs-up.

"We're on it." Tameka salutes me before skipping out of the barn. She doesn't quite make it out the door before her boyfriend snags her, spinning her around once before kissing her laughing face.

Aw. They are so cute together.

I can't imagine a guy ever spinning me around. Heck, even being lifted off my feet for a second would make me feel like a beautiful fairy. I spot Willow flittering near the doorway, passing decorations up to Manu so he can nail them to the wall.

Pressing my lips together, I turn back to the stage area and catch Cam smiling at me. I grin back and check the list on my phone, ready in case he's about to ask me what job needs doing next.

"He can't stop looking at you." Stacey appears behind me, whispering in my ear.

"What?" I spin to face her. "Who?"

She looks at me like I'm stupid. "Cam."

I flush and have to seriously fight the urge not to glance over my shoulder at him. Instead I duck my head and use my fringe to hide my profile. "What are you talking about?" I grit out, realizing that every time I've glanced his way today, he's definitely been looking at me. "Why would he do that?"

"Duh! Because he likes you."

My head pops up and I blink at my sister. "No he doesn't."

"Are you crazy?" She lightly bats my arm. "The guy is gaga over you. It's *so* obvious."

"But why?" I steal a quick glance at him, my insides jittering at the easy way he moves a massive stack of chairs to the other side of the barn. He's so strong and gorgeous. I love how tall he is. "I mean, I don't get it."

Stacey's head jolts back, her look of confusion almost comical. "Bianca, the guy would be lucky to have you."

I scoff and shake my head, unlocking my phone screen so I don't have to look at her while we have this conversation.

"Stop it." She slaps her hand over my screen. "He would be. You are beautiful and kind and intelligent. You don't see that?"

I swallow and avert my gaze, tucking my fringe behind my ear. "Guys don't like me, Stace. They like you."

Her eyes narrow suspiciously. "We're not about to have a Riku conversation right now, are we?"

"No." I cringe and shake my head. "It's not just him. It's

all guys. They don't notice me. They notice you because *you* are beautiful and fun and smart and friendly and sporty and—"

"Okay, okay." Stacey laughs, obviously loving the compliments. But then she takes my hand and looks at me with such sincerity that I can't take my eyes off her blue gaze. "Thing is, sis, this guy likes *you.*"

My breath goes on hold as I glance past her shoulder. Cam catches my eye, giving me another smile and a little wink.

I squeeze Stacey's hand, a thrill I'm maybe just a little bit afraid of jolting my heart out of place. "I still don't get it."

"You don't have to. You just have to *go* for it." Stacey giggles. "Don't turn your back on a chance like this. He's hot."

"What if it's a trick?" I blurt. "What if he doesn't mean it?"

"So score a few hot kisses and boot his butt out the door."

I gape at her. "I can't do that. I'm not like that."

"Calm down." Stacey rubs my arm. "I'm only joking. I know you're not like that, and I don't think Cam is either. He's Tane's best friend. Come on. We know he's not an asshole."

"I know, I just… What if it doesn't work out?"

Stacey purses her lips like she's buying time.

I guess *what-if* questions are kind of hard to answer, but panic's making me punch them out one after the other. It's like I'm looking for excuses not to fall for somebody.

I don't get it. I've always dreamed of having a boyfriend.

But Cam just seems so far out of my league. And I'm not sure my bruised heart can handle another risk, or beating, right now.

"Life's too short for what-ifs," Stacey murmurs. "We know that now. We *have* to live in the moment. And that's not a bad thing. All my moments with Jonas are awesome. They help me forget the sadness. Even just for a little bit." Her lips tug into a heart-wrenching smile. "You deserve to be happy, and if spending time with Cam makes you feel happy, then you should do it. As much as you can."

I love the sound of that idea, but…

"I'm too shy. I'd be so embarrassed. I never know what to say, and I don't think I fit. He's just so…"

"Into you?" Stacey finishes for me.

I whip a terrified look at my sister.

She giggles. "I think all that fitting-in stuff is total crap. And as for not knowing what to say, let him do the work. He seems friendly and sure of himself. Next time he talks to you, just find an excuse to linger. Enjoy." She wiggles her eyebrows at me.

All I can do is cringe. "I'm usually trying to find an excuse to leave. I never know what to say."

"Stop thinking so hard and just be you." She kisses my cheek. "*I* like you. You're fun to hang out with. Why would Cam think any differently?"

"I don't know." I point between us. "We're related. You have to like me."

She giggles and shakes her head like I'm a hopeless case. "You know how Mum and Dad always joked that you got her personality and his red hair, and I got her looks and his humor?"

"Yeah," I whisper, stunned by the fact that Stacey's talking about them.

She swallows, her blue eyes starting to shine. "Well, Mum was one of my favorite people, and Dad adored her more than anything. If you're like Mum, then there's a guy out there who will adore *you* because of who you are. Maybe that guy is Cam."

I want to argue that I don't look like Mum, but the compliment is just so sweet I don't want to ruin it. Stacey's trying so hard to boost my confidence.

I beam her a grateful smile.

She sniffs and squeezes my hand. "Can we stop talking about this now? Crying irritates my contacts, and even though Jonas isn't here tonight, I don't want the world to know I'm blind as a bat."

"You know bats aren't actually blind," I tease her.

"Shut up." She laughs, wrapping her arms around me and pressing her mouth to my ear. "Now I expect some decent flirting from you tonight, Bianca Rose Freeman. Don't let me down."

She pulls away and points her finger at me, her stern look enough to make me bob my head.

Nerves fire through me so hot and fast I feel light-headed, but when I turn to find Cam, I let myself look for a moment. And when he senses my gaze and stops what he's doing to grin at me, I smile straight back.

46

TANE

She held me the whole way back, her chin perched on my shoulder. We didn't say too much. The odd comment about the beauty of our surroundings was thrown out. I agreed with them all. I love this place. I love her and me in this place.

Running my hand down her arm, I press it into my stomach, feeling like the freaking king of the world.

Harper knows I'm good for her.

Harper kissed me like she knows I'm good for her.

I just hope she keeps thinking that way for a really long time.

A giddy thrill catches me off guard, and I'm kind of glad she can't see how big my smile is right now.

As we near the barn, I slow Copper right down to a horse shuffle.

"Everything okay?" Harper's breath tickles my neck, and it's tempting to turn Cop back around and find another quiet spot to make out in. But I don't want to let everyone down. Bianca's worked way too hard for us to bail.

I turn my head so our lips are only millimeters apart. I'd love to kiss her right now—even just a delicate brushing of lips. But people might be watching from the barn, so I jump down before she can make a move.

She gives me a quizzical frown. "What is it?"

I try to ease that look off her face with a smile as I reach up for her. She rests her arms on my shoulders and I catch her against me, wishing I could carry her all the way into the barn. But I do the right thing and place her on her feet, not wanting to spoil the surprise.

"I want to show you something."

"Okay." Her eyes narrow at the corners, so I try to make my smile easy as I lead Copper into the paddock with Jax.

"I'll unsaddle you later, sweetie." Taking off her bridle, I muss up her mane, then kiss the side of her face.

Copper grunts and wanders across to Jax. They're soon grazing on grass, side by side and blissfully unaware of the noise that will dominate the air in about two minutes' time.

"Come on." I take Harper's hand, careful not to thread

our fingers together. This needs to look like a casual leading of a friend, nothing more.

When we reach the barn doors, I stop and grin down at her. "You ready?"

"For what?" She lets out a confused laugh, which quickly morphs into a gasp when the door swings open and a chorus of people yells, "Surprise!"

She slaps a hand against her chest, her mouth dropping open as Willow yanks her into the barn and streamers fly through the air.

People are singing "Happy Birthday" at the top of their lungs and I join them, loving the look Harper throws me. I wink at her and wrap up the song, unable to resist curling my arm around her shoulders and kissing the side of her head.

Hopefully that appears friendly enough.

With a giggle, she pulls the colorful strings out of her hair while everyone crowds around her, taking turns to hug her and kiss her cheek.

Country music starts up as she does the rounds. Manu's playing DJ tonight, and he gives me a thumbs-up in greeting.

I nod, then scan the barn. They've done a fantastic setup in here. Colorful banners hang between beams, and a birthday sign dominates the space above the stage area. Tables are lined with platters of colorful food, and two huge ice buckets sit at either end, overflowing with drinks.

I notice a distinct lack of beer bottles and silently thank whoever sorted out the drinks. Not that I think Harper will touch alcohol tonight, but it's nice that she doesn't even have to look at it.

"Yeah, we figured a beer-free party wasn't the end of the world," Beck mentions over my shoulder when he spots me.

"You read my mind."

He grins and takes a swig from his bottle of Sprite.

"This looks amazing."

"Yeah, they worked pretty hard. When I finally got down here to help, it was practically done." He glances at me, and I try to clear my expression when he asks, "You go all right keeping Harper entertained?"

"Yeah." I swallow. "She didn't suspect a thing."

"The beauty of horse riding, aye? Abby always said it was the perfect way to make time disappear." His eyes glimmer with that sad, loved-up smile he always gets when talking about his wife.

I rest my hand on his shoulder and give it a little squeeze, then spot Zoey and Alaina wrapping their arms around Harper. They better be apologizing for their shitty show last night.

Harper's lips seem to be saying, "That's okay. It's okay."

Their heads all move in together, stealing my chance for any more lip-reading. Instead, I decide to hunt down Bianca and tell her she's awesome.

As I glide past Zoey, she catches my eye and gives me a knowing wink.

I try to play it cool like I don't know what that smile on her face means, but I'm probably giving myself away with a blush.

Steeling my expression, I move through the crowd, saying hi to my mates and trying my best not to keep looking at Harper.

She makes it literally impossible.

Her smile tonight is carefree and golden. She's more beautiful now than I've ever seen her.

Our kiss by the creek has supercharged my heart, and it's pulsing a beat just for her. All I can hope is that another moment in the glade isn't too far away.

47

BIANCA

People are loving the party and I'm stoked.

I stand at the edge of the room, surveying the crowd and smiling. Clusters of people have formed their own little circles, but there's still a united vibe in the air. Beck tips his head back with a laugh while chatting to the neighbors. Even though Harper's never met them—none of us have—they came to help celebrate. It's nice seeing Beck hanging out with friends. He's been so focused on us, it almost seems weird seeing him socialize like a normal adult.

It's good for him.

I grin and glance to my left, where a bunch of Tane's mates are laughing and joshing each other. He grins and takes a swig from his ginger beer bottle while Adonis and Killian make fools of themselves doing Fortnite dances.

Tane came over and gave me a hug before, gushing about how awesome I am. That was really nice to hear. He's such a sweet guy. I love the way he calls me *cuz*. He's like an older brother—a really cool one, with a really gorgeous friend. My eyes skim Cam's back and I rub my hand down my arm, smoothing down the raised hairs. Just the thought of Cam liking me sends tingles spiking over my skin.

I can't get the conversation with Stacey out of my head. What if Cam really does like me? I've never had that before—a guy I think is great liking me. Usually I get crushed on by guys I have no interest in, or flirted with by guys who are after my sister.

But what if Cam is purely after me?

The idea is thrilling and terrifying in the same heartbeat.

Stacey appears beside me, a bubbly grin on her face, her eyes dancing. "We're going to sing."

"What? In front of all these people?"

"Yes! Luka just dared me to go first, and I'm not about to chicken out."

I glance across the room and spot Luka's cheeky grin. Is it weird that she looks prettier without Leon by her side? I don't know why that thought popped into my head, but there's just something relaxed about her smile.

She tinkles her fingers at me and I wave back, but still protest. "If it's your dare, why do I have to be involved?"

"Because you've got the best voice. You can mask my bum notes." Stacey laughs and snatches my wrist, dragging me toward the stage. "This is a karaoke party, isn't it? So far, no one has sung anything. They're all just standing around talking."

I glance over my shoulder as I'm dragged between bodies. "People seem to be having a good time."

Every face I spot is either smiling, laughing or listening. I don't see any bored expressions. Some people are even dancing to the music.

Stacey stops next to Manu. "Time for us to sing now, Moo."

"Choice." He does his funny giggle that always makes me smile.

Stacey and I share a quick grin before scrolling through the karaoke options.

"Should we go for a country-ish one, to stick with the theme?"

"We could." Stacey tips her head. "Or we could go for something that you can belt out so everyone knows how good you are."

"Stop it." I nudge her with my elbow, no doubt turning tomato red.

Singing in front of people is way scary, but I'm also itching to do it. Or just sing. I've been humming along to the tunes ever since they kicked in. I guess I might as well sing into a mic.

"Oooo! This one!"

I glance over her shoulder at the screen and gasp.

Stacey cracks up. "Just kidding!"

She flicks the screen away from "Baby Got Back" and keeps scrolling until she gets to "Footloose."

"This one?" She looks at me and nods. "This one. Yes! This one! Blake Shelton's a country singer, right? Harper will love it."

I grin at her, nervously following her to a mic while Manu takes over setting up the song for us.

"Hey, everyone!" Stacey calls into the mic.

The crowd settles down, and soon every eye in the room is on me. Or Stacey, but I'm standing right next to her, so I'm feeling naked and exposed! My throat starts to close up until I spot Cam in the crowd. He's beaming a smile right at me, and my heart does a backflip in my chest.

Maybe he really does like me.

I bite my lip and smile back at him, dipping my head when I feel the heat blooming on my face.

"…so if you want to belt out a tune, just come up and see Moo. He'll sort you out. Bianca and I will kick things off with a little number I think you'll all know." She gives the room a flirty wink and everyone starts to laugh, then cheer when the music kicks in.

The words pop up on the screen in front of us, but I don't really need them. Like Mum, I'm freakishly good at memorizing lyrics.

Stacey points at me, and not wanting to miss the beat, I start the song solo. Stacey's doing all these *Footloose* dance moves. It was a family favorite. Even Dad used to watch it with us. She's hamming it up for the crowd, which I'm grateful for. It takes the heat off me, and I can just enjoy the singing part.

Closing my eyes, I get into it and Stacey joins me on the chorus, along with a smattering of people from the party. By the second chorus, everyone's getting into it, and I can't contain my smile anymore. The song ends with a roar of applause and cheers. I flush with the praise, then hand the mic to Harper as she jumps up.

"No! You stay." She grabs my wrist.

"We need your voice to make us sound half decent." Zoey laughs while Alaina wraps her arm around my shoulder.

"You got some pipes, babe." She gives me a sloppy kiss on the cheek, which I subtly wipe away once she's let me go.

I notice Cam laughing up at the stage and figure he's just seen me. I wince and he just winks, his eyes so bright with what I now realize might possibly be affection that it's hard to breathe for a second.

Oh man, I hope Stacey *is* right.

Is it worth the risk?

Yes! Because even if Stacey is wrong about this, she's right about having to live in the moment.

I'm not very good at that.

I need to—

The song starts up, my train of thought derailed as I'm sandwiched by a group of girls in order to sing a country song that I vaguely recognize. I know the chorus, and by the end of the second verse I'm sussed, finishing the story with a flourish.

We stay up there for four more tunes, and I'm pretty sure my voice will be hoarse by the end of the night. My final number is a LeAnn Rimes song that Mum used to love. I belt it out like she's standing right next to me. Every person in the room starts to fade until it's just my voice and the memory of my mother's.

Oddly enough, it doesn't make me want to cry.

Instead, I'm filled with this giant... I don't know... joy, maybe? It consumes me. And it must shine through in my voice, because as I wrap up the song, I notice I'm the only one singing, and the cheers and whistles are practically deafening.

I flush and hand the mic to Logan and Tameka.

"I don't know how the hell we're going to follow that up!" She laughs. "That was amazing."

"Thank you," I murmur, rushing down the stairs and covering my boiling-hot cheeks.

I so don't want to look in a mirror right now. I probably look hideous with my tomato skin and—

"You sounded so amazing!" Cam bends down to be heard above the next song.

I give him a nervous grin. "Oh, not really."

"Yeah you did. It was beautiful."

I'm not used to the word beautiful being associated with me. At least not from a guy. I don't know how to respond, so I just dip my head and tuck my fringe behind my ear.

Cam holds out a cold bottle of Coke. "I thought you might want a drink after that. Do you like Coke? Or I can get you something else. There's water if that's better for your throat, or..."

"No, this is good. Thank you." I take the drink and glug

it back, the fizz tickling my taste buds. It's cold and delicious, although I'm pretty sure he could have handed me a glass of mud and I probably would have taken it from him.

He smiles down at me and I grin back, turning to face the stage so we're standing next to each other.

Logan and Tameka are singing "Why Does Love"—a kiwi classic—and when they reach the chorus, Tameka yells into the mic, "Everybody!"

A crescendo of voices fills the air, sending goose bumps rippling over my skin as people belt out the words. Singing en masse always has this effect on me.

Cam's hollering beside me. He sounds terrible. Missy's right, he really can't sing. It makes me giggle, and I quickly slap my hand over my mouth to hide the sound. Cam gives me a sideways glance, like he knows what I'm laughing about. With a wide grin, he turns to face me and just starts singing that much louder.

I laugh, an unchecked sound that I have no control over. Spreading his arms wide, he keeps singing out of tune, and I try to join him between my giggles.

Stacey catches my eye and gives me an enthusiastic thumbs-up before draping one arm around Luka and the other around Willow. They sway next to each other, both singing like they've forgotten to be sad for a moment.

A warmth I can't explain fills me to overflowing. I never want this moment to end. Forcing my brain not to jump ahead to the end of the party or even the next day, I blink a few times and focus back on Cam.

This is the moment I need to be in right now.

This happy, laughing bubble with a gorgeous guy who might just have a crush on me.

48

HARPER

Everyone's left and I'm happily exhausted.

It takes a lot to surprise me—I usually predict these things—but I guess I've been kind of distracted. When I first walked into the shout of "surprise," my only thought (bizarrely) was, "I'm not wearing any makeup." My eyes were puffy. My lips a little swollen. I must have looked a mess.

But no one seemed to notice, or if they did, they didn't show it. They were too busy hugging me and kissing my cheeks and making me feel important.

It was actually kind of nice.

Zoey and Alaina will be back at the motel by now. They leave first thing tomorrow, so I've already said my goodbyes. They apologized profusely for ditching me and then nagged for details on Tane. But I kept my lips sealed. I'm not exactly sure why. They'd be so happy for me if they knew. I don't know... I guess I want that moment by the creek to belong to Tane and me, no one else.

A smile curls my lips as I remember his sweet expression, how husky his voice was when he told me he'd be good for me. Happy tingles shimmer down my spine and are dulled only by my physical weakness. The black headache I woke with is just starting to ease back into my conscious. I'm looking forward to bed. As much as I'd love to dream, I'm pretty sure I'll be comatose within seconds of hitting the pillow.

With a yawn, I cover the leftover food with Gladwrap and store it in the fridge before heading back to the barn to make sure there's nothing else to do. I can't believe Bianca put this all together for me. The others helped too, but she was the driving force. I'll thank her properly in the morning, as I think she's already been ordered to bed by Beck.

As I walk past the stairs, I can hear a little post-party giggling from the twins. It makes me smile. Everyone was just so happy tonight, caught up in this moment where nothing could touch us.

I think we all needed it.

Crossing my arms against the chilly night air, I head down to the barn. The moon is only a thumbnail tonight, so it's not giving me much light. I tread carefully on the path, wishing I'd brought a torch or something. I left my phone in the kitchen too.

Winding down the path, I head towards the lit barn, focusing on the cracks of light shining from the upper windows. I mildly roll my ankle once on a pothole I didn't know was there, but shaking out the pain isn't too bad. It's nothing compared to the mondo bruise on my hip. I can't remember how I got it, but when I leaned against the kitchen counter before, I definitely felt it.

Lightly brushing my hand over the mysterious injury, I nearly jump out of my skin when a large shadow looms in front of me.

"Oh!"

"It's just me." Beck chuckles. "We're pretty much done in there." He points over his shoulder, his face coming clearer when he stops in front of me. "Tane's just cleaning up the last of the mess."

"Okay." I nod, wondering if he's all alone. I can't see any other cars around, and hope fires through me, hot and needy. "I'll see if he needs a hand."

"Right. Don't be too long, though. You need your sleep."

I smile at him.

He pats my shoulder and turns to leave, then stops me with his gruff voice. "Hey, Harp?"

"Yeah?" I spin back, hoping my expression is casual enough. He shouldn't be able to see it in this dim light anyway.

I don't know why exactly, but the thought of Beck knowing about me and Tane just feels weird.

He gives me a gentle smile, the light from the barn highlighting his big bear features.

A swell of affection blooms in my chest. I get why Dad chose him.

Stroking a hand down his beard, he opens his mouth a couple of times, then sighs. "Look, I want to apologize for yelling at you last night. I was pissed off you got so drunk and ended up at the police station, I guess." He shrugs. "Or maybe I was just afraid. You know, of letting your dad down."

I swallow, my throat starting to swell.

"Thing is, I didn't notice, or know, that you were struggling so much. You hide it all so well and…and I know you think you can't do this without your mum and dad, but the thing is… you *are* doing it. And you're doing okay. When I first lost Abby and the boys, I couldn't even get out of bed in the morning." He blinks and looks up at the starry sky. "Your parents would be real proud of you. I know it… because I am." His voice is all thick and gummy, making my heart squeeze.

Tears spring onto my lashes.

Seriously. You cry once and it's like open season on your tear ducts.

I step back across to Beck and wrap my arms around his thick neck. "Thanks, Beck. They'd be proud of you too."

He hugs me, his large hand splaying between my shoulder blades before he gives me a quick kiss on the cheek and pulls back. With a little sniff, he starts walking for the house. "Don't stay up too late cleaning. We can finish the rest in the morning."

"Got it." I wait until his body has completely disappeared into the darkness before slipping through the barn door.

Tane's alone and my stomach fires with giddy jitters. His hands are loaded up with bottles and cans. I race over to open the recycling bag for him.

"Thanks." He grins.

The rubbish tumbles into the bag, clinking together to create a glass-metal staccato that mirrors the beat of my erratic heart.

Tane returns to gather up the last of the debris. I should be helping him, but all I can do is stand here holding open the bag and admiring the view.

His movements are so smooth and strong. I can feel his arms around me again, the protective shield his body created. I want to lean against it, close my eyes and just revel in the feel of him.

Standing tall, he pauses and looks at me, like he knows I've been watching him this whole time. Sauntering over with a casual little swagger, he drops the recycling into the bag. "Hey, can I ask you something?"

"Of course." I nod, the pulse in my neck throbbing as I jiggle the contents of the bag and set it down between my feet.

"That kiss," Tane whispers. "You think it might happen again sometime?"

I press my lips together but can't control the smile fighting to break free.

Glancing up through my lashes, my voice quakes as I softly reply, "I hope so."

His grin is freaking adorable, and I almost hate to wrinkle my nose and spoil it with my condition, but it kind of has to be said.

"Maybe not in front of anybody else, though."

He nods and the knot inside me unfurls. "Probably a good idea. I don't know what Beck would think about us being together."

"Yeah." I wince and glance at the door to make sure we really are alone.

Satisfied, I step over the bag and right up against Tane's chest. His arms automatically come around my waist and I start playing with the short hair at the nape of his neck. Brushing my nose across the tip of his, I murmur against his lips, "So, our little secret, then?"

He captures my mouth, heating me through with an unhurried kiss that basically melts my brain. I let out a soft breath when he gently pulls back to smile at me. "Our secret."

I don't know why that's so thrilling, but it is. Cupping the back of his head, I push his lips down to mine and revel in a little Tane candy. I could get highly addicted to this, and it worries me a little. I still have siblings to care for, and I can't let Tane become a distraction. But maybe we can muddle our way through this together.

He's a really good guy.

And maybe he's right... we will be good together.

49

TANE

"So we're all agreed?" I glance around the dining room table and make sure I connect with each person sitting there.

"Yes!" Stacey groans, tipping back her head before pointing at me. "Although I would just like to reiterate that Bianca and I have always had housekeepers, so we are pretty much useless."

I throw her a withering glare. "Even useless people can be taught to clean a toilet."

"I'm just saying." Stacey raises her hands while Beck snickers and shakes his head.

"Okay, here she comes!" Oscar scuttles back to the table, Rocket locked against his chest, as Harper walks in the front door, brushing off her shoes.

She jerks still when she notices everyone sitting at the table, smiling at her.

"What's going on?" She pads past the couch and stops before reaching the dining room. "You know what, guys... after last night, I don't think I can handle any more surprises."

"It's your final gift." I walk over and take the Four Square bag out of her hand, softly whispering, "To make up for the shit one I gave you before."

"That wasn't shit," she whispers back.

"It wasn't what you wanted. I think this might be." I try to smile, but nerves are attacking me from all sides. I've never needed someone to like one of my gifts this way before.

Her expression softens with a loved-up smile that warms my core, but then she catches herself, her chin lifting a little as she remembers there are other people in the room.

Clearing my throat, I wink at her. My back's to everyone, so they can't see me anyway.

"Come on." I carry the groceries into the kitchen and rush back to the table as Harper stops to stare down at the massive square gift lying in the middle of it. It was too big to justify wrapping, so we just covered it with a blanket.

"You ready?"

"I guess so." She grins, sharing a quick look with her sister as I unveil the whiteboard with a flourish.

Harper's eyebrows wrinkle as she looks at the whiteboard with its columns and rows. Each member of the household has their own column. Willow ruled it up for me. She's freaking meticulous, and when she saw me about to start, she grabbed my arm and practically yelled, "I'll do it!"

I've never heard her talk so loud before. It cracked me up.

"What is this?" Harper chuckles.

"This is our new chore chart." Bianca grins and holds out an envelope.

Harper narrows her eyes and opens it, laughing when she catches the Boss Badge Oscar made for her.

Holding up the circular disc, she reads the yellow block text. "Da Boss?"

"That's right." Beck nods. "We're putting you in charge of us, which means you are no longer allowed to do every single chore in this place like some slave girl."

"We need you to organize us." Bianca grins.

Stacey forces a smile, her voice plastic-coated. "We're all pitching in."

Harper snorts and then narrows her eyes skeptically.

"You guys are going to help me keep this place clean and tidy?"

"You bet. And we've all signed a contract promising that we'll do it complaint free." I raise my eyebrows at Stacey and then Oscar before swinging my arm around Harper's shoulders, hoping it looks casual enough. "You shouldn't have to do it all. We all live here, and we all need to carry our weight. We just need someone to direct us."

Beck grins at her. "And with the free time you'll no doubt pick up, I was wondering if you might like to help me with a little admin work—accounts, bills, things like—"

"Yes!" Harper interrupts him, her expression pure gold. "That would be great. I—I'm really good with numbers."

Beck and I share a quick wink, but Harper's too busy fighting tears to notice.

Bianca catches my eye and wiggles her eyebrows at me. We did it. Looks like our little brainstorm came up with the perfect gift.

Picking up the whiteboard marker, I pop the top and hand it to Harper.

She gently takes it from me, her eyes glistening as she looks from me and then around the table. "I love this.

Thank you, guys. It means the world to have your help."

"We're a team." I bump her with my hip.

She glances at me again, her eyes rich with desire, and I wish I could pull her into my arms and kiss her right there. But for now, keeping this a secret is for the best.

Who knows how the people around this table would react if they found out Harper and I have the hots for each other? Not to mention the fact that I can see myself falling hard and fast for this girl.

I don't want anything to get in the way of it.

Secrecy will protect what we've got going. It's bound to come out eventually, but hopefully by then we'll be solid enough to counter anything that might try to tear us apart.

I'll fight for this girl.

I'll fight for what we've got.

Because it's good. I know it with every fiber of my being.

Keep reading to find out what's going to happen next on the Connell farm.

A secret is brewing. A new one. A nasty one that's going to hurt and destroy.
Can this fledgling family act as a unit to fight against it?
And will Bianca find the strength to fight for what her heart wants most?

Find out in Shy Girl vs Popular Boy

Releasing November 29, 2019

A second-place sister. A first-rate jock. Can the light of love shine through the darkest pain?

Bianca:
Cam likes me. He's asked me on a date.
It's kind of unbelievable. He could have any girl he wants, yet his eyes landed on me.
Can this be real?
Do I go for it?
He's so out of my league. I'm terrified.

I don't think the other girls like it. Their heated glares are warning me away, and now my twin sister's in trouble too. Stacey won't tell me what's wrong, but she's acting weird and I'm worried that her boyfriend has hurt her. I need to get to the bottom of it. I'm all she has left.

Can I really make this thing with Cam a reality? I want him so badly, but I promised Stacey I'd stick with her no matter what. How do I protect both sides of my heart? How do I choose between love and loyalty?

Shy Girl vs Popular Boy **is the third story in the touching Forever Love YA contemporary romance series. If you like sweet high-school settings, sisterhood bonds, and sensitive takes on real-world trauma, then you'll adore Jordan Ford's rollercoaster journey.**

Buy *Shy Girl vs Popular Boy* to find love where the other half lives today!

If you'd like to be the first to know about the release you can either:

- Sign up for Jordan's mailing list, and gain access to a free introductory novella for her Ryder Bay series. (https://www.subscribepage.com/JF_book_signup)

- Follow Jordan Ford on Amazon. (https://www.amazon.com/Jordan-Ford/e/B01D5FL09Q)

- Follow Jordan Ford on Bookbub. (https://www.bookbub.com/authors/jordan-ford)

PREVIEW

SHY GIRL VS FIX-IT BOY

CAM

"So, what's going on with you and Bianca, then?" Tane brushes the black sand off his hands and smirks at me.

I sigh, adjust my sunnies and then shrug.

"Well? Are you are going to ask her out or just keep smiling at her?"

"She's shy. I don't want to scare her off. Sometimes she's really warm and friendly, and other times she ducks her head and hurries away. I can't figure her out. I know she's been through this huge trauma. I want to be respectful of that."

Tane purses his lips and nods. "Yeah, but she still has to live, bro. She needs someone who's going to make her smile."

I squint out at the ocean, checking on the Year 9 students and doing a quick head count.

Our group of twelve is all still messing around in the water while we play lifeguards for their forty-five minutes of free time. It's been a good camp so far. Only one day left to go…and I've thought about Bianca the entire time we've been away.

"Am I the right guy to do that for her? Make her smile?"

"Yes." Tane gives me a pointed look, even dipping his sunnies so I can see his eyes. "You like her. She'd be an idiot not to like you, and she's not an idiot, so maybe you just need to be direct with her. *'Bianca - I think you're gorgeous. I love your hair. Can I take you out sometime?'*"

I give him a pitiful frown and Tane starts laughing.

"I'm just saying, if you want this girl, you're gunna have to put yourself out there."

"I'm not used to chasing girls. It's weird."

"The best ones are worth chasing, mate."

BIANCA

I hear giggling as I enter the barn, and my curiosity goes on high alert.

Is this what I think it is?

With a grin, I creep across the dusty hay floor and peek into Copper's stall.

Thought so.

Harper and Tane are finally together.

Yay!

My romantic heart nearly busts out of my chest. I'm so happy for these guys. They deserve it.

Harper lets out a soft moan and hooks her legs around Tane's waist, drawing him even closer. She's sitting on the gate between Copper and Jax's stalls, kissing Tane like it's her last act on earth.

He glides his hand around her waist, fusing them together.

I wonder what it must be like to kiss that way. I've never kissed a guy. You know, like, romantically. It looks so passionate and enticing.

My stomach knots as I think about my conversation with Cam this afternoon. I should seriously leave these guys to it, but... I kind of need their help, so I accidentally on purpose kick my foot against the wall and then try to act like I've only just arrived.

"Bianca!" Harper whispers, wide-eyed.

"Oh, hey. I was just..." I point over my shoulder but don't actually say the lie that I was just leaving. Instead I settle for an awkward wave and smile.

Harper dips her head, hiding behind Tane's face while he gives me a triumphant grin. I can't help a little giggle.

"Um, we were just..." Harper tries to get down, but Tane holds her in place for a second.

"It's okay. I won't tell anyone." I smile at her.

She instantly relaxes, resting her cheek on Tane's head.

I grin, then bite my lip. "I'm sorry to interrupt you guys. You must have missed each other this week. I should probably let you get back to it."

"Did you need something?" Tane asks.

"Sort of." I cringe. "I mean, I don't know. I mean yes."

Harper snorts. "So, which is it?"

"Help," I practically whimper.

Harper jumps down immediately, pushing Tane aside to get to me. "What's wrong? What's happened?"

"Cam asked me out to the movies tomorrow night, and I said okay. So now I'm like freaking out and literally don't think I can do this."

Tane saunters over. "What do you mean, you can't do it? Cam's awesome."

"Oh, I know." I raise my eyebrows. "It's just… well, I've never been on a date before, and I'm really worried I'll say something stupid or do something silly and I just… I don't know if I can go my own. I need backup."

Harper grins, looking all excited for me. "I'll be your backup."

Tane slides his arm around her waist. "*We'll* be your backup. It can be a double date."

I give him a grateful smile, which soon morphs into a worried frown. "Do you think Cam will mind?"

"Leave it to me." Tane winks. "He'll understand."

"Thanks, Tane." I smile and then point between them. "I really like this, by the way. It's a good fit." They give each other gooey smiles and I spin for the door, feeling light and playful. "I'll let you get back to sucking each other's faces off."

STACEY

The party is lit, just the way we all thought it would be. Nico's acting like the police to make sure no one ruins the house. If his parents find out what we're up to, he'll be slaughtered. But they're not back for a week, so it's not like he has to stress about cleanup or anything. He's got plenty of time.

Jonas swipes his hot tongue in my mouth, gently biting my lower lip before pulling me out of the main living area. The hallway leading down to the bedrooms is a little less crowded, and he pushes me against a wall, his hands sliding all over me as he kisses my neck, my jaw, my chin.

"Let's go to Nico's room."

His suggestion makes me stiffen. I know what he's asking of me right now. "I don't know," I whisper when he gives me enough air to speak.

Jerking away from me, his eyebrows form a sharp V before he slumps his shoulders, resting his forehead against mine. "Come on, how long are you going to make me wait. It's torture."

"I'm not trying to torture you." I skim my finger along the neckline of his T-shirt. "But I don't exactly want to lose it on Nico's bed, at a party, where anyone could walk in on us."

"I'll put a sock on the door or something. It'll be okay." He starts kissing me again, catching all my sensitive spots and making my body buzz with desire.

I close my eyes, wondering if I should give in. He's been hinting at this for weeks, and I guess it is something I want to do. It's just—

The chain around my neck gives way. I feel it slipping into my shirt, and I jerk back to catch it.

"What?" Jonas snaps.

I give him a pointed look, and suddenly sex is the last thing I feel like.

"Losing it on Nico's bed is a no-go," I snip, shouldering past him and shoving the chain into my pocket.

He lets out a disgusted huff and stalks past me into the living room.

For a split second, I think about running after him to apologize.

What the hell is wrong with me?

No. Nothing's wrong with me. If I don't want sex right now, I shouldn't have to have it.

Jonas can be such a dick sometimes.

But he is my boyfriend, and I don't want our night to be completely ruined. This is my first decent party since—

I slam the door on memories from the past and grab a bottle of beer from the ice bucket, which is basically just a pool of cold water now.

"Here." I hand it to Jonas, who is now leaning against the breakfast bar sharing a cigarette with Dee.

"Thanks," he grumbles, glugging back half the bottle before taking another decent drag.

My nose wrinkles as I sniff the air. It doesn't smell like weed, but any kind of smoke is pretty foul-smelling to me.

"Outside with the ciggies!" Nico whines, storming over to us. "Come on, you guys."

Jonas laughs at him and gives the cigarette back to Dee. "It's not mine."

"Thanks a lot." Dee slaps him and stalks outside with Nico, who is playfully telling her off.

"That's gunna cost you a kiss, Dee."

Jonas burps, then wraps his arm around my neck, diving for my mouth with a slobbery kiss that tastes like smoke and beer.

It's kind of gross, and I push him off me.

His eyes glint dark and dangerous before he downs his bottle, then raises his arms in the air with a loud whoop before throwing the bottle away.

It missiles through the air and straight into the TV screen.